M. C. Rudasill

I0668223

Jewel
of the
Mind

Literary Lights Publishing
TALLAHASSEE

This book offers a fictional representation of events that occurred during the occupation of England by the Norse armies under Guthrum the Dane. Many of the events described in this novel occurred, while others exist only within the realm of the story.

Special thanks go to Pilar Delp for her eagle-eyed editing of this book.

ISBN: 978-0-9727127-5-0

I dedicate this book to my wife, Susann, and to our Maker, who created the heavens and the earth, the sea and the springs of the deep.

The Voyages

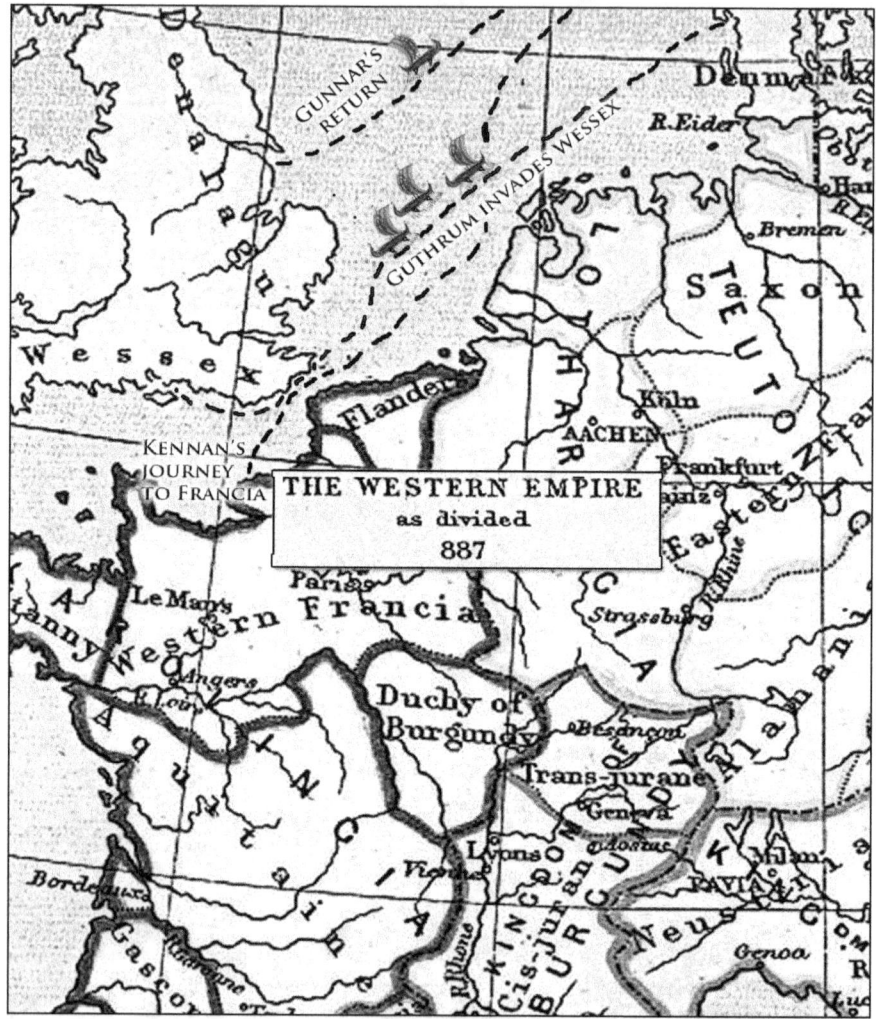

This map depicts the three voyages at the heart of The Gunnar Saga: the invasion fleet of Guthrum the Dane, the journey of Kennan Whitefang to Francia, and the return of Prince Gunnar to the city of Bryne. The saga itself, considered lost until the discovery of a copy in a small monastery in Flanders, is most often attributed to the warrior-poet, Barad-zur.

The Gunnar Saga

Stories are told about the great sea-kings
Who braved bitter strife in the years of our elders:
The sons of the Mighty, not once drawing back,
Their blood-whetted swords stirring war's pyrrhic pitch.

Dreadful in battle, the warriors of old
Poured molten death upon ashen-faced strangers
And built to the heavens good-fires of conquest
That sent crimson sparks dancing upward in triumph.

Spent weapons, once wielded by valorous princes,
Fed fires that feasted on spear shaft and helmet.
Brazen shields, throbbing hot,
Swooned in weak, fevered fealty,
And gushed flaming streams down their pyres of joy.
Burning steel sifted through ruby fingers of flame
And found rest in the earth with shield-bearer and thane.

The greatest of Healf-Scylfs, the chief of their kind,
King Vigmar grew strong in the land of the North.
He hunted the hills of his harsh mountain coastland
And waxed great in wisdom, in honor, and strength.

Hope melted like wax before Vigmar's dread hosts
As if breathed on by fire, and the strength
Of their victims poured out with their lives
Into cold waterways, mingled with burnings.
Detritus of kingdoms - bones, ashes, and blood -
Slid to the sea with the dust of their dreams.

Holding by hand the young and the helpless,
Vigmar sheltered the weak and encouraged the strong.
Leading his hosts to the homelands of strangers
He conquered strong kings
And made sport with their crowns.

Many a good night was spent in the mead hall
Recounting his battles in light's golden glow.
Lulled by the fire, safe from the howling,
As snow-billows roared on the ocean of night,
The mighty men rested within their fair haven.
Moored the food-board, full-stocking their mead-holds,
They took weighty ballast and shared his abundance.
A generous man and a good king was he!

No valiant earl wanted for armor or gems
When Ingeld's son Vigmar shared treasure and mead.

Pitch and Battle

The arrow hissed past his ear like an angry snake, a slender sliver of death that flashed through his field of vision and exploded against a cliff, far ahead. The impact struck bright sparks from the stone: a brief, burning blossom of light that flared for an instant and vanished, lost among the dense forest shadows.

A wisp of smoke, drifting from the site of impact, slowly uncurled in the spray of sunbeams that sifted through the tall forest canopy. The smoke lingered in the still forest air, at rest in the towering pillars of light.

The horseman raced his steed with tumultuous abandon, oblivious to the glories of nature. Crouching low in the stirrups, he focused intently on the trail ahead.

Lanced by beams of morning light, the primeval forest offered a freewheeling feast for the senses: musty earth watered by clean patches of snow, the delicate scent of fir and resin and a translucent shimmer of smoke, at rest in a column of light. The beauty of the forest, like the incense of springtime, belied the deadly business at hand.

The frantic hoof-beats grew louder, pressing hard against the silence. The thin cloud of smoke – offspring of iron and stone – stretched luxuriously in the dusty luminance.

The young horseman ripped through the ribbon of smoke in heedless disarray, hurtling past the sheer rock wall in a fine frenzy of urgency. He drove his horse recklessly, at the limit of his ability, in a desperate dash at breakneck speed across the steep slope.

Ancient trees towered above the rider and his magnificent mountain pony. A dense carpet of needles cushioned the perilous, rock-strewn terrain over which they breathlessly surged, an explosion of haste in the midst of the hushed forest cathedral.

The rider heard the distant blast of a war-horn ringing through the valley, answered by the throaty cries of the bandits. The sounds echoed through the haze, mingling with the scent of the dew, the thud of hooves, the harsh hiss of his ragged breathing.

Hearing the war-horn, he remembered the ambush.

"Run!" his father had cried, and as an obedient son, he had obeyed. He had whipped his pony's flank and sprung away in a dead run, seized by a surge of terror that had surprised and overwhelmed him. He had fled like a frightened child, betraying his childhood dreams of heroic splendor. His brave plans had vanished when the bandits attacked.

The rider veered to his right, rushing dizzily down a steep mountain slope, testing the limits of the gifted pony's sure footing, The pony left a heavy cloud of dust in his wake.

A cruel black arrow hissed past his ear and bit deeply into an ancient tree that he hurtled past without a pause. He heard the cries growing closer now, heard throaty shouts as his pursuers called to one another in a harsh, unmelodic dialect.

Their horses must be fresh, he thought, and an unbidden idea suddenly flashed through his mind. The idea was desperate and hopeless, but he had little to lose.

Far below, a great blast from his father's war-horn soared above the rocks and trees, filling the distant reaches of the vast, open valley. King Vigmar was leading his pursuers north, hoping to lure them away from his son.

If you had been there that day, on a mountainside high above the trees, you would have seen the young rider as he darted across a clearing on his slender chestnut mount. If you had tarried beneath the rim of the valley, meditating in the solemn hush of the ancient woods, your meditations would have been abruptly shattered by the sudden crash and clamor as he fled past: a bright, fleeting vision of pre-medieval Norse nobility, his blond braids whipping behind him, bronze helm low, face peering intently around his horse's neck as he thundered past and was gone.

His name was Gunnar, and today was his seventeenth birthday.

The Wielder of the Lance

The skin began to swell, bulging outward as the sharpened iron pressed from underneath. It grew taut, stressed to its limit, straining, stretching until it split and the well-whetted point burst into view, thrust powerfully through the gap. A vivid crimson stream followed the emerging iron point, forced by the skilled hands wielding the lance.

The bearskin shone rich and lustrous in the morning light, its deep cinnamon hue accented with subtle silver highlights. With elegant understatement, the scarlet needlework provided a colorful counterpoint to the fur's soft, mottled surface.

"What do you think, mother?" the girl asked. "How do you like it?" She held up the ornate hat and looked across the room, a hopeful expression on her face. She was a fair-haired beauty: a pretty, petite child of fifteen with an expression at once whimsical and wise. As always, she gazed at her mother with a glance of affection mingled with respect and not a little awe.

"It's beautiful, Ilse," her mother replied with a smile. "Simply beautiful." Ilse's mother Katla was a prominent member of their clan, known for her insight and her wisdom. Blonde like her daughter but taller, stately and graceful in her simply patterned ivory dress, Katla was an aging beauty whose inquisitive brown eyes showed flashes of a youthful exuberance. The childish wonder in Katla's smile seemed almost out of place on her delicate, dignified countenance.

At this particular moment, no weighty care could crease Katla's brow. Her daughter's handiwork occupied her thoughts.

The ornate stitching was unlike any that Katla had taught Ilse. She took up the bearskin and closely examined the elaborate band of crimson and purple that ran around the bottom. *It's truly lovely,* she mused, rubbing a smooth white hand across the glossy surface.

I've never seen anything quite like it.

"Ivan told me about hats like this. They wear them in Novrogod. Look here!" She took the hat and put it on her head, proudly demonstrating how the side panels folded down to protect the ears. She looked ten years old as she struck this particular pose, small and mischievous in the richly furred, oversized hat and simple earthen-hued dress, looking for all the world like a fair-skinned, green-eyed little elf waif that had materialized fully formed from the fertile imagination of a tale-telling grandmother at story time.

"Ivan is very knowledgeable," Lady Katla said slowly, continuing her pointed inquiry. "But I don't think he taught you that style of needlework." Her daughter's work was remarkable. Ivan, whose fashion sense was limited to blacks, whites, and the occasional gray, had assuredly not taught her the pattern.

Katla and her daughter appreciated Ivan, who was the oldest man in their city: a funny, sincere gentle person as well as the king's favorite counselor. He had an interesting history.

After the armies of King Rus the First had captured Ivan and sold him into slavery, King Ingeld, father of Vigmar, had purchased him in the Stockholm slave market. Years later, freed by Vigmar, Ivan had become the king's companion and his wisest advisor in all matters of statecraft and seamanship, peace and prosperity, honor, love and war.

"Tell me, my daughter. Are you making that for your father, or do you have other plans for it?"

"Mother!" Ilse turned away quickly, her face burning. Katla knew the reason for her embarrassment. *How she blushes at the very thought of him,* Katla mused as she watched her daughter. For years, Ilse had loved the young prince, Gunnar-val.

The two children had grown up together under the exacting tutelage of Ivan Redbeard. Yet in spite of their close relationship, Katla knew that Gunnar was unaware of her daughter's feelings. Now, because she had an advantageous moment, Katla would have pursued the matter further, but Ilse was anxious to redirect the conversation. She pushed back a strand of hair and glanced innocently at her mother, then looked back at her work.

"What do you know about Ivan's family?" She held up the hat distractedly, as if she inspected it. *A subtle change of subject,* Katla thought wryly. *You are certainly your father's daughter.*

"There's not much I can tell you about his family, darling. Even Ivan doesn't know much about them."

"That must have been very sad, to lose them so suddenly."

"Yes, it was," answered a deep, gravelly voice.

Ilse looked up quickly to see Ivan Redbeard towering in the doorway, slightly stooped, as always. He loomed over his two friends like an amiable, rail-thin, moss-covered chimney bowing beneath a drift of snowy white hair. Ivan was a tall, wiry remnant of a mighty warrior dressed in faded black wool clothes, with long white hair and a huge beard streaked in the prime of old age with broad slashes of gray.

His namesake beard had faded in glory since the days of his youth. No longer a vivid crimson, it had aged to a bland shade of cinnamon-bear amber. For the moment, his bushy white eyebrows were knit together in an expression of gentle concern, providing a thatched platform from which his bony brow could overlook his long, hooked nose.

He stared intently at the young girl, his blue eyes sparkling. As she met his gaze, he smiled wryly. His face, weathered with age, displayed a marvelously intricate patina of delicate blue veins barely discernible beneath his tanned skin.

"It was, indeed, very sad to lose track of my family," he repeated. "But the memories have faded. And truly, they disappear altogether when I see your face."

"Oh, Ivan," Ilse answered, blushing. "You should have knocked."

"I see that you have become old enough to say what I should do. Will you also begin to instruct me in the ways of our kingdom?"

"As you heard, Lord Ivan," Katla interjected. "Ilse was asking about your kindred. Why don't you answer her?" Katla had been friends with Ivan for so long that no subject could be considered off limits ... even this issue, which touched upon so many painful memories.

"My lady, I am at your service. But I am afraid that the poor quality of my offering will little justify the curiosity of two such worthy women." He sat down on a low stool and pulled it close to them. "Nevertheless, you both shall hear the tale of my life, if you wish... which life, as you can see, has left me somewhat the worse for wear."

Ilse brightened up and looked at her mother excitedly. They loved it when Ivan told them a story. "So, let us begin at the beginning.

"This," he said to Ilse, gazing piercingly with his pale blue eyes, "is the tale of my childhood."

Dream-Speaker

"Of my family, I remember little save my mother and my grandfather. I have many memories of my mother. I am in her debt forever for her instruction in the value and meaning of loyalty, love, and devotion. She began teaching me when I was only a baby, and by the time I was taken by the Rus at age fourteen, her words had taken hold.

"My father, as you know, was a fur merchant based in Kiev. He was a traveling trader, leaving often to buy and sell his wares... far to the north, or in the south in the markets of Mesech (a growing village back then, nothing like it is today). I was learning the trade as well, but it ended when King Rus the First captured me. He was the grandfather of Rus the Great, who is making war on Novrogod to this day.

"In the spring of my fourteenth year, I was traveling with my father a great distance north of Novrogod. We were trading with the native people on the river. A hardy bunch of wild men they were – people of the old ways: as deadly as sharks, and as tough as ivory. There wasn't an iron sword to be found among them, but they made do with bronze quite well.

"Early one morning, I borrowed a small boat from our camp to do some fishing. To my surprise, one of the raiding parties of old King Rus happened along, and well... there you have it!

"I was captured. I never knew what happened to my father, or to the rest of our companions. I was sold as a slave in Helsinki to King Ingeld, the father of Vigmar. But the capture and the years of slavery were a small part of my youth. Quite fortunately, they made the least impression. I had many wonderful years in Kiev, the city of my birth. During the years of my early childhood I enjoyed many good years with my mother and grandfather.

"By the way," he added, with a whimsical tilt of his head. "My mother was a gifted musician. She used to sing very popular duets with her brother, my Uncle Inved." Ivan's eyes twinkled. "Uncle Inved had a special nickname for me." He paused. "Of course," he added, glancing at Ilse. "You wouldn't be interested in that."

"Of course we would," protested Ilse.

"You're too polite," he continued glumly. "You're only saying that to be kind."

"Oh, Ivan," she said. "You're terrible! Tell us."

"My own dear Uncle Inved called me…" Ivan paused, looking around, embarrassed. "Butterbelly."

"No!" Ilse chortled. "You've got to be kidding!"

"Upon my word, my lady," said Ivan solemnly. "And Uncle Inved earned great fame in our city. He was a smith who made a pair of war hammers, unique weapons that became famous in Kiev. They were commissioned by Prince Gorgoth himself: ornate monstrosities wrought of iron and bronze, inlaid and covered with gold and gems.

"Uncle Inved's gilded battle hammers were given to the Weir-Huns by our great and noble Prince Gorgoth as a gift for his bride-to-be, Zilga the Heavy-Handed. But that is another matter entirely."

"Oh, Ivan," Ilse sighed, rolling her eyes. "Really… are you kidding us?"

"Not at all," he replied, looking at her and then at Katla. "There actually was a Zilga the Heavy-Handed, and she did her best to live up to her name. Fortunately, she left Uncle Inved's battle hammers on the wall."

"Tell us more," Katla said, casting a bemused gaze toward her daughter. *She so loves a story!*

"Yes, yes, of course," Ivan continued. "As I said, my father was a trader from Kiev, and my mother spent her days with me at our home in the city. But my grandfather, Taball, came from the Caucasus Mountains in the south with his friend, Justin Andronicus, who grew up in the famous city of Rome.

"I spent much time with them, sitting and listening and asking them questions. They seemed as ancient as the mountains, although I imagine that they were no older than I am today. I had an exciting youth in Kiev.

"It was a great city, an international city in its way," Ivan said, pausing and shaking his head. "But there was always a shadow on the horizon. The Rus were approaching from the north." He looked up at Katla. "They were traveling in their longboats up the river, beginning to endanger the lands north of Novrogod. We knew that if Novrogod fell, Kiev might be next."

Ivan looked at Ilse and smiled at her warmly. He loved this little girl as if she were his own daughter. "My parents, my Uncle Inved, and my grandfather were the only relatives I knew. Our ancestors, however, had a history that might interest you.

"Of my ancestors on my mother's side, I know only two things. I know that they were exiled from their own land, far to the south, in the ancient days. The other thing, which has set us apart from the nations with whom we have lived, is that my ancestors – and I too, in my old age – believed that there is one God: alive, all-powerful, and all-wise: the Maker of all things, yet Himself unseen."

"But Ivan," said Ilse, looking quickly at Katla. "We believe that, too. Don't we, mother?"

"Well, yes," answered Katla. "And others have also believed this, including our king. But, of course, many in our kingdom still worship the gods of the wind, or rain, or thunder."

"Yes," Ilse replied thoughtfully. "Ivan, tell me. Does God ever send dreams to teach us… or to prepare us for things?" Ivan looked at her soberly. Her mother tensed, suddenly alert, surprised at her own reaction.

"I believe that He can, if He wishes," he said, looking at Katla. They exchanged a glance and then looked back at Ilse.

"Your grandmother was a draumspaki," Katla informed her. "She could read dreams." *I can too.*

"Well, I had a bad dream last night. It kept me up for hours. When I finally fell asleep, I dreamed it again."

"What was the dream?" Ivan asked, praying for understanding. He did not like the sound of this.

Ivan was, indeed, a man who believed that God cared for humankind. He was convinced that God communicated with his creation as He saw fit. But Ivan was a thoroughly pragmatic mystic. If Ilse's dream held a divine message, he wanted to respond to it correctly. If not, he hoped to quickly move on to other matters... such as the beautiful new hat in Ilse's hand.

"In my dream, I was standing by the sea," Ilse began. "I was looking at the waves as they crashed against the rocks. I turned around and looked up the cliff to the King's house. But his house wasn't there, Ivan. I saw two trees where the house should have been. One was huge, but the other was just a sapling. I mean, it was big, too, but it looked very young. Anyway, I saw all of this, and then I saw some woodmen with big axes. They climbed the cliffs and cut down the big tree. They even cut up the stump, and they burned it with fire. After that, they cut the top off the young tree along with its branches; you could see that it was going to live, but they hurt it badly. Then they dug it up and dragged it away!"

Ilse paused now, her eyes gazing off into the distance, out the window, oblivious to the fact that the two adults were staring at her in shock, transfixed by her narration. "I fell asleep, after a while, and I dreamed it again a second time, just like the first." Now she turned and looked at her mother, and then at Ivan, who continued to stare at her in disbelief.

"Tell me, please," she asked, gazing in surprise at their stunned expressions. "What does it mean?"

The Great Stag at Bay

The sky looked majestically blue – deep and cold, framed by snow-capped mountains showing the first signs of spring. Across the vast span of the valley, the earth burgeoned with bright green grass, weeds and buds: meadows sown with a rainbow mosaic of wildflowers, forests full of awakening evergreens, and hardwoods with tender shoots just beginning to uncurl. White patches of snow, almost hidden beneath the trees, seemed out of place in the expanse of this spectacular day, in this beautiful valley.

King Vigmar, furiously driving his spirited chestnut mount, clattered heavily through the cold stream on the valley floor. As he hoped against hope, a plan emerged. He would take his pursuers on a chase up the valley's severe southern slope. There, on a bright green wall of the valley, Vigmar would find a place to make his stand.

"We'll see what these thieves are made of," he said to his horse as they bounded past the great stones and fallen trees that lay scattered about like toys cast aside by careless giants. The horse refused to answer the king, as was his habit, choosing instead to gasp for breath, intent upon survival.

The King, dressed in hunting greens, nimbly clung to the back of the horse as they swiftly raced across the uneven ground. Vigmar was agile in spite of his advanced age and great size, showing no hint of exhaustion, no sign of the searing pain that accompanied every breath or the weariness that tugged at him heavily, dangerously slowing him like a lead chain around a swimmer's neck. He looked wan and haggard, and his white hair streamed from his uncovered head, and yet he rode hard and true.

As they climbed the steep slope, King Vigmar fought off a wave of despair, a powerful, sickening rush of hopelessness that threatened to overwhelm him. With supreme effort, he forced his concentration back to the task at hand.

At the top of the near-vertical incline, he saw a flat shelf of rock strewn with boulders. Vigmar realized that he could make a fighting stand there, possibly picking off the boldest of the bandits with his arrows as they tried to follow him up the slope. His eyes traveled up past the ledge, high above the valley wall. He had to lead them yet higher if he could, further into the barren rocks that offered refuge to the wild goats and the sheep of the mountains.

A sharp pain slammed into his left side, taking his breath away. An excruciating, burning sensation spread into his arm. The agony was unbearable, as if someone had dumped a bucket of hot coals down his leather jerkin. A well-aimed arrow had struck home.

"Great King of the universe," Vigmar prayed. "Help me to fight bravely. Help me to die, if I must, as a man."

As he drew near the ledge where he planned to make his stand, his horse lost his footing. King Vigmar felt the big gelding stumble beneath him, beginning to fall to his left.

Reaching desperately with his good right arm, he managed to seize a branch that grew straight out from the cliff just below the ledge. It was a strong branch from a twisted, gnarled pine of great age, and it held his full weight.

The king's longhaired horse, his companion in many an adventure, screamed in terror as it began the plunge. The light brown mountain horse tumbled end over end, flopping like a huge rag doll, squealing and writhing from blow to blow, bouncing down the steep incline in a hellish journey that ended in silence and a distant cloud of dust.

Vigmar glanced down once as his horse fell and then concentrated on working his way up the wiry branch of the knotty pine, hand over hand. The tough little tree swayed and bobbed wildly under his weight, but he made it to the roots and then fought and clawed his way onto the stony ledge. There, Vigmar rested on his knees and prayed once again.

"Great Creator, high above all gods," he prayed. "Strengthen my hands today. Help me, I beg you. If I should not be saved, please save my son." His eyes were cast heavenward as he prayed in the tongue of his fathers. His sweat, pouring down his flushed face, ran down into his long gray beard. On the slope below him, the strangers drove their horses relentlessly, following his path to the top.

Vigmar's left arm, nearly numb by now, was soaked in crimson blood. He might be able to hold his shield in that hand, but he knew he could not handle his bow. *The bow,* he thought with a surge of despair. *If I could use my bow, I might defeat them all.*

Still on his knees, Vigmar looked down at his chest and seized the arrow where it had come out at the left front side. He broke the arrowhead off and – bowing low – reached behind himself with his good right hand. As he slowly pulled the arrow out through his back, the agony was incredible. The pain slammed home like a battle-hammer, driving him nearly mad with anguish.

He struggled to his feet, slung his shield, and drew his sword in his good right hand. Leaning over the edge, he gazed back down the mountainside at the horsemen, who grew near to his position in their struggle up the slope.

"Come and fight," he cried loudly. "Cowards and brigands! May the One who made the heavens defend my son from your infamy!"

King Vigmar watched as the fastest horseman scrambled higher, drawing near the stony ledge. His heart quailed for a moment and he stumbled backwards, fighting against the terror that surged within him. *Help me, Creator. Save my son.* To his surprise, a profound wave of blessed peace rolled in like a cloud, and his fear vanished like smoke in the wind.

Alone, undaunted, and finally undone, the greatest of the sea-kings gathered his strength. Lurching ahead, his eyes dim and burning, he walked over to meet the messengers of death.

II.

Vigmar the King was unlike any other.

Of the breadth of his kingdom, his bold independence,
The singers have sweetly sung in the wide halls.
The tale of his life and his hour of ending
Has oft been retold in that time of the evening
When Boasting gives place to the pool of Reflection.

At the height of his strength, in the spring of his wisdom,
The hope of the mighty was quenched in full flower.
The root and the branch were both struck together.

The death's-head of darkness,
Smooth tongue of the traitor,
Pierced through the heart of King Vigmar of Bryne.

Like steel slicing softly between the warm chambers,
His own flesh and blood cut the quick of the just.
So cruel Haruk Longknife, father of Kennan,
Rewarded with daggers his king's love and trust.

King Vigmar lived boldly, unbounded by fear.
He was the chief of the Sea-kings of old,
The chief of the Norsemen who battled the Night
In the time of the ancients: the age without hope.

Vigmar forged forward without turning back,
Unyielding, unflinching, unconquered, undone
When at last that dread darkness, cold Chaos, came down.
His son was Prince Gunnar, the hope of the realm.

The days of the Prince and his unfailing vision,
The strength of his youth and the depth of his cunning
Fill up the stories of Prince Gunnar-val.
He was their favorite, the heart of his people.

They mourned when the young Prince
Was plucked from their breast
By the traitor, his uncle: the Dragon of Kuzbi.

The Prince, led away from the City of Bryne,
Bore into bondage a prisoner's dream.
He yearned to return once again to his homeland:
His motherland, fatherland, land of his love…
The essence of longing distilled in his tears
For the jewel in the mind of the Praise of his Peers,
The jewel of the mind
For the slave,
Gunnar-val.

Fall of the Right Front Leader

Lady Katla and Ivan stared at Ilse with her question echoing in their minds. She had asked for the meaning of her dream, and the answer, to them, appeared obvious.

The great tree in Ilse's dream, growing in place of the King's house, represented King Vigmar the Great. The younger tree symbolized the Prince, and the dream meant that the King and the Prince would soon be attacked.

This revelation, however, presented other considerations. The woodmen, who could they be? Had treachery entered their kingdom, or would the assault be the work of outsiders? Would an attack happen soon, or was the dream sent to prepare them, so it could be avoided?

Their prayers had been answered unanimously on one account. Katla and Ivan both held the certainty that this dream held a divine revelation. They paused, weighing the information that had just been introduced into their lives.

"Ilse," Ivan began.

"Ivan?" Katla interrupted.

"Yes?" he asked Katla, surprised. He looked at her curiously as she turned to Ilse.

"Ivan and I must talk, darling," Katla said to her daughter, who gazed at them wide-eyed, beginning to fear their silence. "After we speak, we'll tell you what we can. Please excuse us."

"Of course. Mother?" asked Ilse as they stood to leave the room.

"Yes, my child?"

"Uh... nothing," Ilse replied. She stood up. "I'll wait here."

Ivan bowed with a formal, sweeping gesture more reminiscent of his homeland than of the fjords and coastal plains of Bryne. He truly loved and admired this wise lady and her surprising daughter.

He followed Katla into the library of her spacious home of

hewn oak and fir. Here, in this quiet spot, ancient scrolls were stored on high shelves against the wooden walls. The home was the hereditary household of Ithmar, Katla's husband, the Keeper of the King's Head and leader of his inner circle of friends.

The northern Vikings – those pillaging pirates who lived by the ancient ways – held to a tradition that the Romans called the comitatus. A comitatus was a chosen group of men sworn to total loyalty to their King, dedicated to the preservation of his life at any cost. The members of a comitatus devoted their lives, becoming like brothers, sons, and guardian angels for their lord.

Ithmar was a warrior and a student of the books kept in this library, yet he was also the chief captain of Vigmar's comitatus. He followed the ancient traditions, bound to his royal ring-giver by the brother-bond and a vow of lifetime service. Ithmar had given his all to his king, receiving trust and generosity in return.

It was unusual to find anyone who could read within two hundred nautical miles. And yet, a great number of books and scrolls were stored in this very room... the treasure room of Katla's husband, Ithmar.

King Ingeld, Vigmar's father, had captured these valuable writings during long years of warfare. In an act of royal generosity, he had divided them with Ithmar's father Wendren, the only other man in his kingdom with an interest in learning to read.

Wendren, intrigued by the books, had longed to decipher the meaning of the colorful, intricate markings on the aged scrolls. The purchase of the young Ivan Redbeard at the slave market in Stockholm had given Ingeld the key to unraveling the texts, for Ivan had been trained to read the strange markings in the books.

Ivan's mother and grandfather had taught him this great mystery, both the alien language of the scrolls and the art of deciphering the inky markings. In his youth, Ivan's grandfather Taball had learned the skill from a Roman adventurer named Justin Andronicus. Together with Ivan Redbeard's grandfather Taball, Justin Andronicus had traveled north to Kiev, where they had found wives and settled down.

Ivan had known these ancient men as a boy, and the memories

of their long conversations in the Latin tongue remained with him to this day. His mother had tutored him, teaching him how to read from a Latin book that had come into the family's possession. Purchased by King Ingeld, the young slave Ivan Redbeard had shared this gift with the few who wished to learn it: Ingeld and Wendren, their sons Vigmar and Ithmar, and Katla. Later, as a free man, he had tutored Vigmar's son Gunnar, Kennan the son of Haruk, and Ilse the prodigy.

Katla turned to Ivan with deep concern etched on her countenance. He faced her from the other side of the well-lit scroll room. For a full minute, they stared into one another's eyes. Clear beams of afternoon light, streaming through the opaque western window, painted shifting patterns on Katla's clean woolen dress. Specks of dust, suspended in the air, slowly drifted between them: illuminated by the fiery light of the cool northern sun.

"Do you know what Ilse's dream signifies?" Katla asked.

"I know, as you do. Her dream says that our king will be slain and our prince carried away."

"Do you understand why I interrupted you?"

"Yes. We need to keep this close, at least until we know what to do."

"Ivan... can this be real? Must this event happen, or is it merely a warning?"

"I am deeply troubled, my lady, for I believe it shall happen. When, I cannot say, but I believe it will be soon. Do you remember the sacred texts that King Ingeld took from Son-Velline?"

"Of course. The largest scroll was named after a man... Daniel."

"Yes, my lady. In the story of Daniel, a great king had a dream like Ilse's. That dream, like Ilse's, occurred twice in one night. The interpretation was certain, and the events predicted by that dream soon came to pass. Even the content of the dream was similar to Ilse's."

"Yes, I remember." Katla looked out of the window at the sea. A great distance below them, great waves crashed upon the rocky coast. The sea foamed and frothed, casting up sky-high plumes of spray that slowly drifted back down into the surge and ebb of the restless torrent. "We must tell no one."

"Agreed, my lady."

"There may be a conspiracy involving one of our own. Perhaps, if we watch closely, the conspirators will reveal themselves."

"You are right, of course. But, my lady, concerning Ithmar... " Listening to Ivan, Katla perceived the direction of his thoughts.

"He must be told about this," she replied. "I'm aware of that. But he is famous for his over-protection. No one will suspect a thing if he musters the Ten and rides after the King. We all know how he hates this annual, solitary hunt of Vigmar's. He has long feared that the King's life might be threatened someday when he is off alone, hunting in the mountains."

"Yes, of course. And my lady... "

"Yes?"

"Let's gather our little ones close. These things have been shown to us so we might be prepared. Why? God only knows."

"I'll protect my little ones, Ivan," she looked at him closely. "How about you?"

"You are all my little ones," sighed Ivan. "That, my dear, is the joy and the pain of it." He sat down heavily, showing his age. He looked old: older than the stones of the hearth, older even than the thoughts encoded upon the ancient books that lined these dusty walls. This was only illusion; he was a man of seventy-two years, not even as old as the weathered tree on the cliff's edge, a stone's throw beyond the windowsill.

Ancient or not, Ivan Redbeard was filled with an ancient dread. That dread, compelling and powerful, was far older than he, for it was born of an age-old quarrel: an ongoing battle between good and evil... with the angels of eternal life arrayed against the devils of everlasting death.

"I fear, my little one," he slowly added, "that a serpent is loose among the hatchlings." He thoughtfully gazed at Katla, and his heart caught painfully at the sight of the woman he had tutored from the age of seven.

She had come so far and had learned so much. From a bright-eyed child who loved stories and sweets, she had grown into the greatest person he had ever known. But now, this dear woman and her precious family were beset by danger.

"May heaven help us," he said, speaking words that were at once a prayer and a sigh. Would the battle never end?

A Party of Jackals

The Prince's brave horse began to stagger with exhaustion. The pursuit had been long and cruel, and soon it must end. A plan flashed through the mind of the Prince, and he immediately put it to use.

Turning his horse to the left, his eyes searched for suitable terrain with which to try his gambit. His mouth tasted ashen: dry with fear. His lungs burned, and his back ached, but his hands were strong on the reins as he rode, scanning the treacherous terrain ahead.

Suddenly, he saw it: a short canyon with a wide mouth and a steep mountain slope at the end. He turned his pony into the canyon, and his pursuers followed him furiously, uttering a jubilant cry. He raced swiftly past the boulders and began to gallop up the steep slope at the end of the canyon, striving to climb with his horse to the top of the cliff. It was a near-impossible goal under any circumstances, and under these it was hopeless.

The slender stallion thundered up the slope, sloughing off a steady stream of saliva that fluttered behind them like an opaque banner of delicate lace. The horse's great heart fought relentlessly to drive his body forward. His trail-hardened, shining coat was covered with a fine filigree of sparkling froth that shot off in irregular puffs into the cool, clear mountain air. The frothy specks of foam, swirling in the heavy clouds of dust, slowly floated to earth, randomly circling at the mercy of the breeze.

Ahead of his horse, a great rock towered above the steep canyon, dominating the terrain. With its left side snug against a sheer canyon wall, the massive monolith hid the highest reaches of the dead-end slope. The youth and his pony struggled up the steep trail to the right of the great rock, taking the only passage that might lead to the far-off, hopeless canyon rim.

The bandits, all six of them, let out another cruel cry and

spurred their mounts into a frenzied, heady, helter-skelter blood-rush up the steep incline, hard upon the heels of the desperate boy.

They lost sight of him when he rode behind the rock. They did not see as he wheeled his about and began to charge back down the steep slope.

Gunnar-val caught them totally unprepared. Given his youth and his boyish appearance, the power and fury of his charge shocked the bandits into confusion. He rounded the boulder swinging his mace, closing quickly on his targets.

Gunnar greeted the foremost thief with a tremendous blow that shivered the man's brass helm into splinters and spun him backwards off his huge sable horse. His lifeless body smacked hard to the earth and skidded to a halt in a pile of dirt and debris, sprawled among the rocks of the canyon like an uninvited guest in a garden of stones.

The second rider reined his mount tightly to his left, but to no avail. The young warrior chose his mark well, hurling his mace with faultless timing and catching his victim above the stomach. The death-dealing blow ripped through the rider's too-tight shirt of mail, splitting the strong cage of his chest and bursting his heart asunder. The rider tumbled to the ground clutching feebly at the air, losing his breath as he settled onto his back. His horse fled away: eyes wide, saddle flapping loosely.

The Prince rushed past the fallen warrior, stunned by his own actions and shocked by the faces of the men he'd just killed. He had received training in the martial arts since childhood, but it had been only that: training. Now it was real... as real as the stomach-turning expressions on the faces of the vanquished. With his survival at stake, he pushed the faces out of his mind.

A third bandit wheeled about and turned his back to the Prince, fleeing down the slope. As Gunnar swept past, he delivered a disabling blow before veering sharply to his left. Those who could follow him fell in behind.

Gunnar's lungs seared him with each inhalation. He and his father had been trail-weary before the ambush, and now his weariness started to tell. His pony wheezed loudly with horrible rasping sounds that the Prince had never heard before. *He'll die if I don't give him rest,* Gunnar thought. He focused his mind on the problem at hand; there were still three pursuers behind him, and this time they would not be so easily surprised.

Looking ahead, he saw a low ridge running off to his right, an abrupt wrinkle in the valley wall. It gradually turned into a deeper cleft, but just before it became an impassably steep, a large fallen tree blocked access to the low, rounded ridge.

If he could make it over the formidable tree trunk and reach the top of the ridge, he would buy precious time with which to discover a defensive position on high ground. There, his arrows might even the odds. His pony might live also, if he could find a place to make a stand.

Objects appear closer in the mountains… especially if the one doing the looking is accustomed to viewing the landscape at sea level. So it was that Gunnar misjudged the distance to the fallen tree. Because of this, he misjudged the size of the tree, as well.

His pony, striving mightily toward the mark, would have jumped if the Prince had let him. But Gunnar pulled back sharply when he realized that the barrier was impossibly high.

The well-trained pony obeyed his command, using all of his sure-footed talent, scrambling and skidding to an abrupt, bone-jarring stop in a cloud of dust and pebbles. The skill of the pony surprised its rider: so much, in fact, that he couldn't hold on.

Gunnar pitched headlong off his pony, staring in shock at the mammoth gray log that expanded so immediately in his field of vision. His head was brutally, unexpectedly kissed by a distant, slamming sensation that triggered a celestial confluence of exploding lights: a spray of sparks that trailed heavily downward, bent by gravity like falling embers. The lights cascaded toward the earth like stars falling from the heavens. As he passed out, the shining coals were instantly sucked into a lightless abyss.

The Final Blow

King Vigmar lay on his side, burning with death-blows. His universe pulsed, and his vision dimmed as his hearing began to desert him. His head spun wildly, slipping away. Forcing his eyes to focus on the smooth granite surface a few inches in front of his nose, he tried to rise, but to no avail. His broken body, carved like a butcher's yearling, finally failed his iron will. Vigmar could not see the approach of his childhood friend.

Like a walrus climbing onto a steep floe, the rotund and fastidious Lord Haruk Longknife waddled up the dangerous slope and struggled onto the wide granite ledge. What Haruk saw stunned him. Around the King lay five strong men, dead or dying. The eyes of the dead seemed flat, while the living flickered with a waning spark.

The dying warriors moaned softly, their eyes slowly wandering or fixed in shock: wondering perhaps, like Vigmar himself, what would become of them as their broken lives drained into the ground. Off to the side, three men less grievously wounded panted and stared at the result of their fight. They did not look like victors.

King Vigmar's sworn protector – Haruk Longknife, the Dragon of Kuzbi – slowly stepped over the fallen warriors and pushed past bloody survivors, creeping softly to the side of King Vigmar of Bryne. The fallen King, his eyes fixed in their sockets, saw the tip of Haruk's boot as he stepped into the dark crimson puddle on the granite by his face.

A feeling of hope, a dull pulse of life, stirred deep within the King as he recognized the distinctive black boot. He smiled somehow, the thick-caked blood cracking on his battered face as he struggled with new hope, trying to raise his head. His universe swirled, turning purple and gold as a cloud of light surrounded him. A sensation of overpowering nausea overwhelmed him. He had lost too much blood, and his body had begun to shut down.

"My brother," Vigmar whispered, his eyes rolling in search of the boot's owner. For a moment, wild hopes of deliverance raced through his mind. *I am dead,* thought King Vigmar, *yet my brother has come to save my son's life.* The great King, finding renewed strength, reached deep within. Focusing his willpower, he managed to roll from his side onto his back, the better to see his dear half-brother.

Lord Haruk, staring down at the King, was shocked to see that he still breathed. When the body moved, it appalled him.

Vigmar's body was scored with deep, mortal gashes. He lay in a dark pool of viscous blood – and yet, somehow, he had managed to roll onto his back. A shining light danced in his eyes. Bathed in blood, preparing to die, King Vigmar gazed up at the towering form of Lord Haruk and smiled dreamily, shutting his eyes.

"My brother. My dear one," Vigmar whispered. Abruptly he jerked, and his eyes rolled heavenward. "King of heaven, receive me!" he sighed. And then, with a shiver, King Vigmar breathed his last.

His final breath passed gently, a soft suspiration sent up with prayer that sailed beyond thought toward the heavens: far past the face of the sky. Vigmar felt the warm touch of an invisible hand on his forehead, and there, on a barren hillside, the greatest of the sea-kings quietly passed away.

Haruk felt stunned: overwhelmed and appalled at the sight of this specter of a man, with his pale body drained of blood, whispering a prayer. He did not to react until it was too late. He found himself staring at the empty husk of a man whose spirit had found freedom from pain.

Haruk paused, realizing what had just happened. Slowly, the distinctive boot that had caused Vigmar such joy swung back, and with all of the force he could muster, the King's dear half-brother began to kick Vigmar's blanched face with those beloved, familiar boot-tips. Haruk kicked the King's body again and again, almost weeping with frustration and unfulfilled rage.

"Filthy hero!" Haruk howled. "Mighty Vigmar!" he shrieked.

"Will you cheat me of my joy? I'll eat your son's heart, you pompous hypocrite! I'll kill him! Do you hear me?" He continued to kick the face hypnotically, rhythmically.

"What, can't you speak?" he taunted madly. "Has your spirit fled in fear? Coward! Fool! Idiot! I'll destroy your child, you bag of bones!" But to Haruk's dismay, the remains of King Vigmar could neither feel his blows, nor hear his insults, nor sense a single, solitary thing.

The King had been set free.

Dragon's Gold

"Just look up there," Lendle blurted, wiping the back of his filthy hand across his tangled beard. "Look at them! They're the high and the mighty. You wouldn't know that either one of them ever had to touch the earth."

"Shut up," hissed Nevin. "You know the Captain hates your whinin'. Besides," he added, rolling his eyes expressively toward the other men, "the rocks have ears."

Nevin motioned in the direction of a quiet group of warriors who sat by themselves on a broad, flat boulder at the foot of the slope. These men, subdued and circumspect, had not joined in the riotous celebration after the death of King Vigmar, although they had been involved in the fiercest fighting. They had ridden with Captain Rurik since his earliest years as a soldier, before he became a mercenary. They did not revel in the ways of war.

"Nevin, you have a big mouth," spoke a third man who lolled with seeming indifference on the grassy floor of the meadow. "The Captain knows what he's doing." Most of the men had gathered in a cluster with Nevin and company, reclining in the shadow of a great tree that towered above the stony valley floor. The broad patch of shade provided a welcome break from the morning's heated chase.

The new speaker was a tall young man named Kirioff with slicked-back, dirty blond hair and a hard-bitten countenance that offered no evidence of his age. In spite of his youth, he had attained the lieutenancy of this surly pack of misfits, malcontents, and skilled soldiers gone mercenary, and he hoped to have the Captain's job some day. He gazed around with a sneer.

A temporary snowmelt, caused by the warmth of an early spring, had generously watered the high mountain valley. The riotous rainbow of delicate wildflowers carpeting the meadows danced lightly in the cold east wind, evoking a giddy ripple of color that rolled across the valley. Each delicate blossom danced joyfully in its place, competing for the eye's attention.

A heavy forest covered the southernmost reaches of the deep green valley, which stretched north and south through the jagged mountains. In contrast to the forest, a series of broad meadows covered the valley's wide northern slopes.

The rich land provided a vivid counterpoint to the deep blue sky, leading the eye through a diverse concerto of light and color, an ornate sonata of the senses. The lieutenant looked north, letting his vision travel high above the rocky peaks.

He dreaded what he saw.

A distant black smudge slowly advanced toward them, steadily encroaching on their pleasant afternoon. Soon the cool breeze would turn bitterly cold, and the false spring would show its true colors. *It's snow, or sleet, or both,* he thought. *Before long, we'll taste the worst of it.*

Lieutenant Kirioff let his eyes drift away from the clouds. After looking intently at the broad valley's southern reaches, he gazed up the eastern slope to a solitary rock where two men stood in close conversation. Captain Rurik was speaking with a tall, heavy man dressed in rich leather garments. *What are they doing,* he thought impatiently, *planning the pillage of Rome?*

If the lieutenant had heard the men's conversation, he would have known that his captain's mind was not set on grand future plans. Captain Rurik was in the process of completing a business transaction with the ignoble Haruk of Kuzbi. In short, he was trying to collect the balance of payment from the penurious Haruk, a hard task, indeed... not unlike trying to draw blood from an armored leech with a dull pin.

The captain regretted his decision to take this job, which he had stumbled across in Stockholm harbor. He had added additional men to his troop at the behest of Haruk, and it had seemed like a good choice at the time. The down payment for his services in this bloody affair had been a small fortune. His reputation, he decided with a bitter frown, did count for something – for gold, if nothing else.

Now that the action was over, he had only regrets. He had lost several of his men, including some of his best soldiers and most familiar companions. The whole business had been one sorry mistake. Any one of his dead men was worth a thousand villains like the rogue who stood before him.

"I told you that I wanted them both," Haruk's deep voice softly purred, bringing the Captain back to the business at hand. Rurik scowled at him, angrily twirling his moustache.

To gaze at the two men who stood on the flat, rocky ledge was to observe a study in contrasts. The tall, lean figure of Rurik – with his brilliant red hair and long moustache, cloaked in the robe of a simple traveling man – stood juxtaposed against the rotund yet delicately constituted Haruk. Against Rurik's lean visage Lord Haruk loomed ponderously, like an obese buzzard: weighty and powerful, clad in crow-wing black, clean-shaven, richly dressed, and trimmed with shining gold. Having overdressed for this deadly occasion, Haruk resembled nothing so much as an evil demigod fresh from the underworld, ensconced in a sepulchral shroud of satins and supple leathers.

Haruk spun his argument with apparent sincerity, as if he offered the very model of moral persuasion. His long, pale fingers moved stiffly, like ivory stilettos, as he implored Captain Rurik in the name of plain, honest dealing.

"You remember the proposition that we made in Stockholm," Haruk continued. He looked to all appearances like a man deeply wounded at their misunderstanding. "We made a bargain for the death of the King and the Prince." He gazed steadily at the Captain as he spoke. "That is what you agreed to," he added, licking his lips.

Haruk's dark, beady eyes measured Rurik with the cunning of a serpent sizing up a hawk. He had made a mistake, and he knew it; he was overplaying his hand, and the Captain did not accept his ruse. Their deal had involved the death of King Vigmar only. The presence of the Prince, an unforeseen companion to the famously solitary hunter, had surprised them.

"You lie," said Rurik, looking straight into his eyes. "And you know you lie." He spit on the turf, despising Haruk with all of his heart. "Now," he stated bluntly, "you will pay me. You'll pay us the remainder of our fee, or I'll kill you, free of charge." He smiled coldly. "Have you forgotten why you hired me? Have you forgotten of your need for secrecy? That is why you are here, alone among us."

Lord Haruk snarled at Rurik, his face swelling, contorting and turning purple as it twisted into the countenance of an angry gargoyle. His expression offered a bizarre caricature of his inner being, almost too bad to be true.

"The gold is on the beast," Haruk hissed, "as if you didn't know. Curse you, Rurik, for defying me." Captain Rurik smiled dourly at this display.

"If I am cursed, and justly so, it will be for serving your purpose in this sordid venture. It will certainly not be for defying you, Lord Haruk, worm among men. May we never meet again."

"Well said!" rejoined Haruk, beginning to regain his composure. "For if we meet again, I will drape your bowels around your ears and feed your carcass to my dogs."

"On second thought," suggested Rurik reflectively, "I think I'll kill you anyway." He reached for his sword.

Losing the veneer of bravery, Lord Haruk bolted to his horse and leaped upon it. With the powerful gelding groaning mightily beneath his ponderous bulk, Lord Haruk galloped off heavily toward the south.

On the valley floor below Rurik, the men began to stir as the Captain checked the bags lashed to the mule. They were stuffed with the agreed-upon pay: gold from Haruk the Cruel, the famously depraved Dragon of Kuzbi. Picking out a coin at random, he bit it and nodded approvingly at the golden center revealed by his bite.

"Let him go," he called to his men. "We have our pay." At this, Lieutenant Kirioff stood and stretched.

"We were due for some good news," Kirioff said. The Captain rode down to them on his black stallion, leading the mule by the halter.

"Bury our fallen men under those rocks," Rurik said to Kirioff. "We have to leave right away. We'll travel all night." He nodded at the distant storm clouds. "That snow should cover our tracks."

Kirioff turned and clapped his hands. "You heard the Captain. Get to it, and bury our fallen," he barked. "We don't want to be taking a nap when the royal bodyguards come looking for their king. There's no money in that." Some of the men laughed as they scrambled to their feet.

"What about this dead king?" Kirioff asked the Captain, who lingered beside him. "Should we bury him, or leave his body for the wolves?"

"This dead king, as you call him, was King Vigmar the Great," said Rurik, biting off his words. His blue eyes flashed brilliantly as he stared fiercely, strangely, at Kirioff. "Bury him with full armor, as if we he were one of our own. Do it quickly! We must go."

"You, men," Kirioff said, pointing at Lendle and his companions. "You've just volunteered for the burial detail. Let's get this over with." They rose to their feet and began to struggle up the steep incline behind Kirioff, approaching the bloody site of Vigmar's last stand.

"Was he really a King?" Lendle asked Kirioff as they trudged up the slope.

"He fought like a king," Lieutenant Kirioff replied.

The wind increased, sending a chill message of bad weather ahead.

The Sound of the Trumpet

Ilse sat in front of an intensely interested audience. Before her, arrayed in a tight semi-circle, sat her mother, her father, and her teacher, Ivan Redbeard.

"... and that's all I remember," she finished, seeing the same stunned look on her father's face that she had previously observed on the face of Ivan and her mother. There was a long silence as Ithmar considered her words.

"You were right," he said, nodding first at Katla, and then at Ivan. "The king must be in danger. This dream seems to be a sign from the heavens. And since you both agree with this conclusion, the danger must be real." He tried to conceal it, but inside he was in turmoil, for his lord, his liege, was in danger, according to all signs, interpreted by the two wisest souls in Bryne. This was too awful for words, and yet it had to be dealt with immediately.

"What will you do?" asked Katla.

"I must gather the Ten and go after my king," Ithmar said, deeply distracted. He stood up abruptly, pushing his chair backward so quickly that it tilted precariously on its rear legs, almost balancing on its fulcrum before falling back and hitting the floor with a sharp clatter.

Katla was not startled. She knew him too well. Ithmar's heart was entwined with the life of his king... like a strong, flowering vine might grace an ancient oak, embellishing the beauty of the tree without preying on its robust health.

"Ithmar," she said evenly, hiding a sudden, sharp fear that pierced her like a knife. "Be careful. We don't know what we're dealing with."

Ithmar bent over and took her face in his hands. He stood tall: large but well proportioned, with wind-burned skin and hair as dark as a raven's wing. Due to the implacably advancing years, his hair showed vivid streaks of white. His sea-green eyes sparkled mischievously as he studied her face. For a moment, he forgot the ominous portents of woe.

"If I had known you better when I was a lad, I'd have married you sooner."

"If I'd agreed," she rejoined, smiling as he kissed her lightly on the lips. Ithmar straightened up and stepped over to Ilse. Kneeling, he hugged her tightly.

"Listen to your mother and Ivan," he warned, "and keep me in your prayers, little one." Ilse hugged him back intensely, as if to prevent his leaving by force, if only she could. Tears welled in her eyes.

"Be careful, Daddy," she said, laying her head on his shoulder. He squeezed her and straightened. His expression changed, and he looked tense, preoccupied. Bowing to the two most important people in his life, he gestured to Ivan Redbeard, and together they left the room.

Ilse watched as the two tall men walked out through the dark, ornately carved doorway. She heaved a great sigh.

"This is all wrong, mother," she said, turning to Katla. "We should be preparing for the Feast of Spring, but here we are with all of this trouble."

"At least we're prepared for trouble, when it comes," answered her mother. She reached over and caressed her daughter's shoulder. "Come now," she added. "Let's get back to our work."

Blood Sport

Rurik's men strapped saddles onto their ponies as their companions returned from the burial ridge. Despite the promise of gold in the offing, their mood turned grim as they considered the coming weather. One man, however, still seemed determined to enjoy some bad, old-fashioned fun.

Gilfast – a small young man with a face grown sour and pinched by a lifetime of petty cruelty – hid behind the great tree in the middle of the valley floor. On the other side of the tree, the young prince struggled desperately to free himself from his leather bonds. Gilfast slowly crept up behind him, armed with a hard stick. He cursed when he broke a twig, and Prince Gunnar turned toward the sound.

"You're a prince, are you?" Gilfast whispered unevenly. "You look pretty common to me."

The envious Gilfast believed that he had ample reason to hate the young noble… for Gunnar was the son of a famous king, and Gilfast was not. He did not care that King Vigmar had grown more generous and kind with each passing year, or that he had been loved. None of this mattered to Gilfast the self-righteous. Envy rested like a hot coal in his bosom, burning him up inside.

Envy fuels the pious outrage of the cruel. Envy offers its own bitter logic, spinning a garment of justification from the flimsiest of excuses. In the hands of a practiced hypocrite, envy can weave a priest's robes from the hair of a gnat.

Gilfast knew envy firsthand; he lived it. As he drew closer to the boy, he carried his stick loosely, hefting it as he sized him up. Prince Gunnar's eye looked badly swollen. The side of his head still throbbed from the great rock that had broken his helm; the rock could have easily killed him if the heavy bronze helm had not held up stoutly to the force of his fall. With a start, Gunnar saw Gilfast draw back his weapon.

He managed to duck just in time.

Gilfast swung his stick with gusto, striking a glancing blow against the crown of Gunnar's head.

"Here's a gift, prince of fools," he hissed.

Gunnar's cry of pain roused the attention of the other warriors. Dropping his weapon, Gilfast feigned innocence and sauntered back to his ignoble friends.

"What say you, Gilfast? How is the brat?" Kirioff asked as Gilfast began to help them saddle the horses.

"Sleeping like a baby," he replied.

They laughed, kindred spirits at ease together. Incongruously, their tongues lolled out as they smiled, like a matched pair of well-nourished wolves enjoying a kill.

It had been a good day for hunting. Kirioff and Gilfast felt content to share these wild mountains together, at least while the trail burgeoned with prey and blood: rich with gold and slaves, choked with murderous passion... and paved with the brick-hard souls of the damned.

The Ice of an Early Spring

The men drove their ponies relentlessly, traveling all night through the strong bones of the harsh, broken mountains. They rode past jagged peaks and across smooth plates of granite as ancient as earth itself. The raiding party persevered throughout the following day, a day grown bitterly cold, brittle, and colorless beneath dark clouds that scudded silently overhead.

The clouds poured their diaphanous essences across dips in the ridges: foggy waterfalls cascading over each high mountain pass. Like Valkyries pregnant with pent-up woe, the low-flying clouds crept ominously before the edge of a freezing wind.

The horsemen persisted in the face of the coming storm, fighting off sleep to ride beneath the hard-hammered sky past twilight of the second day. By now, the men had left exhaustion behind and had slipped into that particularly unreal, dreamlike state common to those suffering severe sleep deprivation.

The men grew unnaturally quiet, numb in their saddles, swaying and twitching as they fell asleep and awoke again, struggling along the perilous mountain trail. The ponies were near collapse, yet somehow they plodded ahead, one hoof in front of the other, traveling more on will than on skill. Some of the men carried covered lanterns that they unveiled sparingly in the hostile wilderness. The ponies ignored the light. They seemed almost clairvoyant, finding their foothold on the winding, narrow trail by sheer instinct.

Sometime shortly after dark, the young prince fell asleep and had a brief but vivid dream. In his dream, he was once again in his father's house at Falcon Rock, snug in the King's library as he lay on his side facing a fire in the old stone hearth.

His mother sat beside the fire. When he looked up and saw her, his heart leaped within him. She had died more than eight years ago, perishing unexpectedly after a short bout with pneumonia.

Now, in his dream, his mother smiled sweetly at him. As he basked in the smile, he experienced a powerful sensation of peace. He felt loved in her presence, and he wondered if she knew about the things that had happened since her absence.

"I love you, mother," he tried to say, but could not. He rose to his knees. "Help us, mother." He forced the words out. "We need you." His chest felt tightly compressed, and he could not breathe. Suddenly, it seemed unbearably hot in the family library.

"Mama," he began again, and he started to cry. She continued to smile, as if she understood and knew that all would be well. Once again he felt the overwhelming love, wave upon wave of it. He had so much to tell her. He had mastered Latin since they last saw one another. She had always wanted him to learn to read, and during the past years he had learned the strange language with its mysterious symbols.

Something else had happened recently. He had fallen in love with Ilse, the daughter of Ithmar: a mysterious and whimsical girl, but one worth pursuing. Yet he, Prince Gunnar-val, who had beaten grown warriors in royal games of battle, had found himself tongue-tied when he tried to tell Ilse the truth. Even now he could not speak, although he tried with all of his heart. His mother smiled at him again, wisely, lovingly, and he finally understood.

She knows. She already knows what I'm trying to tell her, he realized. He exhaled sharply, finding great comfort in the knowledge. His head fell forward as the relief flooded through him, leaving him awash in sweet peace, filled with forgetfulness.

The movement of his head falling forward awakened him. He found himself traveling through the dark on horseback, tied to a saddle. He hung his head low and shivered in the frigid mountain wind.

The wind sliced sharply through his cloak, and his hands felt like unfamiliar pieces of wood at the ends of his arms. As he worked some slack into the leather thongs, his fingers began to burn like coals of fire, throbbing under the pinprick assaults of a thousand tiny needles.

A synaptic echo of recent events returned to him in a single, fluid rush of remembrance. They had murdered his father. He could not comprehend it, but he knew it had happened.

Less than ten days ago, when his father had asked him to accompany him during his annual hunt in the mountains, Prince Gunnar had been euphoric. He had managed to keep the news quiet at his father's request, and two days later they had left their small city unannounced in the hours before dawn.

Anticipating the hunt with joy, the grizzled, aging king had led his only heir into the mountains of the wilderness. The Prince had been the apple of King Vigmar's eye. It had sometimes hurt him just to look at the boy.

Now, Gunnar felt the pain of the bitter truth. He would never again see his father... not in this life, on this green earth.

To the ravens in the trees overhead, Prince Gunnar offered the perfect picture of misery. He shivered in the blast, his hands lashed tightly to the saddle where he sat, wrapped in fur so he would not freeze fast to the leather. Trapped in the midst of such suffering, Prince Gunnar abandoned all hope.

Lightning flashed, trapping the mountain in a brilliant blast of light. In that moment, a picture of the travelers was seared into Gunnar's memory. At the front of their group, a tight cluster of shivering ponies threaded their way between two great boulders, leading the way to yet another high mountain pass. In this group rode the men that Gunnar had come to think of as the Veterans. They showed an easy familiarity with one another and with their captain.

Behind the Veterans rode the other warriors, those who obviously lacked the seniority of the former group. These men were unruly, prone to complain, and poor horsemen – with the exception of their lieutenant, the man named Kirioff. Gunnar could see that they were hired men, an unstable crew without the stamina and professionalism of the Veterans.

He had deduced most of this from the actions of the men, without much help from their words. Although many of the men were Battle Scylfings, most spoke with an accent unfamiliar to Gunnar. He had a gift with languages, and for hours he had strained to hear their words, which seemed vaguely familiar to him. He had, by now, become familiar with their accent, and he was beginning to understand their speech. Their language was closely akin to the tongue of Bryne, his small city-state.

Prince Gunnar's head throbbed viciously, and his left eye was badly swollen. *I hope it's still in one piece,* he thought. He had heard the recent hasty return of a scout and subsequent chuckles among the Veterans, and so correctly guessed that they were preparing to encamp.

After a few more minutes, they arrived at the narrow mouth of a cave. Gunnar heard the scout loudly inform the group that they had reached a large cavern with a sand floor and two entryways. In his dazed state he heard an order, and then the sounds of ponies groaning as their passengers dismounted.

As he sat alone on his longhaired pony, the snow and ice swirled around him. Gunnar watched dreamily as the men in the party pulled off the saddles and hobbled their ponies in a sheltered nook beside the narrow entrance of the cave. Facing the storm, the ponies bowed their frosted heads against the bitter blasts of frigid weather that tried to invade their stony shelter. They crowded close together, warming themselves in spite of the blinding snow, the merciless wind, and the hard pieces of sleet that stacked pearl-like strings of pestilential ice atop their manes, foreheads and hooves.

The flakes of snow, whirling around the Prince, seemed almost luminous to him. They danced like sparks ascending from a fire: lulling him, leading him into a strangely disjointed state of mind.

Gunnar's jaw ached from its compulsive twitching. His teeth were numb from chattering and his body sore from shivering, and yet even these painful points of contact with his surroundings were beginning to grow distant and dim. Would these bandits leave him outside in this miserable, frigid blast... in this faraway frozen cluster of dancing lights that flickered and swooned so mysteriously before him? He began to become drowsy once again, but this time from unanticipated warmth that began to wrap him securely in its thrall.

As if from a distance, the Prince realized that he was not alone. An old man was speaking to him, standing beside his horse and tugging on his leg.

"Come on, son," the man said in the Scylfing tongue. "Let's get you out of this weather."

"Leave me alone," murmured the Prince. He liked the way he felt: he was growing suddenly comfortable, and did not see why he should be disturbed at this particular time. The Prince did not perceive it when the old man pulled him from his pony and carried him inside, to the sand beside a huge fire that was surrounded by men who were already asleep. Their mouths were open, and they sprawled carelessly, like dead men scattered across the cave floor.

Gunnar awoke for a few moments and saw the sleeping men. He did not know why, but the sight seemed comical to him. The old man loosened the rawhide thongs that had bound the hands of the Prince and put his own cloak underneath his head.

"Thank you, sir," Prince Gunnar softly whispered to the old man, who had, by now, walked away.

He felt the pain in his hands as the full surge of blood began to return. "Thank you, sir," he whispered, and rolling over, he fell asleep.

The Cockatrice

Kennan, son of Haruk, had gone on the prowl. He left his father's castle and rode into Bryne looking for trouble, and he harbored an unwholesome hope that he would discover it soon. Trouble tended to be in scarce supply in Bryne, however, and this evening was proving to be no exception.

Kennan would have to search diligently to find trouble tonight; there were no festivals in the offing, the mead hall was empty, and the town lay quiet and still. Few windows showed light, although it was only an hour after sunset.

Fisher-folk! These primitive walrus-mongers are asleep already, I'll wager... dreaming about pricking the long-tusked blubber-bellies on the bounding main. The very thought embittered him.

Kennan loathed all fisher-folk, from all backgrounds and locales. He hated their prey as well: the seals and fish and otters, free creatures all. The freedom of such creatures stood as an open offense to Kennan, who wished to dominate and enslave all beings to his perverse and unrelenting will.

Walruses disgusted Kennan. He despised their ponderous grace in the water, their insouciant indolence, and perhaps most of all, their value as a tool for peace through trade in their ivory tusks.

Near the top of Kennan's hate-list swam the behemoths of the deep: the mighty, freeborn whales. Kennan hated their brine, their fins, the very spiracles of their splendor... their quivering bulk and blubber, their bloated look and slimy feel, their whistling sounds and unseemly reek.

Whales, however, could not claim top spot in Kennan's hate-list. Above even whales, he hated the peace-loving citizens of Bryne. Kennan despised all who had forsaken the misanthropic, predatory ways of their ancestors in favor of peaceful lives as fishers, whalers, and traders in ivory and amber.

Kennan bitterly loathed the ancient, egalitarian ways of King

Vigmar and the free men of Bryne. If he could, Kennan would enslave them all. But the rulers of the city, immured as they were in the throes of such pious pretentiousness, still clung to the ancient ways and treated all free citizens as equals.

Although some slaves lived in Bryne, the council had forbidden the taking or purchase of new slaves. By Vigmar's express edict, all babies born in Bryne inherited their freedom with their first breath. And to make things even more unbearable for Kennan, every freeman had a vote in the great Council of Bryne.

King Vigmar had ascended to the throne after a surprise vote of the Council, a vote that had rejected Kennan's father, Lord Haruk. After his election, Vigmar had sought to serve his people through the brotherhood of warriors, the practice of peace, the work of prosperity, and what has been called, in other cultures, noblesse oblige.

Kennan despised noblesse oblige. Along with it, he uniformly despised the chief men of Bryne, along with their noble ways.

We should be sailing for the prey in Francia, he mused, *but instead these idiots are out chasing fish, or sharpening their harpoons among the floes.*

Kennan was repulsed by the change that had occurred in Bryne since his youth. The men had not raided the southern coasts in years. They had become traders and merchants who earned their gold through trade in mundane products such as fine oil, ivory, spermaceti, furs, and amber.

Although their war-waging ways had changed, King Vigmar had preserved other aspects of their traditional culture. This approach had given Kennan little pleasure.

"Vigmar kept the foul, and threw away the sweet," Kennan muttered under his breath. "He kept his false show of honor, his stultifying strut and prance of so-called grace – generosity to fatherless brats, squalling infants and their filthy dams – yet he abandoned the glory: the blood and the gold."

Lord Kennan hissed sharply, abhorring the very thought of what had happened to his once-great city. He looked up into the cloudy night sky. In spite of his phenomenal night vision, he could not see the subtle movement of the snowflakes scudding softly to earth. *This night is deliciously dark,* he reflected.

The storm had settled in to stay, and only the hardiest travelers roamed abroad. The night was dark, freezing and foreboding. Kennan was angered by the storm, and by the thought of the changes that had occurred in his kingdom. *We should be peeling the shoulders of men, not stripping miserable rolls of blubber from some freakish fish,* he thought. *Gold isn't found in the sea, but with men: in piles heaped high for the taking. It's hidden under genteel Frankish floors, not in the tusks of filthy walruses.*

Kennan loved gold.

Brimming with evil thoughts, Kennan fancied that he had the streets to himself. But as he rode and reflected on the object of his desire, a loud sneeze jolted him from his reverie.

"Good evening, Lord Kennan," a strong voice said. "How is the King's nephew on this lovely snowy eve?" Dothan, a watchman, was the speaker. He stepped out of a doorway and walked up to Kennan's horse, unveiling his lantern to let it shine upon the ground. "It's bitter cold tonight, eh?"

"Right," said Lord Kennan, and he shook the reins, causing his horse to jump into a trot that he maintained until he rounded the next corner. *What kind of fool would volunteer for his job?* Kennan wondered. All of the city's watchmen were volunteers who took turns serving the citizens of the city as they walked their appointed rounds. Sneering derisively, Kennan looked above the narrow, tightly packed houses with their tall, pitched roofs, letting his gaze wander up to the top of Falcon Rock, where he beheld the darkened silhouette of King Vigmar's house.

What a fool Vigmar is, he reflected. *He's too fine and noble to invest in a castle. He'd rather feed the pathetic widows and orphans.* Kennan's father Haruk, who mocked the poverty of widows and orphans, had built a castle in the southern European tradition.

Kennan did not care that Vigmar had made a tenuous peace with the mighty King Harold of Norway, or that no number of castles would have protected them from King Harold if the peace had not been negotiated. Because of Bryne's close blood ties with certain Scylfing princes from the nation that would one day be called Sweden, King Harold had allowed their tiny kingdom to remain independent as a suzerainty, a sister state in alliance with Norway. Each year, Bryne's King Vigmar gave a token gift in return for the "protection" of this famous king, who was in the process of welding together the Norwegian nation from a collection of isolated warrior kingdoms.

Kennan's eyes settled on a large dwelling situated just below the king's home. This second house overlooked the only road that led to the top of Falcon Rock. *Hmmm... he thought. Oh, my... isn't the noble Lord Ithmar roaming far afield in his search for our wayward King? The poor, pathetic King... there's no telling what may have befallen him, or his arrogant, blue-blooded brat.*

As the moon emerged from a break between the clouds to cast faint light on the stony landscape, he nudged his horse into a canter up the steep road that led out of town. He stood in the stirrups as he rode, grinning fiercely into the darkness.

"Didn't Auntie say that dear Lady Katla would be visiting tonight? I suppose they've come together for prayers, since they're both such pious old dames. Well, here's the answer to their prayers."

Leaving the town behind, he spurred his horse to a run. Kennan possessed wonderful talent as a horseman. He seemed almost joined, as it were, to the hooves and shaggy legs of the beast on which he traveled.

"It's pleasant night for villainy," he informed himself sociably, "with peace at home and abroad. And who would bother to guard their home in a land such as this, where the hearty fisher-folk dwell in security, abiding in the ancient bond of filial devotion?

"They love tradition?" He laughed. "Well, here's one. A single man who forces his will on an unmarried girl may marry her if he wishes. And if he asks for her hand in marriage, the penalty for rape does not apply!" He laughed again with a harsh, abrupt explosion of air that sounded more like a strangled cry of triumph.

"Ithmar's gone off to hunt corpses in the mountains, King Vigmar is dead, and Lady Katla's visiting my own, dear Auntie

Innocence. They've left the fox here with the chicken," he hissed, licking his lips. "Or, should I say, with the cute little chick? The beautiful little chick." The moon slid behind a cloud, and he slowed his horse to a walk. Even a horseman of his caliber could not gallop safely on such a dark night.

"Oh, Ilse, Ilse," Kennan whispered slowly. "You are in for the experience of a lifetime." Kennan was only twenty-three years old, but he was already wealthy. With his rich inheritance added to the dowry of such a wealthy bride, he would rival his father in gold, lands, and the riches of Bryne.

The icy night cloaked him as he warily rode toward the house of his prey. *No servants keep this noble house,* he reflected wryly. *Ithmar is too refined to clutter his household with slaves. If he had his way, all of our slaves would be freed.*

Things were finally going Lord Kennan's way. He felt strong and invincible. Kennan's magic was strongest in the absence of light, after all... and hadn't Morthric, the wizard, taught him well?

Of all times, Kennan most loved the night. He thought once again of Ilse, the little girl alone in the house up the road. Throwing back his head, Lord Kennan bared his clean white teeth and howled at the hidden moon.

Axes

A hand on his shoulder shook Gunnar awake. He looked up to see the dark shape of the kindly old man gazing down at him in the dim light of the smoky cavern. The Prince did not know it, but he had slept for several hours in the same position, motionless under the heavy bearskin cover. He felt stiff and sore and ravenously hungry.

"Come, boy, let's get you out of here," the old man whispered hoarsely. "Some of these fellows would love to cook you for dinner." He nodded at the slumbering men sprawled out beside the fire like logs scattered abroad after a curling contest. The fire had burned down to smoking coals that offered heat but little light inside the dark cavern.

Gunnar stumbled raggedly to his feet and followed the old man to the back wall of the cave, sitting where he was directed. The memories flooded back, including the sickening memory of his father's death. He had tried many times to push the images away, but they inevitably returned with relentless persistence.

"I'm Val," the frail old man wheezed as he began to retie the leather thongs around Gunnar's hands, not so tightly as before. He nodded at a separate group of sleeping men on the right side of the fire. "Those men are my friends. You don't have to worry about us. We don't begrudge the fact that you killed in your own defense. It was a battle, and you fought well. But those other fellows," he motioned at the other group, to the left of the smoking coals. "They'd love to throw you into the fire." He put a hand on the boy's shoulder and looked him in the eye. "Stay away from them."

The old man turned away and limped over to the fire, sitting down heavily. He dragged a knotted branch from the pile beside him and threw it onto the coals, waking up two of the men, who began to rouse the rest of their band.

Soon, all of the men were awake, sitting or standing around the well-fed fire. A sentry came in with fresh meat that they cut into pieces to roast over the fire on long green spits. They began to speak animatedly as they waited greedily for the meat to cook. When the meat had been thoroughly charred, they shared a noisy dinner, scarcely noticing when the old man sauntered to the back of the cave and slipped Gunnar a well-cooked piece of haunch.

It tasted marvelous: rich and satisfying, almost creamy in texture, more like spiced candy than meat. The Prince chewed slowly, unnoticed by the men as they finished their dinner and began to generously share the potato whiskey they had carried with them from Stockholm.

Captain Rurik sat against the cave wall across the room, far from the warm red fire and opposite the Prince, who was still intensely focused on his food. The men had hung bearskins across the cave's two narrow entrances, creating a haven safe from the bitter cold outside. The volume of their talk, which increased exponentially in direct proportion to the amount of liquor consumed, soon mounted to hitherto unattainable heights. The men on the left side of the fire jeered and jested raucously, filled with noisy hilarity. On the opposite side sat the Veterans, staring soberly, reflectively into the flames. They said little, occasionally glancing up at the giddy antics of their cohorts.

After a while, the tenor of the conversation changed. Those men most soaked in whiskey, who had once been animated and gleeful, now began to cast dour glances in the Prince's direction and murmur softly among themselves. Fortuitously, Gunnar had managed to decipher their dialect, which differed from his own tongue only by inflection. He took careful note of the change in tone, and began to listen closely. The man they called Belaf, a huge, broad shouldered, balding warrior with a pale, shiny face and a filthy red beard, raised his voice above the others.

"We lost two good men to that boy," grunted Belaf. "And Arren is wounded." The big man looked around the fire expectantly, expecting some backing from his comrades. While the men on the left side of the fire stirred angrily in support of his words, those on the other side sat without moving, watching him without expression.

"Two of our best friends, dead," mourned a short, ferret-faced comrade of medium build, "not to mention Rurik's man... dead as dirt. And there sits the murderer." The speaker was Gilfast the Swift-Handed, the same Gilfast who had so recently struck a painful blow to Gunnar's head in the name of good, clean fun. A changeable man of quicksilver backbone and mercurial moral fiber, Gilfast possessed the political instincts of a weathervane. Noting the mood of his companions and the source of their ire, he shook his head somberly. "There sits the princely brat that killed our comrades," he said, mournfully shaking his head.

Some of the Veterans looked at one another uneasily as the drunken giant, Belaf, suddenly staggered to his feet. The few who had been sipping mead set the bowls quietly on the ground. Lieutenant Kirioff, who sat in the middle between the two groups, now joined the general conversation.

"Aye," Kirioff interjected, nodding in Gunnar's direction. "There sits the killer." He cocked an eye at Belaf.

"We made a deal once," answered Belaf, looking around at the men on his side of the fire. "Blood for blood, and death to any man who dares to strike our mates."

Prince Gunnar, seeing Belaf rise, sat up and glanced swiftly across at Captain Rurik. The Captain sat as if he were asleep, his face buried in his cloak. Through the hooded slits of his eyelids, Rurik's eyes flashed with a sharp glint of light as he watched the trouble developing.

Hanging from poles that leaned against the walls, four whale-oil lamps illuminated the wide hall of the sandy-floored cavern, casting light to its farthest reaches. The room was huge, much wider on the eastern side than on their end. The smoke of the fire meandered upward, escaping through a gap in the high ceiling. Through the narrow fissure, a fine, frozen powder softly sifted down into their midst.

"We made a deal, all right," echoed Gilfast the Swift-Handed. "Before we joined this crew, we ran together as brothers." He gestured disdainfully at Rurik's men on the other side of the fire. "You men wouldn't know about that, but not all of us here fought for King Rus, with or without Captain Rurik," he continued. "We were the scum of the city, you see. We were the harbor rats of Stockholm, doing dirty business in the filthiest part of town. But we had a deal. You boys remember it! We all swore an oath, and we all stood fast to the vow."

"I remember the oath. Blood for blood," said Belaf, turning swiftly toward Gunnar and pointing directly at him. "And death to all who dare strike our mates."

"Right!" shouted a voice. "Death to all who dare!" This time the speaker was Lendle, the unwilling gravedigger for King Vigmar the Great. Lendle, an accomplished opportunist, was always quick to spear a wounded trout.

"You're right, men," Belaf replied, almost yelling. "Though we've joined with Rurik, our vow still stands. It stood when we were hunting Slavs to feed our Scylfing rats, and it still stands to this day!"

"If a vow is to stand, a man must give it legs," said Lt. Kirioff, cutting his eyes at Prince Gunnar, who by now had huddled back against the wall, shivering in a bitter breeze that had tossed aside the bearskin at the cave's entrance. At this, Gilfast raised his voice sharply.

"We should have skinned and filleted that royal runt instead of this deer," Gilfast suggested. He stood and flung a well-gnawed bone in the direction of Gunnar. The prince watched warily as it struck the wall to his right.

"The gods' curses on that little bone," said Belaf angrily. "That won't get the job done. Here, fling this at the whelp." He dug a long, thin throwing-spear out of his baggage.

At this point, the old man named Val decided to speak. "Put up the javelin," he advised, rising to his feet and limping around the fire. "The battle is over. It's not wise to show a weapon of war in an hour of peace." He stood in front of the angry giant and reached out his hand.

"Your hour may be for peace," snarled Belaf. "Mine's for war while this yellow-haired brat yet lives. He killed two of our men!"

"I noticed you weeping for them after the battle," said the old man. "Or were those the sounds of celebration that I heard ringing in my ears?" The old man had a bit of a temper, and he felt tired. He knew better than to trade words with a fool, but he did it anyway. "Now, come on," he added. "Let's put up that weapon. Somebody might get hurt." Belaf stepped close to the old man, but the elder warrior showed no fear as he calmly stood his ground.

"Oh, go back and sit down," said Belaf with a dry, brittle laugh and a shrug of his huge, meaty shoulders. "I hear you." The old man smiled at his companions, greatly relieved that the conflict had ended without bloodshed.

Belaf struck suddenly downward with the butt end of his spear, dealing a swift, savage blow to Val's head. The old man slammed into the dirt face down. His attacker stepped back quickly, holding the spear in a defensive posture as he faced the Veterans, who had leaped to their feet.

The old man lay in the dust with his head twisted sideways and his feet askew. He did not twitch a muscle as his comrades came and lifted him, carrying his frail, limp form to the other side of the fire.

Surveying his wounded friend, the warrior named Vangar stepped forward. An athletic man as huge as Belaf himself, Vangar was a legend among the Battle Scylfings and the foremost of Captain Rurik's fighting men.

Belaf licked his lips nervously and tried to smile, his dull, cruel eyes flashing to the right and left as he sized up the mighty champion with his grimly silent group of companions. He looked badly shaken. In the heat of his spite, he had forgotten where he was. Staring wide-eyed at the huge warrior in front of him, Belaf began to realize the ramifications of his actions.

"I don't want to fight you, Vangar," Belaf rasped, trying to force a smile. His face grew pale, and a delicate patina of sweat dappled his brow, oozing from his pores like poison from a puff-toad.

"No," said Vangar. "I suppose you don't." Vangar struggled to stay calm, knowing that rage could hinder his ability to fight. His surprise at the assault had given way to a cold, deadly fury: deep and powerful, as fierce as the love he felt for the kind old man.

"This fight will be to the death," Vangar said grimly, reaching for the sword at his side. But before the stricken Belaf could react, a powerful voice rang out in the silence. The voice addressed them in their own language, but in an accent so strange they could not discern the words.

"Vindriskl sivn sein!" the voice cried. "Eutt beliuskinn, eviss yevluski visk!" The men turned in surprise to see that the boy, Gunnar-val, was the source of this sudden address.

The Prince stood alone at the edge of the circle of firelight, facing Belaf across the group of men. His countenance, fixed and intense with his right eye blackened by Gilfast's stick, had changed somehow. He looked like a man, no longer a child.

"Vindriskl sivn sein!" he repeated. Belaf looked at Gunnar, then smiled weakly at Vangar.

"He's mad," he said, and some of the men behind him laughed.

"He's not insane," said a voice in the darkened reaches of the cavern. The speaker was Captain Rurik. "I understand what he said." The Captain walked slowly into the light, stroking his mustache. The Lieutenant stood up swiftly, suddenly realizing that he had chosen the wrong side in a nasty piece of business.

"Sir, I," he began, but an uplifted hand silenced him.

"This man is my prisoner," the Captain began. "As such, he is under my protection, as you all should know." He pointed at the stricken old man, who lay as pale as a corpse on a cushion of saddles and blankets. No breath could be seen on his thin, colorless lips, and his body looked very small as it lay there without stirring.

Rurik looked around the cavern. "This old man, this honest old man, has fought with me since my first raids as a youth under Rus, the King of the Varangians," he told them. He studied the men who had provoked the situation, finally settling his gaze on Belaf. "If he dies, it will be blood for blood indeed... as you have said." He let his gaze sweep across the face of Belaf's companions.

"Our young prisoner," he continued, "is Prince Gunnar of Bryne. His full name is Gunnar-val, son of Vigmar King of Bryne. As you may know, Bryne is a small but powerful city-state located on a fjord not so far from our homeland. This young man and his kindred are Healf-Scylfs, closely related to our noble Scylfing families. So you see," he observed, "he and I are related... cousins, so to speak. When we killed his father, we broke a bond of peace that has endured for more than two hundred years between the Healf-Scylfs and their Scylfing cousins." Rurik turned to Belaf.

"Prince Gunnar of Bryne has challenged you to single combat. He is aware that Val was defending him. As the unwitting cause of this unwarranted incident, he claims first right to combat. How do you answer his challenge?"

"He's challenging me?" He smiled stupidly. "He's just a runt."

"Will you accept his challenge?" Captain Rurik repeated. At this, Belaf guffawed.

"He must be drunk, Captain."

"Do you accept? If so, which weapons do you choose?"

"Choose?" He looked around stupidly. "Weapons?" Things had moved a little too swiftly for Belaf. As the realization dawned, however, he straightened up to his full height. A cruel expression flashed across his face, and he grasped the opportunity unsheathed before him. He could go to work now on the boy, just like he had started on the old man. Only this time, no one would stop him. Belaf smiled broadly at Captain Rurik.

"Axes, captain," he breathed happily. "I choose axes." The men behind him laughed and nudged one another as Belaf winked at them and raised his eyebrows comically. "A man's weapon to kill a boy," he joked. "What would his mommy say?"

The mood of Belaf's companions grew festive again as they lit long, dry pieces of pine in the fire and drove them into the sandy floor around the broad backside of the cave. The sandy floor would drink up the spilled blood. It was a perfect killing ground, and the presence of the burning torches surrounding their field of battle only added to the possibilities of torment and torture. Prospects of slaughter and gore danced like sugarplums in Belaf's broad, shiny head.

The battle-axe, even in the year of our Lord 885, had outlived its heyday outside the Viking world. But among the Vikings, the battle-axe – that once-popular weapon of war favored among the barbaric behemoths of the megalithic cave bear cultures – had remained a weapon of war. The axe could be thrown with deadly accuracy or wielded with aplomb if a man had the time and the strength to master it. Because he possessed great strength and surprising quickness, Belaf had long ago found that axes suited him well.

Prince Gunnar stood in the middle of the torch-lit fighting ground as the men chattered loudly and took bets on how long the fight would last. He was dressed in the same soiled green clothes that he had worn hunting. He looked small and thin compared to his opponent, who loomed above him like a ponderous siege weapon towering over a sapling. The men in the cave prepared the area for the bloody work ahead, building up the fire and adding new torches to the ones already lit.

As Belaf warmed up with some stretches and a few wicked swings of his weapon, the Captain walked over to his gear and rummaged through it. He pulled out a slim, brightly polished axe that had obviously seen much use, and he walked up to the boy.

"I took this from your father's horse." Rurik said to the young prince as he loosed the leather thongs that bound his hands. He handed him the axe.

Prince Gunnar wore no armor. His hands, by now, had regained their sense of touch. He felt the strength surge through his arms as he hefted the axe, turning it in his hands, loosening his muscles with slow twists and rolls of the weapon. He stared across the torches at Belaf, who grinned mockingly and began his approach. Belaf had donned his breastplate and mail… protection enough, he thought, from the blows of a child.

The huge, nimble warrior towered over Gunnar, outweighing him by more than one hundred pounds. He dearly desired to hurt the Prince, to make him squeal: to smash him, mash him to pulp, mutilate his pretty face until it was as ugly and empty as Belaf's disfigured soul.

Yet in Belaf's eyes, for an instant, there flashed a strange glimmer of something apart from malice and spite. Was it fear?

Revulsion? Regret? Belaf knew, but he was not talking. He would be a hero tonight, he reasoned. He would shut the mouths of these Varangians, these high and mighty companions of the great Captain Rurik. He drew closer to Gunnar, who silently stood his ground.

As he faced the approaching giant, Prince Gunnar of Bryne felt fear well up inside of him. He suppressed it with all of his might and raised the axe to battle position, holding it loosely in front of him, lightly balancing on the balls of his feet. All of the years of training, days filled with mock battles under the tutelage of Ithmar, had prepared him well.

Belaf approached him at an angle, sidling cannily up to his tender young quarry. Surprisingly, Gunnar did not tremble or draw back, but continued to stand his ground.

And then, the giant struck.

With a brutally swift movement – in a tight spin with a shining arc of light flashing from his axe – the great warrior whirled and ripped into his prey.

A Bad Day to Die

This is how Ilse's world changed forever. Her evening began peacefully. Ithmar's great house, the crowning achievement of so many years of loving labor, lay empty and still.

The rooms had grown silent. Fires crackled in two of the house's hearths, fires that burned low, hissing and creaking, audibly complaining, as it were: unhappily expressing the dissipation of their heat as they settled down for the night.

On nights like these, when her father had left on one of his journeys, Ilse still shared a bed with her mother. It was a peculiar indulgence of her mother's to allow – and even to encourage – this last vestige of childish behavior. But Ilse was not in her mother's room tonight.

She sat in front of the fire in the great room, settling back in the deep cushions of a large chair that faced the warm hearth. At her feet, curled up with his back to the fire, lay Seng, their tall, lanky, longhaired Norwegian elkhound. Seng, a hunter by blood and pet by choice, served the family as an independently devoted companion.

As if he knew that she watched him, Seng rolled onto his back and yawned sleepily, stretching as far as he could and pawing at the air in front of the fire. As he yawned, Seng displayed for her inspection a deadly row of canine incisors: long, milky teeth that lined the delicate, pink, symmetrically ribbed roof of his mouth like a glistening phalanx of ivory spearheads. He closed his mouth and exhaled sharply, causing his lips to flop comically as he heaved a windy sigh.

"Stop that, you big rug," Ilse cooed to the shaggy beast, rubbing his side with her feet. "Stop enjoying yourself. Don't you know that Father is out in the mountains, traveling in the snow? But you're here like a big pillow in front of the fire, over-stuffed and overdone."

Seng yawned in reply, stretching backwards ever more precariously: contorting, drawing his long body tautly into a bow as he pawed frenetically at the air. As his tongue lolled out, he seemed to smile, whining comically and rolling his eyes in her direction.

Ilse leaned back in the chair with a mind full of happy thoughts… a lazy stir of pleasant memories triggered by the mention of her father and the presence of Seng. She began to drift asleep, smoothly slipping into that curious netherworld between the keen edge of awareness and the realm of dreams. For a while she drifted: for how long, she would never know.

Then, something happened. Some intuited, unknown influence altered the atmosphere within her happy home.

She heard nothing. She saw nothing. But somehow, she sensed that something had changed.

Seng stiffened and scrambled to his feet. He began to bark loudly, running into the next room as if he were an excitable puppy. He had often jumped and barked in such a manner in his youth, but had outgrown such behavior with age. Or at least, so she had thought.

"Seng, come back here!" Ilse called loudly, rising and following him into the hall. "Come back, Seng!" She grasped him sternly by the collar and tugged, but he wouldn't budge. Ilse was shocked. Seng had never withstood her before. "Come on, you," she said through clenched teeth as she tugged harder. Seng pulled hard against her, his teeth bared, his nose pressed firmly against the jamb of a closed door leading to the kitchen. Ilse stopped and sighed, and then an idea flashed through her mind. She turned back toward the great room with its cozy fire.

"What's that?" she cried suddenly. "What's that?"

Seng responded instantly, running past her with his stiff-legged trot, tense and prepared for action. Now Ilse headed in a different direction and hurried into the short hallway that led to her parent's library. She paused at the threshold while Seng tried to catch up, scrambling for traction on the hardwood floor in a frantic attempt to pass her and intercept the threat to his household. As he drew near, she flung the door open.

Through the great window on the far side of the darkened room, Ilse caught the dark glimpse of a snow flurry that rattled lightly against the pane. Seng charged past her and ran into the room, barking loudly as Ilse slammed the door shut. For a second he paused, and then began to bark more loudly than before.

"I'll let you out when you decide to behave," Ilse said petulantly, tossing her head as she walked out of the hallway and shut the hall door behind her. A double buffer of heavy, well-fitted wood now muffled his barking.

With a sigh, Ilse sat down again in front of the fire. *It will be a while before mother comes home,* she thought.

Her mother's best friend lived almost a mile away, but Katla did not fear the cold. The road home led through the middle of town, and in the event of a late spring blizzard, Katla could practically feel her way to one of the many homes that lined the roadway.

Their house had grown quiet: strangely still in spite of the faint cry and clamor of Seng. *I'll let him out soon,* Ilse thought as she settled down in front of the fire.

The flames writhed before her like swirling ghosts of light and heat: wraith-like specters that twisted and danced above the coals. Tangible heat radiated from the hearth, and the room was well insulated with layers of heath and mud. Ilse should have basked in the warmth, but for some reason she felt incongruously – yet undeniably – chilled.

The Killing Floor

When Belaf struck, Gunnar reacted without thinking. All of the years of training, the ever-intensifying battles with Lord Ithmar, made his reactions instantaneous. He had allowed Belaf to draw close deliberately, knowing that the apparent certainty of a killing blow might cause the huge man to over commit when he swung the axe.

The ancient art of axe fighting had fallen into disrepute, but it had still been part of the Prince's training, for tradition's sake more than for any practical purpose. Gunnar had been particularly interested in the discipline, fascinated by its unwieldy, romantic anachronism. His hours of practice with this very axe had caused Ithmar to shake his head in wonder. Gunnar had become expert in a skill that he thought he would never use.

As Belaf began his surprisingly quick attack, Gunnar read his swing at the first glimpse. He knew instantly that he could not dive backwards; the great man had gained the angle on him.

He dove forward, hitting the dirt to the right of Belaf's feet. He wanted to make a single roll and to come up fighting, but to pull it off he had to move quickly. Belaf was incredibly swift.

Belaf had swung with all of his might. Having drawn so close to the lad, he knew his first blow would kill. His quickness and power had never failed Belaf in a lifetime of bloody conflict and gore. Unfortunately for him, in his haste to shed blood, he had broken the first law of axe fighting.

Belaf had overcommitted.

With shock, he saw his victim disappear from the path of his weapon and dive nimbly toward the ground beside him. Belaf's heavy axe failed in the attempt to marry flesh to steel, slicing the air above its intended as Gunnar plunged beneath it and kissed the earth instead of the blade. The Prince tumbled past Belaf, his axe held loosely in his well-practiced grasp.

Belaf tried to turn swiftly to face the Prince. But his great axe of war, which he had swung with such power and speed, continued on its course, pulling him off balance as he attempted to wheel around and face his prey.

Gunnar had gained his feet and started his attack by the time Belaf could stop the arc of his heavy weapon. The huge warrior stared at the young Prince with pure, dumb shock stamped upon his wide-eyed countenance.

In the split-second pause before the giant could make a backhanded slice at the child, he realized that he had lost the fight.

Belaf began his backward stroke, pulling with all of his might: snatching the axe head into an upward trajectory aimed squarely at the neck of the lad in front of him.

The Prince's attack seemed almost too quick to track. As he rolled to his feet, he tossed the axe into the air, caught it, and swung smoothly with a circular whipping motion. The sharp head hissed in the air as it slashed toward the shocked giant. With all of his might, Gunnar followed through and buried the axe in the big man's powerful arm, close to the shoulder.

The bone shattered cleanly with an amazingly loud crack. It was not a pretty sight.

Belaf watched in disbelief, still trying to swing as the axe severed his arm completely and dug into the muscles of his chest. His axe, moving at a high rate of speed in the direction of his would-be prey, continued on its path.

The heavy axe sailed closely over the head of Gunnar, who ducked at the last moment. The flying axe dragged Belaf's arm along with it, ripping the remaining shreds of flesh clean away from the stump as Belaf's clenched hand clung tightly to the handle.

With uncomprehending eyes, Belaf watched as the boy ducked under his axe. He gaped in shock as the grotesque bundle sailed off to the edge of the fighting circle, whirling slowly: axe and arm comprising a single, weighty package that barely cleared the Prince before falling with a resounding *wumph* at the feet of the stupefied revelers.

As if it suddenly realized its predicament, the severed stump at Belaf's shoulder began to spurt a fountain of blood. Before the huge warrior could respond, Vangar and the Veterans swarmed upon him, forcing him to the earth.

Belaf shrieked, screaming with a startled, almost feline sound, emitting a cry that seemed totally out of character. He struggled powerfully with eight strong men upon him, trying to throw them off. As they subdued him, another Veteran came walking from the fire carrying the heavy spade that had been heated in preparation against such an injury. The spade, made of solid cast-iron heated to its limit in the coals, glowed with an eerie, ethereal pulse: red-hot and luminous.

Belaf saw the glowing spade and squealed wildly, piteously, as a trapped beast might squeal when it sees a predator approach: with a sound at once so terrible and lost that it would rend any heart that heard it, if indeed that heart had any substance to rend. All within the pulse and thrust of that horrid, high-pitched squeal, which pierced their consciences as it wounded their ears, would never manage to forget it, although they buried it within the nethermost holds of their hardened, sword-shocked psyches.

The warrior with the spade drew close to Belaf, seeking the best angle with which to do his work. Those standing several feet away could feel the bright heat from the glowing iron, which lit the faces and singed the hoary beards of those closest to the open wound. The very thought of what was to come curdled the blood of those unaccustomed to such butchery.

At first, it seemed as if the surgeon would never close on the wound. But then he did, and the sound and smell of burning flesh filled the cave as the giant screamed again. He shrieked loudly, madly, thrashing mightily but to no avail as the man probed with his tool, cauterizing the arteries, sealing the wound, pressing his burning spade from gore to coagulate gore until finally the whole wretched mess had been sealed, stump and chest, vein, bone, marrow, and blood; the fountain was stopped and the life of the giant, at least for tonight, was preserved.

They poured potato whiskey down Belaf's throat now, talking

soothingly to him as he gulped it down. In due time, the beaten man descended into a wandering of the mind, from there into delirium, and from delirium into a deep, insensate sleep from which, he might have hoped, he would never emerge.

The whole process took almost an hour. The companions of Belaf had wandered off long before Vangar carried the unconscious fighter to a place beside the fire and laid him softly on a ragged bearskin.

After he placed Belaf on his bed, Vangar arose and checked the status of the limp and motionless old man. After confirming that he yet lived, he approached the victorious Gunnar. The young prince, shivering against the back wall of the cave, hardly noticed that Vangar had brought him a heavy bearskin covering.

"The old man's alive," he said to the boy, handing him the thick fur.

"Thank you," said the Prince, speaking with a Scylfing accent so his words would be understood.

"You fought well. He was a mad dog. He would have killed and killed again until someone put a stop to him."

"Yes, he was a killer," the Prince replied, his expression vacant. "And what am I?"

"You? You're a prince."

"No. I'm a slave."

"Yes," Vangar said, sighing. "You're a slave."

"You killed my father without a cause."

"You're right," Vangar said, and, looking down at the slave, Gunnar-val, he felt a sudden wave of pity. "We are all killers, young slave. Belaf has paid a price. But you and I? We have yet to pay."

"Heaven is just," said the slave. He looked pale and thin. He felt sick, and he was... sick and worn, grown weary of his life.

"The gods measure justice as they see fit," replied Vangar. "Sleep well." Vangar turned and walked back to the fire, showing great control not to stagger from the sudden exhaustion that seemed to well up from deep within. The weariness washed like a great wave against his body and mind. As he walked, Vangar prayed within his heart to his gods. He felt truly sorry that he had begun this last, bloody mercenary journey.

Always, in the past, their forays had seemed justifiable due to the evil wrought by the despots they had hunted and killed. But this mission had been accomplished solely for blood money. They had earned a small fortune by murdering a king famed for fairness and mercy.

Simply put, Vangar and his companions had changed from honorable warriors into bloody murderers. He thought it ironic that the gods of heaven, which must judge them if heaven itself remained just, were the only ones who could pardon their foul deeds. *Only heaven can erase our guilt, if enough mercy can be found... in heaven, or on earth,* he thought grimly. Vangar sat heavily beside the dying fire. He could not fully comprehend the changes taking place within him.

The cave grew quiet. The men, exhausted from the impact of two days without sleep, had once again fallen out around the fire. Belaf snored loudly, mercifully inured to the pain.

At the back of the cave, seated directly across from Rurik of the Varangians, the slave mourned and shivered alone. His mind sank into the depths of sorrow, into profound and icy grief that threatened to drown his soul in measureless depths. Hot tears coursed down his cheeks, mingling with the soft stubble of a thin, wispy beard. He thought of his father, and the dam of grief broke.

His self control shattered slowly and majestically, like a dam collapsing: unleashing a torrent of sorrow that carried him away, sweeping him up in the power of its current, whirling him in the eddies, driving him shipwreck against the rocks, pounding him in the flood as he struggled in vain to hold on.

Finally, young Gunnar let go and was swept into the abyss of utter sorrow. He sobbed wildly, bitterly, frantically into his cloak: curling up into a small, trembling ball and looking – for all the world – like the battered child that he was.

Devil's Work

She heard it again: a sound of some sort, a mere hint of a noise, barely discernable above the rhythmic rise and fall of her own quiet breathing. Somehow, deep within the hidden recesses of the old wooden house, an unknown change in the atmosphere had taken place: a shift so subtle that it could only be perceived at first outside the realm of conscious thought.

Something had changed. She stood abruptly to her feet and slowly turned to face the door.

In the course of one swift, sickening instant, she saw a man standing in the open doorway, leaning casually against the jamb with one hand on his hip and the other hidden within his cloak. The man was Kennan, the only person in Bryne who invariably made her skin crawl. He smiled at her blithely. For a moment, she almost thought she might be seeing an apparition.

"Please, sweetest, don't be startled," he said smoothly. "It's your childhood chum, Lord Kennan the Great. How nice of you to welcome me."

Seng, hearing the strange new voice, began to bark frantically. The muffled sound of his barking, insulated by two securely shut doors, seemed distant and strange... as if another dog bayed behind the doors, not her faithful elkhound.

Ilse turned slowly, attempting to appear calm.

Suddenly, she made her move.

She dashed for a door, but before she could open it, Kennan seized her from behind. His hands clamped painfully on her wrists, as hard and as cold as iron.

Ilse kicked and fought as Kennan slammed open the door to the hallway and dragged her past the shut library in which Seng helplessly raged, baying for blood. Kennan kicked the library door as they passed, tormenting the raging hound.

"Bark, you filthy cur," he crowed triumphantly. "Wreck that

stinking scroll-room." Kennan bitterly envied Ithmar for his famous collection of ancient texts. "Eat those filthy parchments!" he added ebulliently.

Kennan began to feel a rush: a surge of evil power not unlike the drunken spin of a black magic spell. He savored the sense of burgeoning power with unholy glee, as if his soul ascended in the smoke of a whirling, swirling tryst of evil spirits gone mad with joy at the prospect of incipient, rapine brutality. Kennan longed to slake his sick burden of hot, envenomed lust: unwholesome, unholy, unhampered by love, and untainted by human kindness.

"God, help me!" Ilse cried.

"Shut up!" Kennan shrieked. He slammed her body into a wall inside her parents' bedroom, knocking her breathless.

"Owoo!" Kennan howled at the elkhound. The bedroom adjoined the library, and Seng could hear them through the wooden wall. "Rage on, you loathsome brute!" Kennan cried, laughing uproariously as he threw Ilse onto her parents' bed.

Seng, mad with anger, slammed himself against the adjoining wall, knocking an amber cup off a shelf. The hand-carved cup shattered loudly on the bedroom floor.

"Come over and join the party, you mindless brute!" shouted Kennan. "The weather's fine." The bitterly cold snow of the spring's last storm brushed softly against the bedroom window, tossed by a slow but steady east wind that groaned like a ship in a mountainous sea.

Kennan unbuckled his belt, cast off his boots, and plunged on top of Ilse with a wild, boisterous laugh. She came out of her state of shock with a jolt, hitting him hard with a cupped hand against his ear.

Kennan reared back wildly, screaming in pain. Shaking his head in an attempt to silence the ringing in his ears, he drew back his hand and struck a powerful blow across her face. The blunt force stunned her temporarily. She could not quite remember where she was or what she was up to, but she knew that it was important. She could see Kennan, far away, towering over her. She vaguely wondered what he was up to.

"I'll make you pay," Kennan hissed, holding his ear, from which there now poured a thin stream of blood. "You'll pay dearly for that." A loud smashing sound came from the next room.

Kennan grabbed the petite girl by her thick blond hair. A drop of his blood dripped from his ear onto the smooth skin of her cheek as she tried to focus.

"Your precious beast has smashed Mommy's best amber plates," he hissed, lowering his face close to hers. "What would Daddy say?" Ilse's eyes suddenly focused, and she tried to bite his nose, but he jerked his face back just in time.

"You're a clever thing," he leered. "You'll make a good mother for our son."

Kennan never knew what caused him to look up at that precise moment. And yet, he did look up to gaze directly into the window.

The lamplight burned brightly in the bedroom. The pure whale oil brilliantly illuminated the rich tableau: wide bed, dark wooden walls, fire burning low in the hearth.

For no particular reason, Kennan continued to stare at the window. A burst of snow slashed across its opaque surface, yet something else seemed to move behind the swirling snow. In a moment suspended outside of time, Lord Kennan earnestly focused, striving hastily to discover what drew his attention to this narrow opening.

With an explosive crack, the window imploded violently in his face, showering the room with sparkling shards of glass that blossomed like a fountain of ice before his eyes. The imploding glass bloomed in his direction until the delicate petals parted and a mask of horror unveiled itself in the heart of the unfolding bud. A red mouth yawned hungrily, hurtling in his direction, its interior generously draped with glistening stalactites of thick, viscous saliva. The fanged mouth was an ingenious piece of work: symmetrically ribbed with dainty pink grooves and clean white teeth like ivory spearheads answering the call to battle.

Kennan rolled backwards too slowly. He managed to extend one arm in a vain attempt to fend off the elkhound before Seng slammed into him, knocking him backward off the bed. They rolled end over end, the dog holding onto Kennan's forearm as they flipped onto the floor. Kennan fell with his full weight on top of his attacker, breaking one of Seng's ribs.

As the grip on his forearm loosened for an instant, Lord Kennan dove for the door, followed closely by the great dog. Climbing onto Kennan's back, Seng drove his massive fangs deep into the muscles of his neck, sending excruciating, tectonically powerful shock waves of pain through his universe.

Again, Kennan fell heavily, this time deliberately, driving himself and his passenger backwards. He landed with all of his weight on top of the injured dog. The pain caused Seng to loosen his grip, and before he could recover, Kennan dove headlong through the doorway. He grabbed the door as he hurtled past and slammed it solidly shut.

Seng flung himself against the door, pounding his body against the thick boards as the uneven steps of the predator beat an ignominious retreat. The front door slammed, and they could hear a horse galloping away.

Seng looked up at Ilse.

The young girl stood, and then immediately sat down as her legs gave way beneath her. The massive elkhound, his long hair matted with blood, gingerly approached and sat at her feet. He gently nudged her knee with his tender muzzle.

For a long time they sat without making a sound. The icy breeze blew into the house, but they scarcely felt it entering through the shattered window. The wind slowly covered them with a fine, well-sifted dust of delicate crystals, frosting them with an unnoticed filigree of clean, white snow.

III.

Bryne was bereaved by the sword-hands of strangers;
Their brave King lay slain by conscienceless killers.

The snowmelt of spring revealed Vigmar's grave
In a barrow above the fair meadows he loved.

Full down on their faces to weep in the dust
The men fell who found the body of Vigmar.
They laid his sword, broken, across the great chest
That cold stones had sheltered
And snow had preserved.

The bold comitatus, so fearless in battle,
Bowed down and wept like little lost children
Crying his name, so great was their loss.
Ithmar knelt speechless, his soul frozen fast.
All of his might, when he reached for its power,
Would not suffice him to rise from the earth.

The strength of their youths and the joy of their lives
Had fallen at last on his mountains of stone.

Their vows to protect him, declared with such fervor,
Now wounded their souls as they came to remembrance.
Yet luminous peace seemed distilled in his visage.
He seemed but to nap, as if cries could awaken him
To once again light up their halls with his laughter:
The songs of the minstrels delighting his soul

And his loving companions again sharing mead
With Vigmar, their liege who lay frosted with cold.

They returned without herald into the King's city.
The houses were dark as the warriors passed by.

The evil conceived in the heart of the dragon
Had brought forth in sorrow the dearth of that night.
They bore on broad shoulders all that was left
Of the greatest of Sea-Kings, King Vigmar the Bold:
The terror of nations and guide to the weak.

Colder than rain and the diamonds of heaven,
Colder than wind that howls over the snow,
Colder than spray of the numb northern ocean
That softly digs down into marrow and bone
And gives ice to the blood, ice that warms before slaying,
Colder than these were the hearts and the souls
That silently watched as his bier was borne by.

The bitterest of evenings, with stars pressing closer
Began to bring change as our King was borne by.
The weather was turning; a south wind brought clouds
And cold rain that started to fall from the sky.
The brave comitatus now bore our King down
To Azbith, his warship, at rest on the waves.

The City of Gold lay swaddled in darkness.
The sail cast a shroud that enveloped our souls.
Our hearts drifted out with the sure, silent vessel,
So lightly bearing the death of our dreams.

Our people had gathered upon the steep sea-cliffs
That lined the small bay where the longships were moored.
There, from the inlet, out into the fjord,
His treasure ship glided upon the black water,
A great swan that bore her slight gosling of horror:
The moldering body of Vigmar, our lord.

A fire-arrow flew and snagged fast in the sail.
Flames bloomed like roses when Azbith ignited.
Bright fire rushed swiftly from stern unto bow,
Greedily lapping her swan's coat of oil
Before biting into a richer repast.
Ornately wrought sail, her ropes and her masts,
Silver-tipped oars and the form of our King
Broke in the onslaught of light, smoke, and heat
That rose to the heavens as sorrowing, weeping,
The people dissolved in their pyre of grief.

The City of Gold had turned gold from the burning.
Towering flames lit the cliffs and the bay.

Unplanned and unbidden, a deep-throated wail,
Strange and foreboding, arose from the host.
Then, suddenly breaking, the ship, loudly groaning,
Was quenched with a roar that extinguished the flames.
Sinking with clouds of foul steam and disaster
She slid toward the deep that awaited her carcass,
Down into the sound past the mouth of the bay.

Long time we mourned him.
The kingdom was troubled.

Some favored Haruk , but others loved Ithmar,
The dearest of friends to our greatest of kings.

The season of sorrow hung over us, heavy,
Until death's bitter harrow of sorrows passed by.

But God has determined that after the weeping
The dawn will arise upon mourners again:
So all of the people, like sleepers awakening,
Healed with the seasons that passed overhead.

In the fourth year, in the time of regaling,
Once again laughter was heard in our halls
That long had sat empty by order of Ithmar
The Steward of Vigmar who kept the King's crown.

At Ithmar's side sat Lord Haruk the Cruel
Filled with venom — well hidden — and hatred disguised.
Haruk's hooded eyes sheltered foul counsel.
He drank in the scene with a wolf's patient cunning.

The people had gathered to toast winter's ending.
Traveling scops filled the mead hall with songs.

This was the springtime, the Feast of the Elders
When women joined warriors to honor them all.

The Mead Hall

Efron despised barbarians. He loathed their very aura, the execrable cultureless mirth of them: their beards, their swaggers, their complacent smirks, and anything else remotely associated with the untutored cretins who sat before him in the dim light of the smoky mead hall.

Efron considered himself to be an artist. In reality, his art was essentially heartless: alternately cruel and maudlin, but always formulated in strict accordance with the public sentiment. His songs insinuated themselves with the smooth tongue of flattery and the fickle kiss of a moral chameleon. His art was a triumph of form over substance.

Efron was a traveling minstrel, also called a scop. A skilled craftsman, his sophisticated tunes aped the most popular musical forms of the day. His repertoire consisted largely of syrupy retreads of the Frankish hits that had so recently softened up the thanes of Paris for conquest at the hands of the untutored Norsemen.

"Ah, the Franks," sniffed Efron as he surveyed the vast mead hall, overflowing at the moment with the much-despised barbaric hordes. "The Franks truly know how to live." He sneered at the packed hall, the largest of all the northern realms. *I suppose it does have a certain crude, Norse splendor,* he thought, his eyes darting greedily to the great flagons and plates of silver that littered the broad tables. *But even in Rome I could find better food. Or at least, I've heard as much.*

Sylvain lusted heartily for the delicate, fluted candies and subtly spiced wines of the legendary Roman banquets. Why couldn't his travels have taken him to Rome? The fact that Efron, who considered himself a sophisticate, would have been viewed as a hopeless rustic by the leading lights of Rome never entered his mind.

"Why couldn't old Krangmeister have taken me to Italy?" He mourned profoundly, despising the very memory of his musical mentor. Efron did not appreciate the fact that frail old Krangmeister had patiently labored to teach him several languages and the very craft by which he earned his daily bread. *Why must I suffer these accursed barbarians?* He searched his heart for an answer, but as always, he came up empty. He was truly a diamond among the clods of the earth, he decided: a rose among the crude Norse thorns.

Efron looked around the dimly lit hall, studying the people jammed behind the feasting tables. The huge room was rectangular in shape, with one end taken up by the seats of honor and the rest of the tables extending in a pattern that followed the building's lines. All at the tables could watch as the minstrels performed.

The citizens of Bryne had filled the room to overflowing. Even the generous space between the mead board and the outer walls of the room overflowed with husbands, weavers, whalers, warriors, trappers and fishermen, wives and maidens, sons and daughters. The ancient and the new filled the room with color and noise: talking, mixing, laughing and having a veritable mead-bowl of unadulterated Viking fun.

The sight sickened Efron.

In the midst of these reflections, he heard someone call his name and rapidly glanced toward the chief seats in the room. There, in front of the heavy wooden table, a gaunt, gray-haired man announced him to Ithmar, the Steward of Bryne, who nodded in response. The largest and most ornate chair in the hall sat empty beside Ithmar, in memory of King Vigmar the Great.

Efron sneered at the empty throne. As a faithless man, he considered such loyalty to a slain king – or even to a missing prince – an embarrassing demonstration of fanaticism.

The gaunt man who had announced the scop to the Steward now turned and, catching Efron's eye, brought his staff down heavily on the wooden floor. In a few seconds the crowded hall became silent, and the man began to speak.

"Brothers and sisters, fathers, mothers, cousins... and elders," the man began. "I am glad to say that we have two of the greatest poets of our time with us tonight. You have all heard of the man that I am about to introduce. He is truly a legend among the scops of our day.

"He was able to come here this year because of the current wars in Teutonia involving King Otto the Fat, which prevented him from wintering at King Otto's court. He is currently on his way to Stockholm to entertain the court of Aeomer, King of the Scylfings. Be that as it may, King Otto's loss is our gain. I introduce to you the most popular of all minstrels... the great Sylvain!"

As the Vikings cheered, the scop doffed his plumed bonnet. He straightened up, tossed back his long black hair, and saluted the entire room, ending with a deep bow to the King's empty throne. *Fools,* he thought bitterly, *Lord Haruk is the only man of refinement in this pestilential breeding ground of great, bearded oafs.* The crowd became silent: poised breathlessly as he strummed his lyre and began to sing,

His first song told the tale of Vinreng, the first king of the Healf-Scylfs. For more than twenty minutes, Sylvain led them through the skeletal remains of the famous tale. As he wandered through the classic epic, the greatness of the story towered over his retelling like a majestic skeleton overshadowing a thief creeping through a moonlit graveyard for whales. As one not awed by tradition, Sylvain had festooned the story with every bright trinket and scrap of shiny cloth in his musician's bag of tricks.

"Chevalle himself could not have done better," he told himself as he finished to wild cheers and a frenetic round of toasts. He strummed another chord and played an introduction that mimicked a complex French style beginning to come into vogue. And then, pausing dramatically, he introduced his next song.

"We all have seen the rewards of our father's battles made manifest by the jewelry of our mothers. We know and love the traditions of conquest and plunder, traditions rooted in our glorious past. But what were those days actually like? The answer is found in my next song, *The Land of Ere.*"

Sylvain strummed his lyre and plunged into the song:

> In the ancient days the King of Ere's
> Wet-carts traversed the water weir.
> With iron fangs unsheathed in hand
> They plundered many wealthy lands.
>
> The maids his brave ones bare away;
> In the land of Ere they still remain.
>
>> With a Hi-Ninny-Ni and a bold refrain,
>> In the land of Ere they still remain.
>
> There was a brave young cavalier,
> A fighting son of the King of Ere,
> Whose looking-orb was lit, full-bright,
> By a maid he saw one Monday night.
>
> By Tuesday eve they both were wed;
> Her man had somehow lost his head.
>
>> With a Hi-Ninny-Ni and a bold refrain,
>> In the land of Ere they still remain.
>
> You wave-lords on the water-main,
> Invading warmer wedding-thanes,
> You bear them north from balmy lands.
> But what of those who held their hands?
>
> Arrow targets they became,
> Hilts to hold your carving blades!
>
>> With a Hi-Ninny-Ni and a bold refrain,
>> In the land of Nod they still remain!

The Pillage of Glastonbury

Glastonbury fell like an overripe plum into their war-hardened hands. On the night that it fell, two young men sat on a hillside north of town and watched it burn. The wreaths and plumes of fire and smoke swirled upward, carrying constellations of sparks that ascended from the rapidly incinerating thatched roofs of tightly clustered houses in the small, pathetic town.

The battle had ended. The men rested as they watched, suddenly exhausted, wanting not so much to exult as to find a place to sleep. Ironically enough, the best beds in town now fed the fires consuming the hamlet before their eyes.

"Alfred's men fought like lions," said one of the men, a young man in his late twenties. Carelessly well-dressed, he wore the particularly bored, irresolute look of a rich young man who believes he's seen it all, but wishes he hadn't.

"Yes. Brave men," replied his companion. A slight inflection in the man's otherwise-perfect Danish gave him away as a native of the far North. He appeared, at first glance, to be in his late twenties. Only his companion knew that he was twenty years old. "It feels good to win one."

They looked down the steep hillside, where a group of their comrades-in-arms toiled, laboring portentously up the slope in solemn unison. The strangers walked with a humorless, stiffly ceremonial demeanor, evincing an unseemly excess of self-importance.

"Hullo there," a voice cried. "Have you seen a soldier named Draumr-skald?" The two young men looked at each other and smiled. Their faces glowed, lit by the flickering yellow light emanating from the sad little town.

"Don't tell them anything," hissed the younger man. His companion cheerfully ignored this advice, standing up to wave at the soldiers. He stood remarkably tall and thin. As he beckoned to them with an oversized, sweeping gesture, his clothes flapped on his bony frame like a loose sail beating against a mast.

"Greetings, fellow butchers," he said cheerfully. "Good evening to all, both great and the small." The approaching men stopped in their tracks to stare at the strange apparition that had risen to such heights before their eyes.

"It's Captain Julian, Sergeant," said one of the men in a deep, gritty voice, loud enough to be heard by all. "He's the giant scarecrow of the Western flank." The speaker, who led the approaching group, was Captain Dalmag of the Imperial Guard. "Still fraternizing with the pedestrians, Julian?"

"He's talking about you," Julian hissed to his companion. "You're the pedestrian."

"Nice," replied the younger man.

"Brother Dalmag, what makes you so upset?" the tall soldier replied. "Calm down, old boot. I happen to have the very man... uh, the very pedestrian... you're looking for." Julian nudged his friend with his foot. "Come on, Gunnar-val... or was it Draumr-skald?" He bent over and whispered loudly. "Do this for me, and your gaming debt is hereby canceled in full."

"I am your humble servant," Prince Gunnar said wearily, rising to his feet.

"Dramr-skald?" asked Captain Dalmag, huffing his way up to them and putting a hairy hand on the young man's shoulder as if to regain his balance.

"The name is Gunnar-val," he answered. "What do you want?"

"We want you, and we want Julian. Come with us."

Guthrum the Dane

King Guthrum scarcely noticed the two young men who stood before him. Pondering his army's next battle, he leaned over a large table, studying a map in a well-lit campaign tent. The tent was unusual only for the origin of its occupant. It was the sort of tent typically used by the noble princes of southern Europe when they went a-playing in the fields of war. But this particular tent, a spoil of war, was now occupied not by refined European royalty, but by a barbarous Norse king.

Guthrum the Dane was a wide man, but not fat: square-jawed, thoughtful, and surprisingly young. The British called all of Guthrum's men Danes, and in the King's case, the description applied. His followers, however, were a motley amalgam of opportunistic warriors from diverse Norse nations large and small: strong men welded by Guthrum into an army of Vikings, Saxons and Teutons dreaded across the European continent. The English called them all Danes, and they had lately begun to call themselves Danes, too… regardless of their land of origin. The title "Dane" – a token of English opprobrium – had added to their unique esprit de corps during the campaign in Saxony.

Guthrum paused, looked up at his visitors, and blinked absent-mindedly. He gestured to empty chairs across from him.

"Sit down." The new man sat comfortably, relaxed but respectful beside Captain Julian, and Guthrum took note of it.

"Julian, it's good to see you. I would have called for you sooner, but you know how it is."

"I'm afraid I do."

"Your father begged me not to let you come with us."

"I know, my king. But I thank you for your kindness in allowing me to serve." Guthrum laughed at this remark.

"My motives were selfish, I assure you. I didn't want your sister to get involved on your behalf. She can turn a hero's blood to ice with one dart from her word-hoard." They both laughed as they thought about Guthrum's timely escape from the long arm of Julian's sister, a woman every bit as formidable as the King had suggested. "So who's your friend... is this the young warrior, Gunnar-val?"

"He's the one. He has a story that may surprise you."

"I'm already surprised... not by you, of course. I knew what you could do. But I'm surprised by what I've heard about this young man." He leaned forward, closely eyeing the Prince. "You stopped the collapse of our right flank in the counterattack today. I watched it from my position.

"I saw our flank collapse and surge backward as the slaughter began. I've seen a few such slaughters in my time. There tends to be no hope once the line collapses. But this time, I saw a knot of soldiers from Julian's troop taking a stand on a knoll. They broke the charge, and turned the battle. Our line took spirit, surged forward, and we beat back the English until they fled in disarray." He paused for breath.

"You were the leader of that group on the knoll, or so I'm told. Now tell me," he asked, looking into Gunnar's eyes. "Who are you, where do you come from, and where did you learn to fight like that?"

Sylvain the Smooth

The evening had turned boisterous in the old mead hall. As Sylvain took a break, the crowd noisily shared gossip and hearty laughter, greedily guzzling their mead – the traditional, sour honey wine that they served in large bowls better suited for porridge than drink.

To the right of the throne sat Ithmar, and to his right sat his family. His two beautiful women – Ilse and Katla – conversed happily together. Their de facto grandfather, Ivan Redbeard, surveyed the scene blissfully, enjoying the season of mirth that had returned into their lives.

To all appearances, Ilse had bounced back with remarkable resiliency from her near-rape at the hands of Kennan, son of Haruk. Ithmar watched admiringly as his daughter traded jests with her mother: listening intently, pausing suddenly and tossing her head in laughter.

The exile of Kennan, by vote of the council of Bryne, had removed a cancer from the kingdom. Ilse's youth and ebullient nature had done much of the rest, assisting in the restoration of normalcy in the life of Ithmar's lovely daughter.

Often, it seemed as if the attack on the sensitive child had left no mark at all. But appearances can deceive, and Ilse had become expert at hiding her pain. In fact, Kennan's attack still hurt her unspeakably. At night, when she tried to sleep, the memories would emerge from the hidden springs of deepest remembrance, haunting her once-innocent dreams.

Tonight, however, even Ilse could believe that her pain was fading into the past. She leaned forward with one elbow on the mead-board and talked animatedly with her mother, laughing loudly, covering her mouth and ducking he head as she attempted to retain at least a modicum of decorum.

A lump grew in Ithmar's throat as he watched her. He turned

swiftly away, gazing again toward the center of the mead hall where he could see the simpering scop, Sylvain the Smooth, preparing to thrill the throng with more of his labored artifice.

Applause rang out as the crowd realized that Sylvain was standing in the center of the room. He gracefully bowed in all four directions, a veritable runic archetype of the Grateful Entertainer thanking his adored and adoring fans. Then he raised his hand dramatically, holding it high in the air until the crowd grew silent. With a bold, circular sweep of his arm, he struck his lyre and launched into his next song.

If his next musical offering seemed vaguely familiar to the gathered host, it was understandable given the songs formulaic design. The poetic work was, for Sylvain, a true tour-de-force; an unseemly mix of Frankish sophistry and Norse dramatic poesy that burst the repressive bonds of decorum and good taste.

In an attempt to marry his shallow but sophisticated musical style with the age-old poetic forms of the region, Sylvain had created a completely new beast… a sort of Teutonic knight in a tutu.

Sylvain's song presented an incongruous marriage of the delicate, lovely style of early Frankish minstrelsy and the classic masculine form common to epic Norse poems. Sagas from the Viking canon – in their purest sense – told heroic tales cast in blank verse of uneven meter and structure, yet possessing a majestic, unpolished grandeur. When Sylvain tried to integrate Southern European poetic conventions into the heroic Norse saga, he failed. His best efforts invariably resulted in awkward, disjointed hybrids… each song sounding as if he had sewn the head of a hummingbird onto the majestic, lumbering body of a great northern bear.

And yet, one aspect of Sylvain's work caused it to stand apart. During his southern travels, he had acquired a fondness for rhyme. With the exception of Barad-zur, the other scop scheduled to perform tonight, Sylvain was the only minstrel in the North known to use rhyme. And without exception, he was the only Norse scop who constructed poems with uniform meter that matched his rhymes.

The other scop on tonight's bill was a man given to frequent flights from formal structure, rhyming or not rhyming as it pleased him as he created works that fit into the ancient poetic patterns. Sylvain, on the other hand, did not discriminate. He had latched onto the new conventions of rhyme and meter with the death grip of the creatively challenged.

In his next song, Sylvain had once again tried to create an unholy alliance that fused a Norse saga with poetic rhyme and repetitious meter. Of course, as Sylvain's mentor had once said, "Lemmings attempt, but falcons succeed." And so, tossing back his hair, the popular minstrel introduced his tune.

"Behold the dirge, *Woe and Behold*," he somberly intoned, "a somber tale of a woeful grief amidst the stormy seas." And then, to Ithmar's dismay, he began to sing.

> The winter ice my hair-bib froze, and
> Sore festooned with bitter snows,
> I stood at watch and shook full-free,
> My grab-foot iced unto the mast.
>
> Fair land was lost, the storm closed in; no hope
> Was left for hearth or kin.
> For twenty days the storm cleaned house:
> Cloud-clods clocked wanderer on chin.
>
> My sight orbs failed fair earth to see, and thoughts
> Hailed back to seasons past.
> My mind took tiller in her beak and flew
> To pleasant seasons past...
>
> I had to flee, to leave the sea, to sail off -
> Borne by tale-winds past -
> T'when life was warm and I, at ease, was just
> A lad lashed to the mast.

The tears welled up and turned to ice.
They burned like splinters in my eyes.
My mind flapped loose like yonder sail and
Scattered like the wind or hail,
Or maybe not, these present woes.

I said good-bye to sorrows past, to pain
Held fast like walrus pie,
Then, straining, saw beyond the clouds of
Stormy blast a bluer sky.

The sun was warm, and comrade's cries rang out,
And yet I stood, aghast.
How could I flee, and leave the sea,
And sail away to seasons past?

How could I go and say hello except
I die before the mast?

I wrenched me back to here and now, where I,
Who once stood tall and proud,
Shook like green tree-hands in the blow that had
This bull so fully cowed.

Yet I was Regwulf, Son of Argulon,
Bane of Bildash the Red-Beard Scylf,
Scion of Hegelic, Geat-Friend and War-Wielder,
Killer of Dragons, Untangler of Kelp,
Cousin of Threadgild who stole Otto's hammer.
That was a good trick, ye warrior of old!

But my lineage was useless to save me from sea ice;
The cowardly storm's hospitality stank!
Assaulting my post with glass-dart and blow-hammer,
It corked up my bottle: no hope of escape.

I searched the sky, the rain, for signs,
But only yawning gray remained.
And then my eyes fell on the pine: the mast,
Sore lashed by frozen rain.

There I, amazed, rejoiced to find dark runes
Cut deep in hidden folds.

The ice I scraped with frozen blade to
Tell the tell-tale picture-full.
Then to my light-jewels were revealed these simple words,
"Woe and Behold!"

"Woe and behold," the writhing rune declared
Before my flickering gaze.
My neck-ball whirled; I wot that soon
I now was bound to pass away.
Or was I? Still I read these words:

"Woe and behold who reads these lines
If all alone he sails and swerves
Alone,
Unloved upon the brine."

"O, this is me! O wretch!" I cried,
"'Tis I who left my hearth and kin
To take this life-long, stormy ride
Past hope's last reef and back again!"
The bearded mast, still dumb, foretold my foolish end...
"Woe and Behold!"

My sitting-blubber numb, my furs availing naught,
The wind a blur,
I fell upon my padded side and
Forked an eye toward frozen sky.

A mournful rent did dent my stint, and
I in grief prepared to die.

I drifted long as I did die.
Rain-rocks full-clogged my cold face-pearls.
I hardly heard the hearty cries
Of Frisian traders sailing by.
They boarded and bore up my frame,
Then placed me down before a flame
Below their deck, on brasen stilts.
I scarcely saw, or breathed, or felt.

A ruddy prince then bowed to hear
And my lips moved as he drew near.
"An ancient chant," he told his men, and then
Drew close to hear again,
And I, my lips blanched blue with cold,
Groaned in his ear, "Woe and Behold!"

As the song droned on... and on... and on, post nauseam, Lord
Haruk the Cruel cradled his head dolefully in his hands and
thoughtfully stared at the poet. *His scrawny neck would suit a
sharpened axe.*

As always, Haruk sat at the left hand of the empty throne, a
mere mead-slosh away from Lord Ithmar, the Steward of the
Realm. Due to his high position, Haruk now found himself
uncomfortably close to Sylvain, who sought to stand directly in
front of the wealthiest families. This was his pattern, for he hoped
against hope to milk some patronage from the legendary treasure
chests of the Norse pirates.

Haruk's glance wandered around the hall, hooded by heavy
eyelids. His were the eyes of an asp, scarcely human and subtle
beyond words. No one could discern the intent of the rapacious
heart that lay, like a panting wolf, behind Haruk's luminous eyes.
Past a veneer of smoky eyelids, behind his heavy, handsome
features, a dragon coiled, relaxed but bored with the festivities.

Lord Haruk sighed and twiddled his thumbs.

Biding time, he thought. *Just biding time.* Haruk hated this particular minstrel more than all the rest... or more than almost all the rest. He only hated one minstrel more, and that particular minstrel was scheduled to sing after the current, miserable display.

For all of his failings, Sylvain does possess admirable amorality. He's a kindred spirit, albeit of a lower order, Haruk reflected. *And yet, I despise his pathetic yammering.* Suddenly, a novel idea occurred to him. *Perhaps, when Ithmar is dead and I am king, I will invite this man to perform at court,* he speculated with his interest reviving. *When he arrives, I'll feed his heart to my rats.* He straightened up and looked around the room, considerably cheered by the thought.

Haruk's mood immediately soured, however, when he noticed Ithmar beaming solicitously at Ilse. His daughter conversed animatedly with her beautiful mother. At their side, old Ivan Redbeard carefully listened to the conversation.

As Haruk watched, Ivan said something that caused them to laugh spontaneously. Although he could not hear Ivan's words, Haruk's imagination provided what his hearing lacked. *A wholesome jest, I suppose,* he seethed, hotly jealous of their happiness. *How he delights the pious dames of the court.* Haruk despised them with enduring venom, blaming them for – among other things – the exile of his son Kennan.

Turning again to Sylvain, Haruk the Cruel stoically endured the poet's recitation. The Ancient Wavebungler's odyssey droned on, and the plot unfolded at a barnacle's pace as the ruined old sea-goat-cum-hero was carried from ship to ice floe to island to log raft and home again, continually rediscovering the doleful inscription, "Woe and Behold."

Carved in ice, chiseled in stone, moaned by the wind, hissed by the rain, tattooed on the side of herrings tossed by the waves into his boat, the tag line "Woe and Behold" began to drive Haruk mad. The words surfaced and resurfaced throughout the tedious presentation like a distant, barnacled whale blowing rhythmically in the doldrums of a monotonous sea.

By the time the last chant had died and the crowd had wildly applauded, Haruk was busily speculating on various means of execution for the scop Sylvain, including but not limited to carving "Woe and Behold!" into his chest with a red-hot iron. As the applause faded and excited conversation took its place, Haruk the Cruel again gazed to his right, past the empty throne. He watched greedily as Ithmar and friends shared their happy conversation.

"Enjoy the evening, fool," he whispered softly, savoring the words. "Your beautiful wife and child will soon be safely under my protection." He leaned back placidly and entwined his long, slender fingers, resting them in his lap. "Eat heartily, noble Ithmar," he said, sighing blissfully. "A man should enjoy his final meal."

Sweet Victory

Victory tasted sweet, like honey from the comb. It tasted almost as good as Gunnar felt right here, right now, in this place. Prince Gunnar approached the whiskey tent feeling happy and free. At ten in the evening, all was well. He slapped a hand affectionately on Julian's shoulder.

"So who's the captain now, Captain?"

"Don't overreach, noble friend. I have seniority."

Gunnar had known Julian for ten months. It seemed amazing how life could change in just that length of time. Ten months ago, he had been a slave serving Julian's father Presius, an elderly cynic who had considered Gunnar faithful, but odd ('the boy is slightly touched,' Presius would say, 'that prince thing, you see').

On an otherwise unassuming day, Presius had presented Gunnar as a gift to his wayward son Julian, who just had returned home to join Guthrum and his armies in their campaign against King Alfred of England. Julian had quickly taken a liking to Gunnar-val, giving him a chance to fight beside him. After five months of service, he had given Gunnar his freedom, and only one month ago, he had promoted Gunnar to the rank of Lieutenant.

Now, in the course of a single day, Gunnar had become a full captain in the king's service by order of King Guthrum himself. And if that were not enough, after a bloody series of defeats followed by their recent, narrow victory, their army of the Danes faced the prospect of a negotiated peace that could bring a swift cessation to the bloody fighting. If the fighting ended, Gunnar could freely leave for home.

Home... to return home... this seemed too sweet to be true. Home remained the city of his dreams, where – Gunnar hoped – his friends and a certain girl still lived. Home had been his source of hope, and his dreams might soon become reality. A lump rose in his throat at the very thought of it, stifling his power of speech.

In spite of the promise of peace, Gunnar could not immediately leave England. As a captain in the King's service, he did not have that liberty. Home would have to wait for now... and so, for tonight, he planned to celebrate.

Captains Julian and Gunnar, recently transferred by direct order of the King to the Right Royal Guard, careened through the tent flap and entered the packed, noisy tent. At the other end of the large tent-room, on a board resting between two barrels, they beheld the siren, the conscienceless temptress that had lured them into this tempestuous reef of drunken humanity. Against the furthest wall of the tent, next to a bow-legged, pinch-faced old warrior armed with a wooden ladle, sat a mysterious, brass-bound barrel of dark, musty fluid; curiously harsh, yet seductively smooth.

This was Scotch whiskey, or its pre-medieval equivalent. A great storehouse full of the mysterious liquid had been captured at the beginning of their campaign, and now they gazed at the murky remnants of that once-mighty stockpile, the last swallows of a dizzy river that had fueled enough drunkenness to make a strong sailor blush... or, at least, to make him reach for another glass.

Battle brought with it nightmarish memories. In contrast to the glamorous image of warfare portrayed in the poetic tradition of his people, Gunnar-val had found war to be the very incarnation of evil. He had been caught up in the passions of war, and had tasted her treasures. In so doing, he had found it to be a hotbed of all that abases and defiles: a rotting bower of death bedding down in the midst of a fallen universe pulsing with the passing heartbeat of temporal life.

As an unintended consequence, war made life seem more precious – and the brotherhood of warriors more intense – when contrasted against the violence. After a battle, the air seemed cleaner, the colors more vivid. The sounds seemed surreally sweet. The innocent play of village children seemed to mock the tumultuous heat of bloody war with its predatory, rapine, inquisitive sword-thrusts and its soul-sickening slaughter.

The golden, heroic portrait of war, a glamorous image that had historically enchanted the men of his culture, had taught them to leap into the bloody bosom of their own disfigurement. But Gunnar had learned in these last few months that the ideal of heroic war was a lie, a seductive song from the insatiate mouth of the mother of sorrows.

War was the playground of death.

Through the ages, the Serpent of Death had sung War from the depths of its pit; singing through the mouths of his mortals, hungry for wayfaring souls. Death had cast a wide net for warriors and fools, serenading the mighty from its desecrated deathbed; there the evil ghosts waited, there the glory was rolled in blood, there lurked war's hungry demons, waiting to savor the taste of lamb and goat alike.

Scotch whiskey, on the other hand, seemed to provide a soothing antidote to war's nightmarish remembrances. During the alcoholic honeymoon period common to new abusers, Scotch acted a wonder drug: a marvelous balm for the blistered soul, an effective narcotic for the tender consciences of even the most rapacious of plunderers. Haunting images of warfare, when men fell under the spell of the enchanting, burning broth, were completely forgotten... along with manners, inhibitions, wisdom, common sense, decorum, and the drunken evenings themselves.

For these reasons, or simply for the thrill of the chase, the flower of Danish manhood had given its strength away to the Scotch. Dane after ruined Dane fell nightly under the sway of a smooth whiskey stupor and slipped into lively conversation, or debauchery, or random violence, or the sleep of the dead.

It was with much anticipation, therefore, that the two friends walked into the dirty gray tent and gazed hopefully at the rough-hewn whiskey barrel.

Set 'Em Up

The two captains bellied up to the drinking-board and smiled at the short, hairy creature behind it. Julian's silver piece rolled around the board in a tight circle on the board before finally falling down with a rattle.

"Set 'em up and we'll kill 'em, soldier," said Julian with a nod at the empty mugs stacked beside the barrel. The furry barrel-troll leered back at them. He was a curiously stocky, unsightly concatenation of European manhood, reeking of stale whiskey, red eyes blurred with toxic vapors from the potent brew that he had stored in his own inner keg. A tiny fleck of something brown and shiny perched on his cracked lower lip, bobbing up and down as he answered them.

"One piece of silver won't do, boys, although it would for me, but I'm not leading the charge, you see. It'll take an uncut gold piece to buy a cup of this brew. The price has been set by order of the Captain Galwin hisself, the Lord of Stores and Weaponry."

The man gurgled in laughter as if he had said something clever, his face screwing up like a squeezed sponge. As he guffawed loud and long, the little brown fleck on his lower lip fluttered like a tiny flag: flying high and proud amid the hot gusts of alcoholic wind. Julian turned to his younger companion and lifted his eyebrows with a feigned expression of shock.

"This fellow can't be referring to dear old Cap Galwin, the Lord of Broken Swords. I thought old Galwin was out wandering the fields, stripping the armor of the slain. I didn't know he had the authority to set the price of drink."

"Oh, heh heh heh," the gargoyle wheezed. "you must be a captain yourself, sir, to speak so freely and fondly of dear old Cap Galwin. He is a great man, indeed, larded and pasted with bloody honors: one who we'd all love to fight with." He paused to catch his breath. "Well, for you noble gents," he wheezed, "I'll give you two full mugs for the cost of one. That'll fetch you lads under the table, proper-like."

He leaned over and drew close to the two young men, as if he were about to share a secret. They instantly regretted this move. The man's befouled, be-whiskeyed breath, exhaled from the rotten depths of his innermost regions, oozed sour fumes as he shared his confidence.

"Don't tell the others that I'm giving drinks to you for half-price," he slurred, nodding at the crowd. "They'll all demand the same bargain. But I won't give in, and it won't go well. I'm a man of peace, you see."

"A man of peace?" Julian asked skeptically.

"Right you are, sir. I'll gut them like proper pigs before I'll yield to their violent ways."

"Hey, hurry up in front!" an impatient voice called from the back of the line that had formed behind the two captains.

"Here are four gold pieces," said Julian, placing the coins in the man's hand. "Pay Galwin his two, and you keep the rest."

"Yes sir, and many more besides." The soldier bowed comically as he hurriedly poured two very large and very full mugs of whiskey.

"I like a generous fellow," he added. "Especially one who's richer in gold than wit. The human intellect is overrated, I say."

"Indeed?" Julian asked skeptically.

"Indeed, young master. The intellect leads to all kinds of social infections… such as bear baiting, silly poems, and war.

"You really think so?"

"Indeed, sir. And I hate bear baiting, not to mention silly poems, which should be punished in a capital manner. As for war, let's hope this nasty conflict soon displays its memorable end, so we can swiftly kick it behind us where it belongs, since it's been such a pain to you noble lads. After that, we can count our stolen loot and shove off happily for home!"

Bearding the Lion

Sylvain – quite mercifully – had completed his final song. After a round of vigorous applause, the people began to circulate in the crowded mead hall: talking, singing, and generally displaying irreverent Viking glee in ways both great and small.

Ithmar, distracted by the night's festivities, had drunk more mead than was his wont. His head felt tight as an unfamiliar warmth crept stealthily across his consciousness. Looking around, he pushed away his mead bowl. *No more.* He rubbed his eyes and glanced to his left. To his surprise, Haruk was staring at him.

Haruk smiled smoothly and spontaneously, lighting up with apparent happiness as he met Ithmar's gaze. Given the degree of warmth emanating from his countenance, one would have thought that he greeted a well-beloved brother. Haruk's thoughts, however, favored envy over joy.

Ithmar, you noble bastard, Haruk mused, grinning like a fool. His capaciously greedy heart overflowed with sentimental hatred. *At least he's made a worthy opponent for all of these years. I suppose I'll miss the thrill when he's gone, and I'm king!*

Ithmar smiled tightly at Haruk, nodding and lifting his cup in a silent, ambiguous toast. *He's always suspected me,* ruminated Haruk, *but he doesn't have proof, and he's too bloody noble to accuse me without it. Well, I did it, old boy. I killed the pious idiot Vigmar. And I'll kill you soon... sooner than you can imagine.*

Haruk smiled and raised his golden cup. He leaned toward Ithmar and spoke loudly enough to make his voice heard above the cacophonous din from several hundred drunken Vikings.

"The scop gave a workmanlike performance, wouldn't you say?" Haruk asked.

"Workmanlike. That's the proper term," Ithmar rejoined. "His songs are like stylish shoes made by a lazy cobbler, all tongue and no soul." Haruk and Ithmar shared two common traits: an appreciation of a song well sung and a loathing of second-rate minstrelsy.

"His lyrics are somewhat predictable." Haruk observed.

"I suppose," answered Ithmar dryly, "if you call 'my grabfoot iced unto the mast' predictable. Predictability would be preferable to such a dreadful turn of the tongue."

"He's predictably insipid," Haruk smirked. "He predictably butchers our most majestic poetic conventions."

"Indeed," Ithmar replied, smiling at Haruk in spite of himself. Haruk, Ithmar, and Vigmar had grown up together in this town, and Ithmar still held out hope that Haruk had not been involved in the murder of his sovereign. He had shared his suspicions about Haruk with no one except his wife, Katla.

Ithmar did not want to suspect any citizen of Bryne. And yet, the fact remained that the ambush of Vigmar could hardly have been a coincidence. The King's murder in such a remote and mountainous region, by a large and well-armed band of men, had to be more than mere happenstance. What hope of reward, what kind of treasure could have lured those warriors into the barren heights? But in spite of his suspicions, Ithmar could not quite believe that Haruk, his long-time comrade in war and peace, was capable of such treachery.

The deliberate betrayal of hospitality – the breaking of the sacred blood-tie, of the bond of brotherly honor – this was the worst sin imaginable among the Norse people. Ithmar refused to impute such villainy to Haruk, but something troubled him deeply about the man; he sensed, on a subliminal level, that Haruk was to blame for the murder of the King. He could not shake the feeling. Haruk, for his part, acted as innocent as a lamb… as if he had no intimation of Ithmar's suspicions.

"Of course, there are not many minstrels as wonderfully inept as Sylvain," Haruk added. "That 'grab-foot' line… that was so bad, it was good." He rubbed his hands together, warming to the subject. *After tonight*, he thought, *I'll have no one in Bryne with whom I can discuss the finer points of Art, the most popular idol of the masses. That's quite a pity, I suppose.*

"And what did you think about the 'whirling neck-ball' metaphor?" continued Ithmar. "Was it a new low in the history of the saga, or a stroke of genius?"

"Genius having a stroke. Or rather, genius deserving of strokes." They laughed together.

For a second or two, it seemed as if there were no tension between them, as if they were once again children playing in a field, or skipping stones by the water… free of the adult baggage of position, duty, or bloody murder that crouched like a dragon behind Haruk's luminous eyes.

In the middle of the room, the master of ceremonies once again thumped the floor with his spear butt, getting the attention of the happy throng. "Dear friends, brothers, sisters, and neighbors, I'd like to present the second and final course in tonight's musical feast. He is a local thane, as we say, born and raised right here, in the City of Gold. And if that isn't enough, some people say that he's become the foremost Scop of the North. Ladies and gentlemen, I give you the greatest of the traditionalists, the legendary Brynish singer and poet, Barad-zur!"

A tall, impressive-looking man struggled to his feet and limped into the middle of the room, pausing in front of the chair that had been placed there. His face was handsome, an early middle-aged face with a white, close-cropped beard. A narrow scar ran across his forehead from the left edge of his hairline to his right eyebrow.

He bowed at the people, and the crowd grew silent as he leaned on his cane and proceeded to bow toward all points of the compass with the traditional minstrel's salute. Finally he ended with a profound sweep of the hat to Ithmar and an even grander salute toward the empty throne. Haruk, however, received no such tribute. Barad-zur paused for an instant and stared at Haruk, angrily, fearlessly staring deep into his eyes. Then he turned and sat down and picked up his lyre.

In front of the whole kingdom, he dares to snub me? Haruk seethed, stung by the slight. *I hope he's planning on staying in our city. I'll bleed him with vipers… that will cure his insolence.*

The crowd grew quiet as the poet strummed upon the

instrument, beginning a prolonged musical presentation that would precede his first song. It was a special moment in the City of Bryne as the brilliant scop, a native son so recently returned from his wanderings, somberly began to play. The intricate interlude resonated richly in the silent hall.

Mysteriously, persistently, the subtle voicing insinuated itself into their consciousness, strangely enchanting them with its beauty. The melodious sounds hung in the air like embers. Glowing sweetly, they floated across the hall before drifting apart and dispersing: settling to earth with rich, poetic resonance, like cooling ash from a fire-drake. Each delicate note submitted to gravity in its turn, returning gracefully to earth within the circle of their hearing.

Like children they listened, enraptured. With awakening hope, they dared to believe that the season of their bereavement had passed... and that joy, like a long-awaited friend, might at last have returned to stay.

The Scots' Revenge

They felt empowered. They knew all, and feared nothing. In spite of their bravado, however, they found themselves unable to manufacture Scotch whiskey from the stuff of their dreams. So it was that Julian and Prince Gunnar of Bryne leaned against the splintered drinking board and stared vacantly at one another, dolefully pondering their predicament. They had been prepared to beg for more drink, but all was in vain; the last barrel had been tapped, drained and rolled aside; the hairy barrel-troll had left for parts unknown, and their cups mocked them… empty at last, and bound to stay that way.

"Tell me again, Gunnar," slurred Julian. "What is your city like?"

"Again? Why do you want to hear it all again?"

"Because it's a nice city. Not like this dirty tent, that's why," Julian answered, straightening up in an attempt to appear assiduously sober. "No Weir-Huns or Healf-Danes in your city. Tell me again, Gunnar, old boy."

"Well, first you must know that it's a great city," he began, trying to focus in spite of his swimming head. "Not great in size, but great of spirit. It's beautiful and generous and bloody civilized… not with fancy manners, but with faithfulness and heart. Lots of heart. The people all smile and bow and say hello. There's a special girl back there. I love her, Jules. You know I do, you know… I hope she isn't married yet... but if she is, I know it won't be to a Weir-Hun. No Weir-Huns in Bryne. Not a single one." Neither of them cared for Weir-Huns, a cultural group about whom they had heard the worst sorts of things. They had heard that Weir-Huns fought with poisoned arrows… and even worse, that they had no honor.

"Where is Bryne? In the mountains?" Julian knew the answer to his question, but he wanted to hear it again.

"It's where the mountains merge into the sea," the Prince said, striving to speak clearly. "The bays are as deep as the summer sky. We're pirates, we men of Bryne. Like you Danes, you know. We have the longships… big, beautiful, open ocean ships. In Bryne, we build ships that swim like swans on the swells. The best sailors around, too. Navigate their way out of the North Sea in a blind snowstorm and make landfall at the city docks. Beautifulest girls in the world in Bryne. Beautifulest. Is that a word, Jules? My girl is the beautifulest one." Gunnar had begun to grow maudlin. That can happen when you are sold into slavery as a child and have not seen home in years.

While they talked, and listened, and laughed at one another, they did not notice that a stranger had sidled close to eavesdrop on their conversation. This man was at least as tall as Julian, but heavier: a powerfully built, dark-haired fellow who appeared to be intensely interested in what they said. He, too, had been drinking the whiskey, and his cheeks were flushed with one-hundred-proof Old Dreadnought, the Scots' revenge upon the armies of the Dane. As soon as the two friends noticed him, the man cleared his throat and began to speak.

"Excuse me, gentlemen," the man said, addressing them with unexpected courtesy. "Did I hear you talking about the city of Bryne?"

"I suppose you did. My friend was born and raised there."

"I'm very familiar with that city. In fact, I had a man from Bryne in my unit until recently. I hired him as a mercenary, and they assigned him to my boat. He was my navigator during the Frisian campaigns." Gunnar straightened up and thrust out an empty sword-hand.

"Gunnar-val is my name. I'm from Bryne… Brynish through and through." They shook hands.

"I'm Telgar Roentner. It's good to meet a man from Bryne. I know something about the city. My wife is Brynish."

"Is she fair?" Julian queried. He was keen to verify his companion's claims about Brynish women.

"As a spring day is fair," Roentner replied. "All of those Brynish girls are fair. Haven't you heard?"

"That seals it," Julian declared fervently. "I'm going to that city when this mess is over."

"What was your friend's name; the navigator from Bryne?" asked Gunnar. "Did he talk about our city?"

"Well, I'll answer you, if you don't mind hearing the whole story." They looked at him expectantly, and Gunnar gestured for him to continue. "Kennan was his name. He was a very good navigator, but a very bad man. We didn't realize it at the time. In fact, my men trusted their gold to him. The men all kept a common purse, you see, and they appointed Kennan their treasurer. Anyway, after we took the land around Grimsby, their common purse got very heavy.

"We sacked a small castle kept by those English wizards... some sort of robed magicians... monks, I think they call them. The locals said that they were holy men. That means that they are different from the rest of us, I suppose. I don't know about that.

"They didn't resist us, and we took their stronghold without a fight. The men wanted to bash a few heads, but I stopped them. Wasted energy, I told them: dull sport, killing men who won't fight.

"The castle of those wizards was packed full of gold. I picked up two gold statues over two spans tall. Shaped like this, they were," he brought his hands together, putting his index fingers together in the shape of a cross. "They had the likeness of a man being killed, right in the middle. That's an awful way to die... worse than an executioner's axe, I'd think. Hung to death, nailed to a tree."

"That night, we got drunk with all of these piles of loot just laying around for the taking... and in the morning, our noble navigator was missing along with our gold. For good measure, he stole my lieutenant's personal slave, killed two of King Guthrum's harbor guards, and got away clean in one of King Guthrum's longships. That ship was worth a fortune! When you add in the gold, he stole a king's ransom. And the miserable part is, if anyone can sail that ship back across the North Sea with a one-slave crew, it's that rascal Kennan. He's a top-notch sailor; although I must admit, it turns out he's an even better thief. Well, now, that's what happened to our group just ten short weeks ago."

Gunnar had listened transfixed, hardly believing what he heard. Kennan? What was Kennan doing in England, so far from Bryne? What had happened to cause him to leave? The thievery Gunnar could easily believe, knowing Kennan. But why had Kennan left Bryne in the first place? He had a princely life in Bryne as Lord Haruk's son, and Kennan highly valued the prestige of his noble name. As for treachery, Kennan had shown himself a thief... but was he also a killer? Did he know what his father, Haruk, had done to Vigmar?

"Did he ever talk about Bryne?" Gunnar asked, talking quickly, excitedly. "Did he mention anyone? What news did he bring?"

"Oh, he didn't say much about it. He was just too careful a man to share any details. But one night we got very drunk together, and he opened up; that was the night when he told me about his fondest dreams. Of course, I thought that they were long-term plans, or maybe just wild dreams. But I guess his scheme is affordable now."

"What scheme?"

"Oh, he wanted to take revenge on the Steward of the city. He claimed the right to a blood feud. He wanted to sail into Bryne with a longship and offer the men of Bryne a chance to go with him, raiding up the coast of Francia. He said the men there are natural born warriors, and he thought that he could get together a raiding party in no time at all. Then, he said they would go to Francia, where his father had an ally. They'd kill the Franks to get their bloody gold, and then he would sail back home with a wild crew of rich Bryne-men. He said he could get elected to the throne after such a success. But first, he said, he wanted to kill the Steward."

"The Steward... that's Ithmar. He's a good man; the best. Why would Kennan want to kill Ithmar?" Roentner attempted to take a swig from his empty cup. When he came up without a drop of Scotch, he held the cup upside-down and looked up into it, eyeing it suspiciously, and glanced ironically at his two companions as if to say, 'at least I tried.' Then, he answered the question.

"Kennan said he was seduced by the Steward's daughter. He claims they exiled him for it. This part of his story I didn't believe for a second. My wife's Brynish, remember? There had to be more to it, or the city council wouldn't have exiled him. So I pushed him, and I pushed him, and I got him mad, and then he spilled his guts. And, let me tell you, what came out wasn't pretty.

"It turns out that he attacked the Steward's young daughter, and he got the worst of it. He claims that he raped her, but I think he was lying. Whatever happened, it did not turn out like he had planned. The little girl fought like a cornered badger, and then her big dog got hold of him. He barely escaped with his life.

"So he brutalized a little girl. That's what they exiled him for, the pig. He's lucky I didn't drown him on the spot, but I needed a navigator, so I let him live. To my regret, as you see."

Gunnar stared at Roentner with his mouth wide open in dismay. He felt as if his blood ran in hot waves from his head to his feet: as if a foul hand pressed upon him heavily from above.

Captain Julian turned to look at his friend and saw him standing there, lost and unbelieving, bleached a sickly white hue and shaking like a luffing sail on a struggling ship confronting a strong headwind on high seas. A flash of insight informed him about his friend.

Oh, no, he thought as he watched his friend. *Poor Gunnar! The Steward's daughter... the one the Brynish navigator attacked... she was his girl.*

Barad-zur

"Mother," Ilse whispered. "Isn't the music beautiful?" She turned her face and gazed at her mother with little-girl expectancy shining from her eyes.

"Hush, dear," Katla quietly replied.

In the middle of the room the poet, Barad-zur, finished the lengthy musical introduction to his first song. Like delicate white butterflies above an outsized black flower, his supple hands floated lightly across the dark, polished face of an Old Norse Lyre.

Lyres of Norse lineage were large, unwieldy instruments, difficult to play and cumbersome to hold, and yet – in the hands of a master – they could sing with rare beauty: resonant with curious, lilting, almost hypnotic power.

With the instrumental passage completed, the poet began to sing:

> The mighty men of ancient days
> Now slumber in the dust.
> The kingdoms of the earth have sunk
> Into the great abyss
> Where worms forsake the carcass
> When there is no savor left.
> What is man that he should glory
> In his fleeting hour of breath?
>
> I was a man who held the trust and honor of my lords.
> In bloody fight amidst the reek I added to the gore.
> I was a servant to my king;
> May heaven bless his name!
> A nobler soul I never knew, nor saw a bolder thane:
> In battle swift as any wolf to shatter crowns and kings.
> I fought beside him at the iron gates of Son Velline.

At Son Velline the city fell
With stones upon our heads.
Their women's cry, a banshee's wail,
Foretold what lay ahead
While we, the pirates, heard their screams
And laughed against the stones
And vowed to grind their men to dust
And burn their pleasant homes.

We fought that day in autumn snow.
Long summer's siege had smoked them out.
My sword stained crimson, dripping, gleaming.
We fought: our breath and blades both steaming.

Many an eye went dull, transfixed,
Mouths gaped beneath our sharpened scythes.
We pressed until the battle pitched before the walls
That hid their lives.

The carnage stoked to fever pitch,
We stormed the massive iron gates;
Our Vigmar pressed the boldest fight,
Collapsed the flank and couldn't wait.
He bit into the desperate host until, in fear,
They wheeled about.
As any cornered beast might do,
They turned upon us with a shout.

And then I saw my Lord, my liege
Cut off upon a barren ridge
With wounded friends, and no one else
Beside him on his day of fate.
And I, so young and so untested,

Found my heart between my teeth;
Yet if I fell, or I was bested,

Knew it must be at his feet.

With sudden strength I gave the cry,
"For Vigmar, brothers, live or die!"
I led the charge into their swords and used
Slick bodies as a bridge
Across the rill that once had run
So clear,
Now red: defiled and still.

I ran upon the giant Lod, and
Smote and spilled his steaming bowels.
I saw dumb shock upon his face as
He beheld them slipping out.
No time to stop; a dart hit hard;
I whirled and slashed another man
Who found himself without a leg and spilled
Hot blood into the sand.

Mighty lions, little sheep:
I slew the valiant and the weak.
Ten wounds I took, and each may tell the total...
If I battled well.
At last our brothers drove them back
And rushed the gates to ram and crash
While warm, soft sleep stole over me.
No battle swirled there in my dreams.

The years have fallen like the leaves,
And I have learned to play and sing.
I never since have done a deed so great
As when I saved my king.
Yes I, unworthy, served to save
Our best and bravest lord and liege.
Those days are past.
Now, Vigmar sleeps,

And I must wander for my keep.

Hear me you people and mark it well:
You'll never know a greater king,
Who loaded you with gold and jewels
And stormed the gates of Son Velline.

At Son Velline the mighty fell;
The blowflies crawled on every face.
You still wear filigree and rings
Borne all the way from Son Velline.
Borne to you by this great king -
At cost of lives from Son Velline.

Young fools dream of wealth and glory;
Old fools recount fame and gold;
Wise men turn from youthful dreams
To mourn the bodies now left cold.

Who can make the widows glad?
Who can make the orphans sing?
Wise men turn and feed the weak,
Yet none can rebuild Son Velline.

Kingdoms pass, and minstrels sing,
But none can heal their fitful dreams.

None can give their fathers life
Or raise the gates of Son Velline.

A Dangerous Brew

"Look, Telgar," interjected Julian, trying to draw his attention away from the stricken Gunnar-val. "Who are those guys?" A group of several tall, red-haired men had just entered the tent, which by now was almost empty. The newcomers were a distinctively dressed group of warriors: quite dapper, considering that they were in a war zone. Each one resembled the others so closely that they could have easily passed for cousins.

"They're mercenaries," Roentner told Julian. "Weir-Huns."

"No!" exclaimed Julian. "They're the dreaded Weir-Huns?" He grinned lazily. "I don't see what all the fuss is about. They look scrawny to me." Of course, he did not acknowledge that by comparison, his own scrawny form made them look stout.

At that moment the leader of the group, having determined that the last of the Scotch whiskey was gone, happened to turn and look at them. Unfortunately for Julian, it appeared obvious to the leader of the newcomers that the two giants standing beside the bar were busily insulting himself and his men. This did not shock him, for Weir-Huns were accustomed to disrespect. But it did not make him happy.

If the truth were known, this much could be said for the Weir-Huns as a cultural group: they were not as bad as described in the popular oral tradition. However, the truth should also be told that, when they wanted to be, Weir-Huns could exceed the claims of their most vocal critics.

Tonight, Ixtalaban was a Weir-Hun in a particularly foul mood. Like Julian and Roentner, he also happened to be a captain in Guthrum's army... the leader of a group of men who had done some of the dirtiest fighting of the war. His battle group had spent most of the long afternoon in the heated core of a blood-curdling, tumultuous battle. They had gone hand-to-hammer with the die-hard English, and had lost more than one good man. Simply put, they had survived a bad day, and were in no mood to tolerate insults.

Now that the battle had been won, Ixtalaban and several of his best men had taken care of their wounded and slummed down to the whiskey tent in a vain attempt to find relief for their souls. They had hungrily yearned for the memory-purging somnolence that whiskey could bring, hiking four miles across the darkened, war-torn countryside to get here. And now, after all of the dust and the dirt and the black-caked blood festering in their boots, after all the bloody clothes and the bloody long hike to this rancid watering hole, they had just learned that the malingerers in this smoky tent had finished the last of the whiskey.

The Weir-Huns felt frustrated and foul: used and abused by the wily Danes who had beaten them to the liquid treasure. Now, as Ixtalaban saw the skinny giant staring at them impertinently from across the room, he felt his hackles rise.

"A Weir-Hun!" Julian said excitedly, nudging Roentner. "This is my first sighting." He winked drolly and glanced back at Gunnar-val.

Gunnar stared vacantly at the tent wall, still unable to fully comprehend what he had just heard. *Ilse... attacked by Kennan?*

Julian hoped to draw Gunnar out of his state of shock with the fact that actual, live Weir-Huns stood within spitting distance, in plain sight of all who cared to look. Now, this was news!

"Gunnar, look!" he exclaimed more loudly than he intended. "Look at the Weir-Huns!"

Several of the warriors accompanying Ixtalaban heard Julian's unwise comment. These were tough customers, but they were also a well-disciplined fighting team. They turned and looked at their Captain.

Captain Ixtalaban sighed deeply and placed his right hand over his face, rubbing his eyes and slowly shaking his head. Seeing this reaction, his men smiled and nudged one another. Their misery, so complete a mere moment ago, was instantly dispelled. They stood in the dazzling glow of a glorious new day.

Nothing warmed a Weir-Hun's heart like a good, foul fight.

Moments of Truth

The packed hall resounded with throaty cheers as appreciative citizens of Bryne – men, women, and children – voiced their approval to the uttermost decibel, well pleased by the song that they had just heard.

"Wasn't that really something?" asked Ilse, impressed by the tone of the work, but not quite knowing how to evaluate the grisly content. She had never particularly cared for the grim, blow-by-bludgeon descriptions of battles that typified Old Norse poetry. "Is the story true?" Hearing her daughter's question, Katla smiled sadly.

"I'm afraid it is. Barad-zur was a young man when he fought beside King Vigmar. He saved the King's life at the battle of Son Velline. It was one of the cities Vigmar conquered before he stopped sailing off to war."

"I can see why he stopped," said Ilse. "War must be dreadful. No, it must more than dreadful. It must be a living nightmare."

"I'm sure it is."

"You are right," added Ivan, leaning in and responding, uninvited and unannounced. Katla smiled at him, but Ilse frowned as she considered the riddle of human conflict.

"Why do men go to war?" she asked Ivan.

"Our people traditionally went to war for glory, or vengeance, or gold," he replied with a wan smile. "And of course, lately the emphasis has been on the gold and the glory, with less said about vengeance. War can be very profitable for the victors."

At this moment, their attention was drawn to the minstrel, who began to play another song. Ithmar, having just finished talking with a local citizen, returned to his seat beside Katla and gently squeezed her hand. They smiled at each other warmly, not needing to speak. Within a minute, Katla was the only one of their party not fully absorbed in the minstrel's entertainment.

Katla let her glance wander around the hall, past the faces of bearded, long-haired men and rosy-cheeked children, past various strong, thoughtful women enjoying a chance to socialize communally with their men. The mead hall was inordinately packed with swarming humanity, for the Feast of the Elders honored not only the patriarchs of Bryne, but the women and children of the land as well. All of Bryne's citizens who could walk, limp, or trundle to the party had crowded together into the huge, rectangular room.

Tacitus, the Roman general and historian, had marveled that the barbarous warriors of northern Europe married one spouse, remained faithful for life, and publicly honored their mates as equals. This social structure differed greatly from the stratified hierarchical system prevalent in Roman society, in which husbands ruled imperiously and mistresses were common among the rich. The armies under Tacitus had never made permanent inroads against the northernmost tribes, and had finally given up.

The traditions of the city-state of Bryne still followed the pattern described by Tacitus several hundred years before. However, in spite of the fact that the Norse people's concept of spousal equality was deeply ingrained in the culture, there were three noted limits to familial and marital egalitarianism in Bryne.

The first redoubt of Norse paternalism remained in final decision-making regarding their families. The second endured in the governmental council of freemen. With rare exceptions, only men sat the council, although women could speak or hold a seat if they headed a family. But even in these two exclusive spheres of influence, men received guidance from their spouses. The third stronghold of male dominion, and the most insular of all, was that last, fast bastion of brotherly camaraderie – a treasured refuge from refinement, civility, and table manners – the mead hall.

The traditions of Bryne were unusual in that, during the annual feast of the Elders, women and children joined the men in the mead hall, their innermost chamber of male revelry. Katla, with not a little irony, appreciated the unusual honor – albeit at arm's length. Once each year, she had the dubious honor of watching as the male citizens of Bryne, or at least most of them, reduced themselves to mead-soaked, inebriated lumps... as weak as lard-carvings, pathetic renderings of their usually strong-minded selves.

She shook her head, glanced to her left, and rested her gaze on Haruk. For once, the cautious Haruk did not notice that he was being watched. *Good,* she thought, *he's unaware that I'm watching. Maybe I'll see some honest reactions for a change.*

For reasons not involving Haruk's son Kennan, Katla had never trusted Haruk. She somehow sensed that he was dangerous, vile, and up to no good. But the man was too subtle, too careful not to get caught, presenting a polished and practiced facade to the world. She had never been able to confirm her suspicions.

She had prayed for insight into his scheming... for some sort of proof to confirm or dismiss her intuitions. Her prayers remained to be answered. Still, she had not given up her hope that she would eventually know, with certainty, the truth about Haruk.

At this very moment, as she mulled these things over, Haruk turned his lion-like head around and looked directly at her husband. For some reason he did not see that Katla was watching him from where she sat, almost hidden from his view by Ithmar, who had just leaned forward to get a better view of the performance in the middle of the room.

As Haruk sat and stared at Ithmar his face underwent a startling transformation. At first it was smooth and emotionless, but then it began to change. He turned darker: first red, then almost purple, and the expression of his countenance changed from benign complacency to a passionate mask of envy and hatred.

Katla stopped breathing. Her heart leaped, lodging in her throat, and then she saw something that sent waves of insight, mingled with shocked despair, washing over her body, already tingling with the blood that been drained from her face.

Lord Haruk the Cruel, his countenance contorted into the very picture of loathing, began to smile. The smile began slowly and spread across his broad countenance like a blemish in the heavens, a concupiscent evening star. An evil moon rising, the foul breadth of his face's waxing luminance haloed his crescent grin with an unclean moon-glow of shining, death-barrow gray.

The dawn of Haruk's smile cast a pall on her soul. The evil gaze went unnoticed by Ithmar, but it appalled Katla. With a flash of insight, her prayers were answered. She finally understood Haruk the Cruel.

He hates Ithmar... he despises him... how has he hidden it so well? He must have hated King Vigmar like this, too. He must be the killer, and Ithmar will be next. Oh, God, she prayed, her head swimming with grief. *Please don't let him succeed!*

The Last Scotch War

"What are you looking at?" The question was at once hostile and pugnacious, more challenge than sincere inquiry. Evaluating the intent of the stranger who had issued the challenge, Julian squinted quizzically and slowly scratched his ear. This was a Weir-Hun indeed… with a chip on his shoulder the size of a narwhal stranded on a floe.

The hostile stranger offered a shady character study in perfectly bad behavior. Clothed in recently stolen English woolens, he seemed the archetypical Viking warrior. His unkempt beard, stained with stale wine, hid a pale face tattooed with faded red freckles, crowned with bushy brows and framed with kinky, brick red hair. His eyes were neither brown, nor blue, nor yet green, or any other color of the rainbow. They looked black: as black as onyx, black as the tar that stained the North Sea waves. The black eyes flashed with anger as he tapped his foot impatiently, waiting for a reply.

In this, Julian's hour of need, his Danish kindred abandoned him to the Weir wolves. Seeing that they were badly outnumbered by the newcomers, the last Danes in the tent quietly vacated the premises. *This Weir-Hun speaks excellent Danish,* thought Julian, resisting the drunken haze that threatened to overcome his impaired wits. *Perhaps he's not such a terrible fellow.*

"Pardon us, good fellow," Julian replied convivially. "We've never seen Weir-Huns before. You're our first." His heavy tongue slurred the words in spite of his best efforts. His last few swallows of Scotch had begun to take effect.

Julian could not have known it – since this was his first campaign with King Guthrum – but the man who stood before him was a deadly mercenary with a very thin skin. Moreover, this man and his companions, infamous mercenaries from the Weirs of Northern Teutonia, shared a childish but dangerous fault. They bitterly hated to be called Weir-Huns.

They may have called one another Weir-Huns in private, but they did not want anyone else to use the term. Among Guthrum's armies, Weir-Hun had become a pejorative term due to the prejudicial assumptions of provincial – if doughty – Danes.

The truth did not need an interpreter; it could be seen on their faces. In this particular place, at this particular time, Captain Julian could scarcely have uttered a more foolish term than 'Weir-Huns.'

"Tell me this," Ixtalaban queried as he quickly closed the distance between himself and Captain Julian. "Are you drunk?"

"Drunk? Sure, I'm drunk," replied Julian with a charming smile.

"Are you stupid?"

"Stupid?" he asked. "My word! There's no call for that talk." He had been trying to be agreeable, but now he felt his temper rise. "Why do you ask? Are you an expert?" Julian asked.

"What do you mean?"

"You sound like an expert," Julian observed. "Your stupidity must be very advanced, since you feel free to critique mine."

"What did you say?"

"Let me put it plainly, speaking slowly," Julian replied. "You must be as dumb as a salted sea-slug."

The insult jolted Ixtalaban, warming his belly and exciting his senses. *This is going to be fun*, he thought, sizing up the small group that leaned against the bar.

Three men stood before him. Captain Julian was a towering cornstalk of a man, well dressed and well spoken, but lacking in solidity. If did not appear that he would offer much trouble in a fight. Standing beside him, however, was a dark-haired man even taller than Julian. This man was muscular and well proportioned, a fighter born and bred. As a point of interest, he possessed the most spacious proboscis that the Weir-Hun had ever seen. *That must be Captain Roentner*, Ixtalaban mused. *I've heard of him. No one else could fit his description… not with that nose. He'll give us trouble, and plenty of it.* After these quick assessments, Ixtalaban turned his head and focused his gaze on the last of the three men.

The third man wore his blonde hair long and loose, in the style of the uncivilized savages of the far north. He was not dressed as richly as his companions, but wore simple, practical Viking clothing that did not hinder movement. He was staring, transfixed, into space. He had not even noticed what was about to happen.

Although dwarfed by his giant companions, the third man was also tall. He wore a bushy blonde beard on a handsome face set with an aquiline nose and thick brow wrinkled in perplexity. He was heavily muscled, but not too heavily: wiry but relaxed. He looked as if he might be a hard man to beat.

All told, it looked like good news. It appeared to Ixtalaban as if the pending conflict might be interesting, after all. These three Danes might give them a good, dirty fight.

"I repeat: are you drunk, or stupid?" Ixtalaban asked loudly.

"I told you I'm drunk. As for stupidity, you've already established that you're the expert," Julian declared, stubbornly setting his jaw. "Your supremacy remains unchallenged."

Julian could be pig-headed. Given this man's rudeness, he had decided not to relent, even if a swarming horde of angry Weir-Huns waved their bloody meat axes in his face.

"Are you calling me stupid?" asked the Weir-Hun. This was just a formality, to establish his excuse for a fight.

"Let's put it this way," replied Julian, waxing impertinent. "If the perfect image of stupidity were carved out of walrus blubber, it would look exactly like you. In fact, I think that's what you are: the very image of stupidity rendered in lard, brought to life by an evil wizard with a sick sense of humor!"

"Thank you," replied Ixtalaban, grinning broadly. "Your insult is well taken. Since we cannot agree, I suppose we'll have to settle our disagreement the old fashioned way. Which weapons do you choose?"

"No weapons," replied Julian curtly. He had not entirely lost his senses. "We have fists. Let's use them like gentlemen."

"Okay," Ixtalaban replied, bitterly disappointed. Loudly enough for his men to hear, he stated the rules. "No weapons, men. We will fight hand-to-hand."

His men moaned with dismay. Nevertheless, in obedience to their captain's command, a cascade of heavy thumps and clatters rang out as various and sundry swords, daggers, maces, clubs, knives, dirks, and hammers were dropped to the tent's wooden floor. The rattle and clank of falling weapons continued for quite some time as the lanky Weir-Huns dug knives and weapons out of the most improbable places. When the last warrior had pulled the final dagger from the innermost depths of the last head of wiry red hair, they were finally ready to engage their adversaries.

How can they pack so much armament on such meager carcasses? wondered Julian.

"You see: no weapons," said Ixtalaban finally, holding out his hands toward Julian with the palms facing upward.

"No fighting to the death, either," replied Julian. *Let's hope they like this idea.*

"Oh, come on!"

"Nope. No killing."

"Okay, no fighting to the death." Ixtalaban drew back his hand to strike Julian, but was interrupted once again.

"Three against three?" Julian offered hopefully. Ixtalaban looked at his men, who looked back with sour expressions.

"Why don't we just have a pillow fight?" a grizzled old veteran asked gruffly.

"I'm sorry," Ixtalaban replied. "I can't go that far. My men must have their fun. Nice try, though. Eh, boys?" He turned halfway around to face his group as he spoke.

Without further ado, Captain Ixtalaban, Hun of the Northern Weir, backhanded Julian with a crushing blow that sent him spinning through the makeshift bar head-over-heels, scattering barrels and boards like grapeshot launched from a catapult.

The fun had begun.

The Dangers of Fidelity

The second lay of Barad-zur had ended, and, once again, a tumultuous roar of Viking glee erupted in the crowded hall. Ithmar stood and bowed close to Katla, speaking in her ear.

"I've got to leave for a while. Somebody has to spell Thayard and the men on watch down at the docks." Katla, distracted by her thoughts and by the current uproar, looked up at him, not immediately comprehending what he said. "You're the greatest treasure that ever graced our city," he whispered. She rolled her eyes as he gave her a hug. This man could charm honey from bees.

"Hurry back, Papa," called Ilse, and suddenly Katla awoke as from a dream with the sharp realization that danger was at hand. Every year during this feast, Ithmar, as dependable as the shadow on a sundial, delivered fresh mead to the men on the dock watch, giving them a much-appreciated break from the monotony of their duties.

He's as dependable as the tides, Katla thought. *Dependable as Vigmar, who left every spring on his solitary hunts... on which he was caught and killed. Hunters, like murderers, feast upon the predictability of their prey.* With a jolt she recognized the danger facing her husband.

"Ithmar!" she cried, standing up suddenly. Her voice was lost in the riotous din as she watched him disappear into the crowd.

A Good, Foul Fight

Like a slim human javelin announcing the beginning of the festivities, Julian crashed backwards through the middle of the rough-hewn drinking board. This gave Roentner some valuable (if hard-gained) elbowroom as he enthusiastically joined the fray. Because Ixtalaban was considerate enough to swing wildly, Roentner generously assisted with his follow-through, ramming him headfirst into the original object of his displeasure: the empty whiskey-barrel.

The other Weir-Huns joined in the fun with hearty glee, rushing Roentner in a single pack. Ixtalaban, with his head spinning like a top, tried to stand, but promptly fell back onto the floor.

In the corner, Julian rolled over and moaned. This did not contribute much to the fight, but it was the best that he could muster under the circumstances. In all fairness, it should be noted that his moaning added authentic background noise, contributing to the ambiance of another foolish battle in Wild West Saxony.

Prince Gunnar, deep in thought, happened to look up as a hearty Hun smashed a fractured barrel-stave across his flinty forehead. The blow staggered Gunnar, rocking him back on his heels.

He stared at the attacking man with a hurt, stunned expression, as if to ask, 'Why did you do that?' The Hun followed up with a vicious kick that Gunnar blocked reflexively.

Finding himself in the middle of a fight that he had not provoked, Gunnar ducked as a stool whizzed by, missing him narrowly before smacking an attacking Weir-Hun squarely in the face. The man dropped like a rock as the Prince looked around the room. "Stop it!" Gunnar cried. He did not particularly like what he saw. Worse than that, he had begun to get angry.

Gunnar's greatest fault was his wretched, lethal temper.

Because he was aware of this fact, he tried to avoid situations that might provoke his wrath. As he had matured, he had labored mightily to control himself and had generally managed, by avoidance, to keep his temper in check.

Now, a foul temper stirred deep within him. The Weir-Huns had begun to get under his skin. Another flying stool clipped him on the shoulder, and as he spun away from the pain, he glimpsed Julian lying unconscious on the floor.

That did it.

Gunnar got mad. And as usual, once he lost his temper he was all business.

Striking swiftly, Gunnar smashed the stool-thrower in the face, putting him down and out of the fight. He spun to his right, ducking a barrel stave swung by another angry Hun. Knocking this new assailant to the earth with a backhanded blow to the head, he kicked him unconscious and whirled to face the men attacking Roentner.

Roentner had hammered his assailants in vain. He lay helplessly on the ground, with three strong warriors using him like a sealskin kicking bag. Other Weir-Huns had begun to work on the prostrate Captain Julian.

All except Ixtalaban were fully occupied, kicking their victims at will. The booted blows seemed to slow down to a snail's pace as Gunnar, in airborne descent, hurtled towards the center of the mob surrounding Roentner.

"AAAGH!" Gunnar cried as he slammed into their midst. As they reeled from the shock, he proved to be quicker than any warrior they had ever seen. Unfortunately, to add pain to indignity, his strength exceeded his speed.

The anger that contorted his face was terrifying; his knowledge of martial disciplines encyclopedic. All of the tricks the Huns had learned in a lifetime of fighting were too predictable against Gunnar, all of their movements too slow.

Before they could begin, he struck, and the men, one-by-one, awoke on their knees or their backs, or flat on their faces. Regaining consciousness, they emerged from the void into a ringing, swirling universe. They felt sick and dismayed, and their heads hung limply as they stared insensibly and struggled in vain to remember their own names.

As Gunnar unleashed his fury, Ixtalaban was smart enough to step back and watch, assessing his opponent's skills with professional interest. Within seconds, Gunnar had dispatched his best fighters like a grown man spanking wayward boys. *Oh, no,* Ixtalaban wondered. *Who in the world is this?*

With his adversaries fallen like trees before the woodman's axe, Prince Gunnar-val stopped and turned toward Ixtalaban. He stood panting as he warily watched the last Weir-Hun standing.

"Okay, big man," Gunnar hissed. Due to his anger, a heavy Brynish accent colored his normally impeccable Danish. To Ixtalaban, Gunnar's accent sounded uncouth. This was a true Viking inflection, brutally abrupt and chillingly primitive.

"It's your turn," the Prince added.

Gunnar's face had turned purple. Although no man had struck him, his nose poured blood released solely by the pressure of his rage. Bright red liquid streamed down his lip in a thin line that disappeared into his beard to feed a growing, crimson blot. He shook his head suddenly like an angry bull, spraying tiny droplets of telltale blood in every direction: a gruesome ruby rain that pattered upon the wood-slat floor in the sudden, utter silence.

This was one scary guy.

Rejecting fear, Captain Ixtalaban sighed wearily, and then smiled. In this, his moment of truth, only outstanding bravery above and beyond the call allowed him to do his duty. Ixtalaban Heinmich, Captain of the Third Battle Group of the Loyal Order of Teutonic Knights, stepped bravely into the whirling saw-blade of a sound and certain thrashing.

He closed on Gunnar with his fists warily poised in front of him in a brave but futile show of force. Compared to Gunnar's oversized fists, Ixtalaban's resembled bony toys. *At least we're not fighting to the death,* he thought hopefully.

He never saw the punch that took him out.

When Ixtalaban awoke, he heard someone shouting. Someone

was yelling loudly enough to cut through the dizzy sea-chantey of crashing waves that rhythmically surged and ebbed within his ears. It was Gunnar, and he was still fighting mad.

"Get up, you scum!" he cried, beside himself with rage. "Get up and fight like men! Get up, you gull-brained lemmings! Rotten whale meat! You want to hurt me? You want to hurt my friends? Then show me what you've got! Get up and fight like men!"

By now, all of the Weir-Huns had regained consciousness, but none dared stand. They remained without moving where they had landed: upside down in a corner, under a board, on belly or back, sprawled over barrels; wherever they had fallen, they stayed, turning their eyes to behold the fierce warrior who had whipped them like fuzzy-cheeked novices.

Gunnar picked up a split board from a broken barrel stave and broke it over the top of his head. Splinters and wood scraps flew in all directions, unleashing a spray of cellulose that rattled thinly on the drinking board, audible in the sudden, profound silence. He shivered like a swimmer in frigid water.

"Get up!" he roared. "Get up and fight!" Finally, in answer to the defeated warriors' prayers, Captain Julian struggled to his feet and stepped unevenly across the floor.

"Gunnar? Gunnar," he said. "It's all right. They've given up, old boy. Good job! I don't think they want any more."

"Well, I do," Gunnar growled. "I want some more." He looked at Julian wonderingly, stupefied as the tide of his anger began to recede. He looked down at Roentner, who gamely tried to stand. The left side of Roentner's face was swollen, but he forced a smile through the pain.

"That was some fight," he mumbled.

Gunnar looked around the room. The recumbent Weir-Huns eyed him with awe and unvarnished respect. He shook his head more slowly this time and passed his hand over his face. The room had become very quiet. He sighed, and looked at Julian again.

"Not a bad fight," Gunnar finally agreed. "These boys are pretty tough." Now that the fight was over, he trembled in the aftermath of the rage that had demolished his composure so completely.

Roentner laughed in spite of his pain.

"I wouldn't have known they were tough," he chortled wryly. "Not from the swath you cut through them." Captain Ixtalaban, hiding behind the broken whiskey-board, held up his hand.

"Excuse me, gentlemen" he asked courteously. "May I speak?"

"You're a free man. Do as you please," offered Julian, reveling in the joy of victory… as if he had contributed to it. Ixtalaban stiffly unwound his legs and stood shakily to his feet, offering his empty sword hand to Gunnar.

"Please, shake my hand," he said to the Prince. "You are, without a doubt, the greatest fighter I have ever seen. And I've seen some of the best."

"Let's find some mead," responded the Prince as he shook Ixtalaban's hand. He had, by now, almost returned to normalcy. "The night's still young," he told the badly battered Huns. "Come on, boys, let's go! Rise and shine! I know where we can find some more whiskey."

The scattered men gathered their wits, or what was left of them, and struggled gamely to their feet, biting their tongues to suppress the moans of anguish that tried to leap from their mouths as bruised, banged, cracked, stretched, pulled, and generally mangled joints, muscles, ligaments and bones tried to function again. They painfully filed outside, following their newfound friends and leaving the tent behind them.

"Rise and shine!" echoed the youngest Weir-Hun, a resilient, fresh-faced lad of sixteen who had suffered the least in the fray. "Maybe we'll be lucky enough to find another fight."

Nobody smiled.

Word of Warning

K atla left the table without a word and vanished into the crowd. She pushed past reveling thanes and boisterous wives, ignoring their greetings as she struggled to catch up with her husband. She saw him walk out the door in front of her and quickened her pace, following him out into the freezing cold, finally catching him by the arm as he passed under the eaves of the building that adjoined the hall. He turned around, his eyes wide with surprise.

"Katla. What?"

"Just listen. Don't ask any questions. Do you trust me?"

"Of course." He searched her eyes for some clue of what she was up to. She grabbed him by his hands, now resting on her waist.

"You're in danger!"

"Obviously."

"No! I mean it," she said urgently, digging her nails into his wrists. "You're in danger!" His expression changed as he absorbed what she was saying, and his eyes narrowed.

"What do you mean?" he asked, looking around the empty street.

"Just believe me. I'll tell you later." She knew that he would trust her insight, but she also knew that she couldn't tell him about Haruk, not immediately. His love for King Vigmar was so profound, and his suspicions regarding Haruk were already so inflamed, that Katla was afraid to tell him what she had seen.

She knew that, if she told Ithmar about Haruk without properly choosing the time and place, a summary, one-man execution would likely be the result. And such a bloody murder, without solid evidence to justify it, could lead to a cycle of vengeance and retribution that would tear their city apart forever.

Fresh Blood

More than two miles away, Gunnar and his companions expected to find the only encampment left – among all the Viking hordes – with a supply of Scotch whiskey on hand. They had no way of knowing that their hope would prove unfounded. So they mounted their steeds and trotted off towards the empty potable at the end of their feckless, alcoholic rainbow.

Along the way they paused at a stream and let their horses drink deeply from the swift-flowing waters. Ixtalaban peppered Gunnar with questions, wanting to know all he could of his background... in hope of discovering how he might learn to fight like him. To Julian's surprise, Gunnar opened up and told them about his home city, even mentioning the murder of his father and his plans for returning to Bryne after the end of the war.

The prospect of peace has loosened his tongue, thought Julian, remembering their meeting with King Guthrum of the Danes. *It's made him giddier than the Scotch ever could.*

A short time later, they tied up their horses outside of the rumored final resting-place of the army's last barrel of Scotch. The English armies, in confused retreat, had abandoned a lordly manor that had served as their field headquarters, and the doughty Danes had converted the central dining room into the likeness of a Norse mead hall. The room had required no extensive makeover, merely a reconfiguration of its tables plus a few well-gnawed bones strewn across the polished wooden floor.

On this particular evening, brain-impaired barbarians had plastered themselves around the room in various stages of debauched inebriation: face down on the floor, draped on the table, sitting, leaning or even standing... all diehards to the end. Here, the mead flowed as abundantly as bitter water at an alkaline spring. But mercifully, Scotch whiskey was not on the menu.

Captain Julian swung open the door and walked in, closely

followed by his newly adopted bosom buddies, the doughty Huns of Weir. Conversation ceased when they walked in the room, picking up gradually until it soon regained its frenzied pitch. Indeed, this was a lively drunken pesthole of jabbering, drooling dolts.

These were their people, and they intended to fit right in.

Visitation of the Watch

"I hear you, darling," Ithmar replied, giving Katla a quick kiss. "I'll be careful."

"Don't go alone."

"What do you mean?" The fervency of her concern surprised him.

At that moment, a door opened at a house directly across the street. Out of the house, a thick-limbed, broad-shouldered warrior stepped into the street.

"Just trust me, Ithmar. Don't go alone."

"Look, there's Rollo," he answered, pointing at the man. "I'll take him with me."

"He's faithful," she responded. "But he's not the most experienced man in Bryne."

"He's a good fighter. A good sword-hand for a dark night."

"All right," she replied, hesitating.

"Rollo!" he shouted, waving his hand.

"Lord Ithmar, is that you?"

"It's me. Be a good fellow and come over here." Rollo walked up to them gladly, radiating good will. He was a young, roly-poly rune-stone of a man, a gentle soul who seemed as wide as he was tall, and who always seemed to be apologizing for something. From his guileless joy at seeing Ithmar, anyone could see that he held him in great affection and respect.

"Hello, Lady Katla," Rollo said, doffing his bearskin cap and bowing low. A brittle white dust of frost had already begun to form on his unkempt auburn beard; the night was growing bitterly cold as the wind died down and the chill settled in.

"Rollo, would care to join me? I'm headed down to the docks to relieve the watch."

"Of course, Lord Ithmar. I'd be honored."

"There, darling," Ithmar said, looking soberly at his wife. "Rollo is the second-best fighter in our city. Second to me, course," he added humbly. "If trouble comes our way, I don't like its chances." They walked back to the mead hall, where he stopped to say good-bye to her. "I'll be back soon."

"Be careful," she whispered fiercely, squeezing his arms and kissing him. Then she turned and, without a backward glance, entered the hall. Ithmar stood there, staring for a minute at the door, deep in thought. Then he turned to Rollo.

"A good woman is worth more than all the gold in Francia, Rollo," said Ithmar, scratching his beard as he reflected on this truth.

"No! Sir? I mean... really... sir?" The Chief Captain looked at him and smiled, nodding slowly in affirmation.

"Yes. Really."

"Oh."

"Are you drunk, son?"

"No, sir."

"Good. There might be trouble tonight."

"Trouble? Tonight?" Rollo did not always pick things up quickly.

"Right. Let's go on down to the main pier and give those men some mead. But let's be ready for trouble. Just look sharp, avoid the shadows, and keep your sword-hand free. Are you armed?"

"Of course, sir; I was going to relieve Eric. He's on the tower watch."

"Well, come on with me," he told him. "Eric can wait." They began to walk back down the street toward the edge of the plateau on which the city had been built. Bryne was a city built without walls, except for the single short wall with an iron gate that sealed off the path that led to the city docks. The small houses of the city, built with stone sides and tall, steeply-sloped wooden roofs, were crowded closely together, perennially huddling for warmth against the ever-present, invasive cold.

The city's founders had built Bryne without walls for a readily apparent reason: a sheer wall of cliffs, with only two navigable paths to the top, separated the waters of the fjord from the broad, fertile plateau on which the city was built. At each end of the Plain of Bryne, the plateau could be accessed from the fjord by a single, dangerous path. One of these lay at the eastern end of the plateau, where Haruk's castle securely controlled access to the shallow, treacherous waters below. The other path was at the southwestern corner of the Plain of Bryne, where a steep, stony concourse led from the city down to the pier.

The warriors of Bryne kept two chief watches: the tower watch, and the watch of the city pier. These watches helped ensure that any fight against invaders would take place in the open waters of the fjord or at the tops of the cliffs... not in the streets of their city. On such treacherous familiar ground, the warriors of Bryne held an advantage. They routinely navigated the steep path down to the city docks – a path better suited for wild goats than for men.

The iron gates at the top of the path had been strategically placed directly below the watchtower. During the clear days and moonlit nights when the pier watch stood down, the tower watch remained to raise the alarm in the event of trouble.

The top room of the watchtower afforded a spectacular view of the bay, including the sound just past its mouth and the great fjord leading out to the sea. On a clear day, the tower watchman could see to the east, west and south for league upon sea-tossed league. Tonight, as always, a watchman manned the tower.

"Who's there?" The watchman called when the Steward rang the bell beside the gate. Ithmar looked up though the falling snow.

"It's Ithmar, Eric. Can't you see me?"

"I'm afraid not, Captain. None of us have your night eyes. I can barely make out the gate."

"I'm with Rollo. We're going down to the docks."

"Go on," he replied, "but be careful. The path is heavily iced."

The wind picked up again, painfully assaulting them as they pulled their hats down tightly over their ears. Without another word, they slowly swung open the frigid, ironclad gate and stepped into the awaiting darkness.

Waiting for Light

"Since today's fight with the English came down to us or them, I'm extremely glad that it was them," Julian stated wearily. "We've suffered too many losses lately." He offered his comments without hope of a reply.

The Huns had returned to their encampment. Roentner had taken the road back to his own outfit, and Julian now found himself sitting once again with Gunnar, lounging near the top of the same rocky hill where their evening had begun.

To Gunnar, it seemed as if this night had lasted for eons. *Things were different in the old days... back when I was a lieutenant,* he thought wryly.

Without warning, the bad news from Bryne returned to his memory. *Did Kennan really attack Ilse? Did he hurt her badly? Is she all right?*

Gunnar became nauseated as he tried to shake the unbidden images that returned to his mind against his will. In the innermost recesses of his heart, he could feel the deep anger rising: pushing powerfully against his consciousness, trying to assert itself as he struggled to overcome it.

For now, he could not allow himself to feel such anger. The time for vengeance would come soon enough. He could not allow the rage to run unchecked, lest it drive him to madness. But the grim anger remained within him… like molten rock seeking a rift through which it could erupt, raining fire and death upon all within range.

It was not enough that Haruk Longknife had betrayed his father to death. To add to the outrage, Haruk's son had assaulted Ilse. If he dwelled upon it, the very idea could unhinge him. *My father told me that God is good... but how can a good God allow such things?* he wondered. *God,* he prayed, *if you hear me, please show me the truth. Why are these things happening?*

After he prayed, he suddenly felt weary. He did not notice that Julian, having given up on trying to distract him from his woes, had leaned back and covered himself with his heavy woolen campaign cloak, a handy shelter from the morning dew.

"Let's rest for a while," he murmured. "It's rumored that if you wait long enough, the sun will eventually rise." The Prince did not respond to Julian's feeble attempt at humor. Instead, he replied from the heart of his hidden travail.

"Do you mind if I talk?" Gunnar asked.

"You never talk."

"Well I want to now. Okay?"

"By all means, Captain Gunnar. Let the word-spears fly."

"What Roentner said tonight really bothered me."

"You? Bothered?"

"Yes. I love my city, Jules. To be back in Bryne with my friends and Ilse... that's the dream that's kept me going. For three years, I was a slave, most of that time with your father. He wasn't a terrible master. But there's the problem: he was my master. When I told the other household servants that my father was the famous King Vigmar of Bryne, they thought I was crazy."

"You can't really blame them," Julian replied sleepily. "They never saw you fight."

"During that time I kept my mind set on Bryne, and on Ilse." Julian tried to rouse himself and listen. His young friend, normally so taciturn, had begun to open up.

"Tonight, when Roentner told us about Kennan, I felt like I was dying inside. That girl he attacked... that was my girl. That's the one I told you about."

"Dreadful," Julian replied quietly, as if he spoke to himself.

"I don't know what I should do now. I don't know how to help Ilse, or how to help my people. Will the city welcome me back? Will they even remember me?"

"They'll remember you. Trust me." Julian's eyes had become heavy, but he managed to speak in a vain attempt to comfort his friend.

"Everything changes, Jules."

"Mm, hmm," Julian replied sleepily, beginning to drift.

"It all changes. Everything we can see and touch and sense, all the people and the places. It's as stable as snow in the sun."

"Hmm."

"Even the ideas, the reasons that nations fight for; even they change. We see it through history. The nations, even the strongest, are temporary. They flourish, they grow great: they have their moment and then pass away, like ice melted by the rain.

"Who remembers the ancient nations? Who knows the stories of those before us? Why do we fight for glory, kill for glory, and dream about glorious riches when this glorious life is so short and so cruel?

"It's too much, Jules... all of it: the life, the death, the things we do to each other. Bryne, Kennan, Ilse... I can't cope. It's all too much." He fell silent, afraid that he would cry. If he started, he might not be able to stop. He leaned back against the hill and stared at the stars.

Julian began to snore softly. Gunnar raised himself on an elbow and stared incredulously at him. *I finally pour out my heart, and my audience falls asleep.* In spite of himself, he smiled.

Far off, beyond the foot of the hill, the remains of the city of Glastonbury snapped and popped and glowed dimly through the smoke. A sad little town even before the war, it had now been rendered into a scattered heap of coals that burned slowly in the darkness.

The remains of the ill-fated hamlet glittered and shimmered below them, sparkling with fiery diamonds of roseate light. The smoldering city lit up God's good earth like the stars that shined so brightly above them: untouchably distant, sunk deep in the darkened heavens.

The Cost as Measured in Blood

Ithmar and Rollo began their precipitous descent down the stony path, carefully navigating with their hands and their feet. Heeding the wisdom of Katla, Ithmar had opted not to use a lantern as a precaution. To minimize the chance of a successful ambush, he wanted their eyes to become acclimated to the eerie, almost-total darkness. An occasional glimpse of starlight as the clouds briefly parted provided the only illumination as they made their way down the cliffs, wending their way to the docks.

Below them, the open waters could be sensed, but not seen. The bay, the sound, and the North Sea beyond insinuated themselves into their consciousness with the ever-present roar of the waves on the rocks, the tang of sea mist, the sense of open air and the bitter blast of cold salt spray on their aching cheeks. They proceeded at a snail's pace down the icy path, as quietly as they could, stopping often to listen. They had grown extremely tense.

"Sir, can we stop?" Rollo whispered hoarsely.

"Of course." The stars had come out for the moment, affording a glimpse of the dark, mysterious waters below the sheer face of the cliff. This path was nothing if not scenic. For centuries it had served their city well, giving passage across the craggy face of the cliffs… a thin, zigzagged crease in the flinty walls. The cliffs were so abruptly perpendicular, so fiercely vertical, they appeared to have erupted from sea to sky taking the shortest route possible.

"Do you honestly think that our Prince might return, Lord Ithmar? Is there any hope that he'll come back?" The speaker, Rollo Broadface, had always been a guileless soul. In keeping with his honest nature, he had broached a question that others wondered about, but were too polite to ask. Ithmar's response was frank and to the point.

"I think he will. I'm quite sure he wasn't killed." With a pang,

Ithmar remembered that Rollo was not much older than the Prince. He suddenly felt pity for Rollo, the quiet, kind, gentle soul that so many men mocked in spite of his martial prowess.

"Rollo... you were his best friend, weren't you?"

"Yes, sir." Rollo's voice sounded strained.

They stood silently for a minute, watching the starlight on the waters of the bay. Then, without another word, they resumed their descent to the docks. They proceeded tensely, walking lightly, turning their heads often to look from side to side. Something seemed awry in the too-still evening air.

They drew near to the bottom of the cliff. In spite of this, they heard no sound of men. No light shined from the base of the pier, where guards should have been gathered around a watch fire. Ithmar saw that Rollo shared his unease. The younger man began to slow down and stop often, following the example of his captain.

We're the fearless warriors of Bryne, mused Ithmar. He felt scared now, and the butterflies in his stomach felt like they were trying to escape from their cage by way of his mouth. The night seemed to grow colder by the minute.

As they neared the docks, the trail broadened and became flatter, skirting the edge of the cliff between a wide ledge and a sheer drop to the rocks below. A short distance below, they could see the sable outline of the docks and the sleek, wide-bellied dragon ships, fitting symbols of the deadly profession that had made their kingdom one of the wealthiest in the North.

Rollo walked ahead of Ithmar, surprisingly nimble for a man of his bulk. He pointed to the ships and turned to speak.

"We're home free, sir," he said blithely.

At that moment, the murderers struck.

Jewel of the Mind

Gunnar opened his eyes in the center of the street and looked around to see a dazzling vision of unexpected clarity. He beheld a city full of people, bustling and happy. The sight seemed to be alive: a bristling mélange of crisp, clean colors set apart by a strange, ethereal brightness under a cloudless sky, awash in a surreal shade of limitless blue.

It seemed too good to be true.

He was at home, in the city of Bryne. The day was painfully clear; the colors, scents, sounds and even the edges of the buildings seemed exquisitely defined, each set apart from the other. The city radiated life, bathed in the cool, clear rays of the northern sun. For quite some time he stared and wondered, his eyes thirstily drinking in the city of his dreams.

He found himself walking down a rocky path and was shocked to see his father walking beside him. The way had grown dark, and the city had disappeared.

His father looked scared and shaky, as if he were about to collapse, but Gunnar felt the urgent need to press ahead. He felt certain that they could make it through the darkness safely, if only they refused to give up.

For some inexplicable reason, the Prince grew angry with his father as they struggled down the dim pathway. He did not understand what was happening in this strange, contorted universe where his father looked sick and weak and tired and ready to quit... where the palpable absence of light enshrouded them, wrapping them tightly in threads of hopelessness as surely as a spider wraps its prey.

"Don't give up!" the Prince said sternly to his father. "Don't quit!"

King Vigmar looked as if he would break into tears. For some unfathomable reason, this angered the Prince.

"Don't give up," he said urgently. "Follow me. We'll make it." He spoke forcefully, loudly, desperately trying to lead the King out of the growing darkness.

At this very moment, King Vigmar's body jerked and spun around. His head snapped back, and his eyes looked upwards. Casting his hands toward the heavens, Vigmar gave a great, rattling exhalation and fell over hard against his son. Gunnar caught him in his arms.

Vigmar's corpse felt as light as a goose-down pillow. His soul had left the soft body that now lay cold and lifeless and pitifully limp in the arms of the stunned Prince of Bryne.

"No!" Gunnar wailed, lifting up the corpse. "God help me!"

His horror was complete. He had seen his father alive again, only to see him die before his eyes. Vigmar had died in terror, collapsing into his son's useless arms.

The Prince awoke with tears flowing freely down his face. He cried like a baby, his body wracked by soul-wrenching sobs. He rolled onto his side and curled into a ball, trying desperately to stifle the sounds and to forget the hideous images. *God, help me, it hurts! The horror, dear God... the horror!*

The hope of the Prince had been brutally broken, scattered like chaff to the wind. The dreams that had nurtured Gunnar through years of captivity had been savagely bludgeoned by the news from Roentner.

How could Bryne remain unchanged and untainted by the crimes arrayed against it? How could he return to the city of his dreams, to the jewel of his mind... the golden city of Bryne?

Oh, Ilse, my love, his heart mourned in the darkness. It was more than he could bear.

Gunnar wept. He wept for himself and for Vigmar, for Ilse, for his city and the fallen state of humanity: brutalized, murdered, deceived and weak... lost, wandering, torn by dragons like Haruk the Cruel, sold for profit, ripped like sheep by the wolves and abandoned as food for the ravens.

God, help us, he wept in the dark. *Help us, for without You we are lost.* His hope was dying, and he had no ability to revive it.

His only chance for restoration and renewal lay completely outside of his control. This was an unwelcome concept for a young man accustomed to living by his wits.

His father had been killed, and he had not been able to stop it. For now, he could only wait... and weep as he prayed for revenge.

Slippery Footing

As the stars came out from behind a cloud, Ithmar looked in Rollo's direction just in time to see a shadowy figure lunge up behind the young warrior and plunge a dagger into his back. Rollo's eyes widened in disbelief, and Ithmar's hand flashed to his sword-hilt, too late.

Excruciating pain bit into Ithmar as a garrote of elk-sinew slammed tightly around his neck. His left hand, with which he had been straightening his helm, was trapped in the deadly noose.

By instinct, Ithmar lunged toward the ledge to his right and fell onto his knees between two stones at the edge of the precipice. He heaved mightily against the braided cord, ignoring the pain. He could not reach his sword with his free hand; his attacker had wrapped his legs around his waist in an attempt to control him for the kill.

From his kneeling position, Ithmar rose with the assailant on his back; slowly, excruciatingly standing as he desperately fought for air. Twisting his body like a breaching dolphin, he leapt into the air and landed on his back.

They landed on top of a sharp boulder. He heard a low-pitched snapping sound, and the noose instantly loosened.

Fighting off the dizziness, Ithmar struggled to his feet. The man lay without moving, his neck broken cleanly in two.

Ithmar glanced up just in time to see a dark human shape swing something his way. Falling backwards with his legs extended towards the new threat, he hooked the attacker's feet and snatched them from under him. The man fell heavily, hitting his head with a loud crack. He did not move again.

Ithmar struggled to his feet and staggered over to where Rollo had been ambushed. He found his friend beside the path, hanging his head, sitting next to the man who had knifed him in the back. The attacker lay face down, motionless.

"It burns like fire, Captain," Rollo said matter-of-factly.

"Where did it go in?"

"Mid-back," Rollo said, gasping as he was smitten by another wave of excruciating pain. "Maybe he missed my liver, eh?" He tried to grin and sucked in a sharp breath as another thrust of pain struck him, like a jolt of lightning mixed with burning sulfur. "It feels like somebody's stuck coals inside the wound," he hissed.

The captain knelt beside him and lightly touched the wound. It was not bleeding too badly, although the internal bleeding could be horrendous. He slid his arms beneath Rollo and slowly helped him to his feet. He led him to a small indentation in the cliff face. There, hidden in a cleft of the rock, he covered Rollo with his own crimson cloak.

"Stay quietly here, in case they come back. I'll be back soon with help."

"I hope so," Rollo said, forcing a smile.

"Whatever happens, don't make a sound. Not until we come for you. Do you understand?"

"Yes sir."

Ithmar the Mighty, the bearer of the King's royal seal, stealthily backed out of the narrow hiding place and began to hurry down the path to the docks. *Are the men at the docks alive?* he wondered.

In the darkness, he did not see the man blocking the path until he almost ran him over. He drew his sword reflexively

"Captain, it's me!" The familiarity of the voice was reassuring. It was a voice that Ithmar had known since the speaker was a toddler.

"Kennan?" he asked, momentarily shocked and bewildered.

Too late, his mind made the connection.

Kennan's blade slid in smoothly beneath Ithmar's ribs, leaving a trail of fire and ice and melting flames that caused his sword to clatter limply to the ground. His knees collapsed beneath him, and the earth cracked him sharply on the cheek. He felt himself being dragged to the edge of the cliff. He tumbled roughly down the rocks, slamming to a rest on a narrow ledge.

Ithmar managed to tear his sliced shirt and fold it into a

bandage. He rolled onto his stomach beneath an overhanging ledge, using the weight of his body to push the compressed material hard against the wound. *This is what Rollo meant... the fire... the burning... oh God! Please... please help Katla.*

Thinking these things, wracked by more pain than his consciousness could bear, Ithmar fell asleep.

The Messenger

"Captain Julian!" a voice called from the foot of the hill. With a groan, Gunnar sat up and shook his friend.

"Holger's calling for you," Gunnar rasped. "He must have some kind of news." Captain Julian woke up and yawned loudly. *Why am I so sore?* he wondered, and then he remembered their recent adventure. *We had quite a fight in that whiskey tent.*

"You're needed in camp, sir," Holger called from below them. "A lieutenant from the King's staff has come to pick you up… you and Gunnar, that is. But they've got his title wrong. They're calling him Captain Gunnar."

"They're not wrong. He's been promoted." Julian mumbled. "What's this all about?" he added gruffly, trying to sound authoritative in spite of his inability to fully gather his wits into one bundle. He staggered to his feet and shook the dew from his cloak, showering Gunnar with a fine, icy mist. "What's the hour?"

"About two hours before dawn, sir," the earnest Holger replied.

"Really? No wonder I feel so bad."

"We've only been here a little while, Jules," croaked Gunnar dryly, without sitting up. "Of course, you wouldn't know that. You've been out like an ox hit by a hammer." Gunnar stood up, and they slowly walked down the hill to join Holger.

"What's this about, soldier?" Captain Julian asked.

"I don't know, sir," Holger replied with wide-eyed wonder. "I only know that King Guthrum's messenger has come here, and he's waiting for you. It's something about King Alfred, I heard, but just what I don't know, sir, not at all."

"Guthrum has business with the King of Wessex? Now, that's interesting!" exclaimed Julian. "I've often fancied that I would enjoy meeting the thane of these dour West Saxons. In fact, after more than one bloody battle I've imagined myself giving Alfred the gift of a sword… hilt-end last, if you know what I mean."

Closing the Circle

How sweet, Kennan thought, savoring the moment. *Ithmar is gone like a well-speared seal. He's sunk among the waves, drifting in the surf like a dead fish.*

Kennan crept up the path, bound for the city gates at the top of the cliff. He chuckled softly as he stealthily crept along. When he had traveled a short distance, he heard something gurgling on the left side of the path, which was open to the bay. At the same moment, his feet stepped on a soggy lump that almost caused him to stumble.

"Kennan, is that you?" a strained voice asked out of the darkness.

"Yes... where are you... is it you, Eber?"

"Yes, it's me. Brulef and Briles must be dead. You stepped on one of them. Here I am... just ahead of you." Kennan could now make out the cowering shadow of his hapless manservant. "I can't get up," Eber moaned. "I think I broke my back." Terror could be heard in his thin, quavering voice.

"Put up your head so I can see you," Kennan responded, his voice tinged with concern. The slave obliged Kennan just as the new moon peeked out from behind the clouds. He could see the outline of the slave's trembling head and neck: a black silhouette at the cliff's edge, set starkly against the glimmering backdrop of majestic, rippling water.

"This will help," offered Kennan as he slowly thrust his sword into Eber's throat. He quickly sheathed the blade and rolled his gurgling victim off the cliff to plunge into the roiling surf below.

Eber's two companions, Brulef and Briles, lay with their dead weight squarely in the middle of the path, as limp as a pair of skinned bears. They proved more difficult to move than the murdered slave; but soon they, too, were drifting in the surf and Lord Kennan had resumed his majestic ascent to the iron gates at the top of the path. He stopped when he heard the sound of footsteps, and the first man almost ran over the top of him. It was Eric, closely followed by a small group of men. In the darkness, the size of the group could not be readily determined.

"We had to leave early," Eric said. "Something was happening in town, I could see it up the street at the top of the hill. Some angry citizens looked like they were headed this way. Did you see Ithmar? He came down ahead of us."

"Oh? Well, never mind about Ithmar. He must have taken to ship. He wasn't on the docks when I landed. Listen, Eric," Kennan added, changing the subject. "If the stout blubber-mongers of Bryne are coming, we'd better get out of here. How many recruits do you have?"

"Fifteen. They're all younger than us. It's amazing that they all kept their mouths shut, but they did. Nobody in town suspected a thing."

"Fifteen? That's a number that will serve us well," purred Kennan. "You did well."

"I can't let down my cousin," said Eric. "Let's hurry. The citizens looked like they'll be coming this way soon."

"All right, follow me, men," Kennan called out. "And watch your step." He smiled with a wicked grin that was invisible in the darkness, and then finished his thought.

"The path is slippery."

Against Hope

She stood at the iron gates of Bryne and watched as the last of the fighting men passed through on their way to the docks, shutting the door behind them with a weighty, definitive clang. Her knees tried to weaken, but she fought off the sensation and stood there without a visible tremor for quite some time.

Things had gone badly ever since she had left Ithmar with Rollo in the street outside of the mead hall. Back in the midst of the joyful festivities, she had been unable to shake the grim cloud of foreboding that had descended upon her. She had waited for Ithmar in the hall for what seemed like hours: until enough time had passed for him to run his errand twice. Ithmar, who was as dependable as the sundial, was never late for anything. *Every year he visits the watch during the feast,* she thought, *but never for this long... never.*

She had felt foolish about her worries at first, but when more time had passed without his return, she had shared everything with Ivan Redbeard. He had taken her worries quite seriously, even going so far as to interrupt the festivities, which had been scheduled to continue all night.

He announced to the throng that he needed a group to go with him to the docks, explaining that he had good reason to believe there might be trouble. Ivan immediately had more volunteers than he needed. Aside from their genuine affection for Ithmar, the wealth of Bryne itself was tied to those docks. The manufacture of a dragon ship was an extremely time-consuming and expensive process, and, for these reasons, the men did not take danger to their ships lightly.

Within a few minutes, the mustered citizens had prepared to descend down the path to the docks, their torches casting flickering red light on grim faces. They had filed dourly through the gate, slamming the huge iron door with ominous finality. They left Katla behind them, just inside the gate. A voice spoke out of the darkness.

"Do you want to go back to the hall?" Katla turned and noticed Ivan Redbeard. She felt relieved to see him slouching nearby, hanging his head toward hers with an expression of profound concern. Snowfall had frosted his white brows and his long silver hair, turning him into the very image of antiquity.

"You did not go down?"

"I'm too old and slow to be of use if it comes to a fight. They said they did not want to risk losing me." He sighed and put an arm around her shoulder. "Come, little one," he said softly. "Let's go back to find Ilse."

She leaned against him gratefully: suddenly weary. *Little one.* He had not called her that in years... not since she was a small child and he was a kind young man teaching a class of four gifted students. Ivan had become such a dear, trustworthy friend over the years. It comforted her to know that he, at least, was alive and well, ready to walk with her up the street to the mead hall. By now, the hall would be filled with the anxious faces of people waiting, like her, for news of what may have befallen the men who kept watch on the docks.

Leaning against one another, ignoring the snow that fell in great flakes upon their coats and hats, Katla and Ivan walked back up the broad central street of the City of Bryne. In their hearts, they hoped against hope that their concerns would prove ungrounded, and that tonight's events might turn out – somehow – for the best.

King Alfred the Great

The meeting had been set for late afternoon, all parties having agreed to the time of day. The locale was a country estate outside of Wedmore. Guthrum arrived accompanied by nineteen men from his armies, including Captains Julian and Gunnar. There was no frivolity associated with today's occasion; at the appointed time, they filed into the great room of the manor, sober and ready to parlay.

In the center of the richly paneled room were several hastily commandeered feasting tables arranged in the traditional rectangle. Twelve Englishmen were seated at the tables when the Danes walked in, and one of these was Alfred son of Ethelwulf, the King of the West Saxons.

Alfred sat, as it were, alone in the midst of a crowd. He alone bore the heavy burden of care for the last undefeated portion of the English race, whose very lives and identities were at stake in these proceedings.

Alfred's recent victory at Edington had not gained the strategic advantage that he had anticipated. To further compound his troubles, yesterday's disastrous loss in the fields of Glastonbury had taken away the momentum built by Alfred's men during the difficult spring campaign, when his armies had successfully waged war against the Danes from Athelney, their fort near the marshes of Somerset.

The scholar-king of the English race had surrounded himself with a distinctly colorful assemblage of soldiers, officials and religious representatives. A dark-haired man with clear blue eyes and a countenance that spoke of profound patience, Alfred somberly watched as the Vikings arrived.

At his left sat a sour-looking ghoul of a man in a dark red robe, warily watching the Danes from a high perch in an oversized, ornately carved chair. The man clucked with disapproval, moving his head slowly from side to side like a vulture in the throes of sweet anticipation. His cold yellow eyes, set like lifeless agates in a gray, cadaverous face, glumly appraised their guests with a hint of dismay, as if he were disappointed at the sparseness of the meat on their bones. Enhancing the curious effect provoked by the emaciated gentleman's dour mien, a great, polished badge – hanging from a pendulous chain around his neck – glittered at them from its perch on his chest. The shiny golden symbol seemed so weighty in its prominence that the sheer, massy heft of it threatened to bow his spindly neck down to the earth and pin him there forever, trapped in an enduring frieze... like a voracious mosquito snared in a jewel of amber.

At Alfred's right hand sat a man garbed in even stranger fashion: covered from head to foot in a dark brown, hooded robe bound at the waist with a single twist of rope. Gunnar looked carefully at this man with wonder and not a little skepticism. *This must be one of the English wizards that Roentner talked about.* He was surprised to see how plainly the man was dressed. *Most wizards dress as if they were trying to clothe themselves in the Northern Lights,* he thought. *This looks like a new breed of magician.*

Alfred and his men waited patiently as Guthrum's entourage walked into the room. The Danes, having conquered almost half of England, took the initiative in setting the meeting's agenda, and Guthrum's representative stood to speak. Because it was known to the Danes that Alfred was fluent in their mother tongue, Guthrum's speaker addressed the Englishmen in Danish.

"We have accepted your invitation for a meeting, Alfred King of Wessex. As a result, King Guthrum, the ruler of all Danes, has come to hear your words. Accompanying him are the chief princes of his realm and chief captains under his command. These have come to counsel their king regarding any offers that you may set forth. We will spare you the introductions of all parties, which may come at a later time. Now, we await your communication regarding your intent, so we can discover the reason for this gathering."

After the speaker finished, King Alfred stood to reply. If he looked saddened and dismayed, he had good reason. His armies, as mighty and fearless as any the Danes had faced, had long fallen prey to the superior tactics and experience of Guthrum and his Danish predecessors. Until Alfred's recent string of victories, the Danes had hounded and hammered the English from shire to shire in a bloody, brutal war of attrition that had led them to the unpleasant prospect of a negotiated peace.

"Men of the North, enemies, friends, and brethren," Alfred began. "It is not for some minor purpose that I have called you together. For many years, your Danish legions have bested our forces by land and sea, schooling us bitterly at the sword's iron edge. As a result of these years of hardship, a newfound humility has displaced the arrogance that once grew like a rank weed in our native hearts. For this, at least, I am grateful.

"I have requested this gathering that I might offer you the right hand of friendship and peace. This is advantageous: not only for us, but your own interests as well, for we are not ignorant of the high price in Danish blood with which you have purchased the most recent additions to your estate. It is not in fear that we propose a peace, but in the sincere desire that the killing of our brothers, and even of our enemies, might end." Alfred looked around the room intensely yet somberly, impressing upon those watching no single effect quite as powerfully as that of a high nobility of spirit, more closely allied to serving than to being served.

"Our armies, which have been considerably strengthened since our victory in Wiltshire, have regrouped after yesterday's setback. But I have issued no orders to prepare another attack. If we must, we are prepared to fight to the last man… until, if need be, we are lodged in the high hills of Wales, fighting side-by-side with the native Celts who have made those mountains their last redoubt.

"We do not wish to continue fighting. We want to negotiate an honorable peace. This, therefore, is my proposal: if your armies halt where they are, we will not challenge Danish rule in the English territories you have already conquered. I pledge this on my honor. The details of a peace can be worked out as among friends, not enemies.

"There is, however, one key term of peace that I require. It may seem unreasonable, but I must ask it as a cardinal matter of conscience." There was a pause after Alfred spoke these words and then Guthrum answered Alfred directly.

"What is this 'matter of conscience' you speak of?"

"Our requirement, King Guthrum, is this: the sacred Christian faith of our English brothers in the conquered territories must be nourished and preserved under Danish rule. To ensure this, you must become a Christian, and be baptized into the mother Church.

"Only in this way can we assure ourselves that a persecution of our brothers and sisters will not occur... as has happened so often throughout history, since the early days when we Christians were slain in great numbers in Jerusalem and Rome, and later were hounded from nation to nation when we were ruled by strangers who did not share our faith."

Boating for Profit

The sun had started to slide down toward the endless horizon, setting the stage for a sudden, dramatic exit. The sails were trimmed on the three sleek crafts: one stolen from Guthrum the Dane, the other two from the city of Bryne. The wind, with the perfection of design, pushed them powerfully past wave upon rolling wave, smoothly and swiftly hastening their progress as they slipped across the surface of the sea. But for all of this, they did not move swiftly enough for Kennan. He obsessively monitored the push of the wind on the face of the deep, keeping his crew jumping with razor-sharp orders delivered in his uniquely piercing, annoyingly nasal voice.

The Bryne-men can't trail these boats like harts in the hills. No tracks are left on the sea, he thought, nervously eyeing the northeastern horizon. *But Brynish sailors are the best. If anyone can sniff me out in the middle of this open water, they can.* If he had known the truth, however, he would not have worried.

The men of Bryne, having taken to ship before dawn, had searched until mid-day to find some sign of the stolen longships, seeking at least some hint of a distant mast-top flickering above the flat horizon. After long hours upon the sea, they had finally given up the search as hopeless and had returned to port. They felt sure that the identity of the thieves would be revealed in time.

The thieves had stolen two of their best ships, and they felt confident that the successful theft would be boasted about. They would test the wind for news of such boastings. Once they identified the murderous thieves who had stolen their ships, they would descend on them like a plague of northern locusts. Their swords would devour the flesh of these bandits like a bear laps up honey. They would leave no home unburned, no neck intact until they had slaked their souls with the cold meat of vengeance.

The Bryne-men who searched for stolen ships did not learn the extent of the treachery until they returned to the docks. It was then that they learned that young men from all over the city had turned up missing, and that Rollo had been found, gravely wounded.

In a tragedy above all others, Ithmar and the men assigned to the dock watch could not be found and were presumed dead. The search for their bodies had already begun, and one corpse had been discovered in the rocks past the entrance of the bay. They assumed that the others had been swept out to sea with the tide.

Kennan, piloting the lead ship in the barren reaches of the North Sea, scrambled to maximize his speed. He sailed all day in a highly charged state of frenzy akin to panic. Wrapped up in the details of navigation as they skimmed across the waves, he did not know that the search had been abandoned. He continued to drive his men without mercy until finally, just before dark, Kennan signaled his captains to rest their crews. Relaxing in the glow of success, he collapsed happily beside Eric, who was manning the rudder of his flagship.

"Have you guessed where we're headed?" he asked Eric slyly, tossing back his black hair and scratching his chin.

"From the course we're plotting, I would say that we're headed for England."

"That was a deliberate guise to keep us clear of a Brynish posse. Too many citizens of Bryne may have remembered my dreams of visiting Francia. Tomorrow, we'll change course for the northern coast of that fabled land. There's a city-state there, and a certain Frankish king with whom my dear father has long had a discreet and highly profitable alliance.

"We will stay there for a while... and then, we'll begin to raid. We'll get rich, my cousin," he clasped his shoulder in a greedy, possessive grasp. "Rich beyond your sickest, most disgusting dreams!" Kennan laughed spontaneously, freely expressing his glee. The rasping shadow of Kennan's laugh startled Eric. He looked up in surprise as Kennan emitted a sibilant series of curious, hissing chortles, his dark eyes strangely aglow with a demonic delight that Eric could scarcely begin to understand.

Window of Awareness

Months ago, they had replaced the window that Seng had shattered while saving Ilse's life. In her bedroom, Katla sat motionless beside the window, staring out at the sea. The sun would set soon on this, the second day since Ithmar's disappearance. His body had not been found.

Katla heard a knock on the door.

"Mother, are you all right?"

"Yes, darling. Come in here, please." With Seng padding closely behind her, Ilse quietly entered the room. Since that fateful night when Kennan had attacked her, Seng had rarely left Ilse's side. "Sit down, darling."

Ilse sat in the chair across from her mother. The fire popped and creaked in the hearth as Seng lay down heavily at her feet with a prolonged and windy sigh.

The longhaired hound placed his head on her foot and gazed somberly around the room, his eyes flashing as they roved from the fire, to Ilse, to Katla, and back to Ilse, the young woman who had not long ago been a little girl. His eyes would pause, aflame with love as he stared at Ilse, the radiant youth he had barely saved from the man-devil who had come calling one snowy, nightmare's eve.

To this day, Seng kept watch for the return of the predator. Night after night, he listened and looked and tested the air with his nose, following Ilse from room to darkened room, here in their once-happy home.

"Mother, what will we do?" The cutting pain of her father's disappearance felt unbearable to Ilse. Since Kennan's exile, it had seemed as if she could feel the accusing glances of his friends whenever she walked through town… as if she, somehow, had provoked his assault. Her father and mother had been a steady source of strength. Their quiet faith and unfailing support had kept her from blaming herself for the tragedy. Now, true to form, her mother's answer was brief and in character.

"We'll keep hoping and praying, darling. We won't give up," she replied. Ilse knew that this was good advice, yet she felt that there should be more that they could do.

"Yes, we should pray, but can't we also *do* something to change things for the better? Can't God use *us* to find father – as easily as he could use anyone else?"

"Yes." Katla mulled over her daughter's words. "You're right. What is your idea?"

"Let's go to the docks. We can get some of father's soldiers to go with us... maybe even the guards that have been keeping watch outside of our house. Let's go there to the docks, and let's take Seng with us."

"Why would we do that?"

"Can't you see, mother? There aren't too many things that could have happened to father. At first I thought that they may have taken him away, but that's no good. He's not a man to hold for ransom because the whole city would go to war against his kidnappers, even if we paid to get him back."

"Yes."

"So, father must either be injured, or dead." Her eyes began to water as she finished the sentence, but she would not allow herself to indulge in grief.

"If he's dead, it can't be helped. But if he's injured, perhaps he crawled into a cave, or hid somewhere else where our men couldn't find him. And if our men can't find him, perhaps Seng can. He doesn't have to see father. He can find him by his scent."

Katla's heart picked up its pace. This was not much of a chance, but it was better than none. She leaned forward and answered her daughter.

"Soon it will be dark, and we'll go."

The Light through the Window

The great room grew quiet. Ruby rays from the recumbent sun streamed through tall windows on the western side of the hall, etching a delicate pattern upon the room's interior. A crosshatch grid of shadows - interspersed with jagged, diamantine shards of light - slid like quicksilver across the robe and face of the man who rose to speak.

"I will tell you a story," he said. "It is a story unlike any other. It is a tale filled with power... for good, not for evil. My story holds the power of truth, and the might to change lives."

The cloaked and hooded man who stood before them was speaking at Guthrum's request. He spoke carefully, addressing the gathering in perfect, uninflected Royal Danish.

The King of the Danes had agreed to hear the Christian proposition in detail, but had not, by any means, agreed to become a Christian. He was not certain of what a conversion entailed, but was curious to hear the man out. *This ought to be good,* he reflected grimly as the monk continued to speak.

"The beauty and order of the heavens above us," the man said, "and of the earth beneath our feet, show a level of craftsmanship that far exceeds the finest work of the most talented human artisan. All humanity combined could not cobble a mouse together, much less the earth, sky, and sea."

The holy man paused and gazed around the room, his face half hidden in the heavy folds of the hood. He was a square jawed, muscular man. *He's not the wizardly type,* Guthrum thought, *but he looks like he'd be handy with a sword.*

"In their hunger to understand creation, and in an attempt to influence the power that made the universe, our fathers told stories about the gods of the northern nations. They attributed traits to these gods that they themselves shared, and created epic tales of struggle and strife... the songs of the gods of the North.

"In the ancient kingdoms of Greece and Rome, the people also told tales of such gods. In these nations, for political reasons, the gods and stories of the different cities were combined into pantheons. In this manner the leaders tried to unite their nation spiritually, accommodating the local gods by giving them a place in a national family of gods and goddesses, heroes and heroines.

"In the sacred literature of these nations, the gods behaved much as if we would if we had been given god-like power. In short, they tended to behave badly."

Julian burst out laughing, but stifled himself instantly as heads turned in his direction. *How true,* he mused, smiling at the monk apologetically. *Give mortals the power of gods, and we would pollute the heavens.* Surprisingly, the monk smiled at him briefly before turning away.

"As the nations established their political pantheons, one people have stood separate from the rest. From the ancient times unto today, the divine stories of that nation have been unlike those found anywhere else on earth. That nation is called Israel.

"Israel, alone among all of the nations of the earth, was chosen by the great Creator of the universe as a distinct people separated unto himself. He did this not by permission of men, but by his own choice and for his own good reasons.

"By means of prophets and seers who foretold the future, the one Creator – who alone is God – was directly involved with the people of the tribes of Israel. By mighty signs and fearful wonders the Mighty God revealed his power unto his people, proving to them beyond a doubt that the Creator of the universe dealt with them. Prophets told the nation that one day another prophet would come, a Deliverer who would save the people from the enemies. This Savior would rule the nation forever."

"You speak of signs and wonders that were shown to these people," interrupted Guthrum. "What were the signs, and how do we know these things are true?"

"When Egypt, the most powerful nation on earth, enslaved God's people, He sent a man named Moses to save them. After Pharoah denied freedom to Israel, Moses declared great plagues upon Egypt. During each plague, Pharaoh pledged to release the Israelites. After each plague ended, he changed his mind.

"As a final plague, Moses declared that God's spirit messenger would kill all the firstborn sons in Egypt. The Israelites were told by Moses to kill a lamb and to place the blood above their doors and on their door posts. That night, the firstborn sons of the Egyptians were slain but Israel was spared: not a male died among them, for the spirit messenger sent to kill the firstborn of every household saw the blood of the lamb and passed over their houses.

"As for whether this story is true, that is for each man to judge in his own heart. I know, however, that if anyone asks God whether this story is true, God Himself will show that person. For this I have learned of the God of Israel: He is good.

"Many promises were made to Israel that they would be saved from their enemies and from death itself. These promises are found in the holy scrolls of the God of Israel, which have been preserved for millennia.

"Israel received a promise that their deliverance would come by God's chosen Messiah, the Anointed One. Jesus of Nazareth was, and is, that Messiah. He is the King of Israel and the Shepherd of his people, and for his sake we bear the name *Christian*."

"Their Messiah – your Christ – was a man? What kind of man?"

"A carpenter."

"A carpenter?"

"Yes, O king. God, having and knowing all things, did not need to clothe himself in earthly splendor. When the invisible God came to earth, he was born into a humble household. Though he owned all things, he took on Himself the form of a servant. In so doing, he showed that the highest calling is not to rule men, but to serve God.

"God, in his kindness, has always blessed us, the just and unjust alike, giving us rain and sun and causing our grain to grow. But now God, desiring to deliver us from this world of death, has commanded that all men hear his Son, whom he has ordained as the only door into heaven. In Christ, God gave his own life to share eternal life with all who believe."

"Eternal life?"

"Yes. Eternal life."

"How can a mortal man hope to gain eternal life?"

"By the power and goodness of God, O king. When men were gathered together without a cause against His innocent Christ, God allowed them to murder his Son by nailing Him to a cross. But death could not hold the Prince of Life.

"Jesus arose from the dead and visited his followers, showing His unlimited power and keeping his promise to rise again on the third day. The murder of God's Son was allowed because it provided the only perfect solution to the conflict between justice and mercy... giving the very key to eternal life.

"You know, O King, how hard it can be to administer justice. To give to justice to a victim's widow, you must make a widow of the murderer, thereby doubling the misery. But in Jesus we see the perfect solution revealed; in Him, mercy and justice were reconciled. For out of a pure and guileless love, Jesus willingly took on the judgment of all who believe, delivering them forever from the power of death. He is the sacrificial Lamb of God, and when His blood is applied to the door of our hearts, the angels of judgment pass over, and spare us. As he was resurrected, so will his believers arise, for He is returning at the end of our age to judge the world. He will gather his own unto himself."

"Look," Guthrum replied thoughtfully. "I am a practical man, but no fool. This makes sense, metaphysically speaking. If God is just, he must punish the unjust... yet if he is perfectly good, who could be just, compared to him? This qualifies us all for exile from his company. It's logical that a kind and merciful God would provide a way for us to avoid this just punishment... a way to satisfy the need for justice while opening the door to heaven.

"But I need more than that. I need some proof; that's all I say, and I'm willing to ask for it. In fact, while you were speaking I prayed to this Jesus, this Son of God you preach. I asked him for a sign. I asked him, if He could hear me, to show me the truth. If he is the Son of God, he surely heard my prayer."

The holy man smiled at his words. For a moment he almost looked youthful, showing a spontaneous happiness that belied his years.

"God is very kind, King Guthrum," the man answered. "He heard your prayer when you asked him to show you the truth. In fact, he prepared a powerful sign for you before you ever came to England." The robed man paused and looked around the room, lit by a multitude of candles and the fire roaring in the massive fireplace.

"Do you remember a young man who once lived in the royal city of Denmark? A man named Tagin?" At this, the king was taken aback. *How does he know about Tagin?* He cleared his throat and leaned forward.

"Yes, of course I remember him. I was a young boy when he lived in my city: younger than him by several years. Tagin was mad: terribly, pitifully mad. He was the teenage son of a minor noble. One day, his mind just snapped. Tagin the Lost, we called him."

"What do you remember about him?"

"Oh, I recall him quite clearly," Guthrum answered, intrigued by the sudden introduction of such a curious subject. "He used to walk the streets late at night with a dead look in his eyes, accompanied by his great mastiff... his hair askew; he couldn't speak clearly. I was very young then, and I was a clever sneak. I often stayed out late at night. My friends and I crept about, hoping not to encounter Tagin because of the late hour and our dread of his piteous madness.

"I don't know where you heard about him, but I must admit that he made quite an impression. The other children mocked him, but I pitied him. I would even talk with him sometimes during the day as he sat by the fish gate, hanging his head in woe and mumbling incomprehensible things. He seemed desperately glad to have someone to talk to, but his words made no sense... his mind was totally gone... it was quite pathetic.

"He lived like that among us for years, and then, one day, he was gone. Nobody knew where he had gone, or how he had managed to leave us. We knew that he couldn't have sailed away... it was well known that he had difficulties navigating any course other than a shaky circle." King Guthrum stopped talking, surprised that he had spoken so freely to a man that he had only just met, here at a gathering that carried such portent.... not only to the gathered men, but to their armies and nations.

The monk drew closer to the King. He was a handsome man of over fifty years who wore his hood loosely over his head. White hair showed from under the hood, and a look of quick compassion and intelligence flashed in his clear brown eyes.

"Look closely at me," he said quietly. He drew back the hood and leaned towards him. "God has certainly given you a sign," he continued. "Don't you recognize me... the poor, sick young man who talked to the little boy beside the gate... don't you remember me... Guthrum?"

The King of all Denmark turned as white as a sheet. His mouth dropped open spontaneously, and he let out a long, audible sigh. In the silent room, the fire was a roar in his ears.

"No, it can't be!" he cried. "You're him! You're Tagin! But you're not him... you've changed... it can't be," he added wonderingly.

The lords and captains of Denmark were taken aback. They gazed at one another, not knowing what to think.

"This is indeed a sign," Guthrum sputtered, pausing for several seconds. "Far beyond my expectations," he added, looking at his men, and then back at the man who stood before him. "If I hadn't seen you... you, of all people... like you are now, as a totally different man... as a man of learning, so eminently sane... if I hadn't seen you like this... and here, of all places, right here before my very eyes... I never would have believed it!"

The Down Side of Death

"Oh, sailing we will go, boys, out on the frothy sea!" their noble leader sang boisterously. "We'll trim the sails and trim the French and trim the girls of glee!"

Kennan was sailing, indeed. He found himself in incredibly high spirits, higher than Eric had ever seen him. In the hours before dawn, Kennan and Eric had sprawled carelessly atop a spare sail in the stern of the lead boat. They had stayed awake by talking through the night as Kennan savored his victory.

As was his wont by dint of habit, Kennan kept a sharp eye on the hapless tiller man. Even as he indulged in jests with Eric, Kennan periodically lashed the unfortunate sailor with his well-whetted tongue, barking viciously at the least appearance of error. This verbal abuse happened with predictable regularity, not unlike the spouting of the northern whale, that rotund fountainhead of trade… the blubber-bound butler of commerce that had ushered in the peaceful prosperity so despised by Kennan.

Like a sounding whale, Kennan's ill will would disappear from sight when he quit talking, retreating deep within the murkiest reaches of his inner being. It would remain there until another flash of memory from his recent, bloody betrayal of Bryne would trigger an explosive burst of sadistic glee. When the hot surge of glee began, Kennan's consciousness would swim upward from the unplumbed depths of his cloudy heart, seeking an outlet of self-expression. His emotions would ascend to the shallow surface with a blast of unseemly joy. He would sound off with a putrid plume of tasteless jest: a coarse, unseemly spray of exuberant jokes and songs. His words steamed like smoke in the crisp evening air, bearing with them the faintest whiff of brimstone.

In his heart, Kennan roundly rejoiced in Ithmar's murder. He felt as if he had accomplished some mythic feat of arms.

The great Kennan Whitefang was drunk.

"Gi'me a song, Eric. Sing a song of Bryne. Come on." In response, Kennan's cousin ducked his head uncomfortably.

"I'm not much of a singer."

"You're no fun," Kennan sniffed loudly. "You're a sour squid in the mead-bowl of life. Sour squid! Do you hear me?" He laughed hysterically at his own sharp wit. "Have you a song? Gi'me a song of Bryne. Come on, come on. Give it up."

"I can't Kennan... we just left yesterday. Bryne is my home. I'm going to miss it."

"Oh, well. Go gut yourself and pull out an eel, sour-squid man. Then eat it. Maybe the taste will cheer you up!" Kennan looked around the boat out of the corner of his eyes. Most of the men had fallen asleep. Seeing this, he leaned toward Eric and spoke in a whisper: a curious, hissing sound that his cousin could hardly understand as he eyed Kennan warily. Kennan looked like a stranger to Eric, an alien creature almost, like an enraptured satyr with his eyes flashing and his tongue darting quickly between his teeth.

"You needn't worry about the city of Bryne... there's no point in being homesick. You're never going back. Of that, I'm certain."

"What do you mean?" Eric sat up suddenly.

"You aren't going back to Bryne, my dear cousin. And neither is any one of our crew. None of these men will go back. Ever. Not unless they want to commit suicide."

"Why not?"

"Because of the good men of Bryne, that's why. Because of their sickening love for their heroic ancestral code. They'll kill you without sparing if you ever show your face there again. They'll show no mercy. They'll recognize no blood tie with you anymore: no friendship, no brother-bond, no love, no house or hearth or precious home. Never. Never again. Forever."

"What?" Eric stuttered, aghast. "Bryne will disown us? Our brothers will kill us? For stealing ships and returning later to share the wealth?" Anxious to reply, Kennan leaned close and wrapped his arm around his cousin's neck, breathing foul fumes of sour mead into his wincing face.

"They will kill you on sight, and for a damnably good reason, dear cousin. Because I killed the bloody idiot, that's why," he whispered loudly now, excited with his own admission. "And Bryne is sure to think that you were all in on it. Or that you knew about it. Or they just won't care. You know the men of Bryne and their accursed code of honor. They'd kill their own brother to revenge their distant cousin, if their brother betrays hospitality and breaks the bond of peace by shedding blood."

"Shedding blood? You killed someone? Who did you kill?"

"The stinking Steward, that gutless Ithmar, that's who." Kennan laughed cruelly. "Gutless, yes, that's it. I ran my blade into his guts, up under his ribs, just like I was carving up a calf for daddy's home-cooked dinner. Only it was a man, not a calf. That's more fun, Eric. That's lot's more fun." Eric was stunned by the news.

"You killed Ithmar? Oh, no... no!" His voice trailed off weakly, a piteous wail that fluttered like a butterfly pinned to a wall.

"Shut up, fool," Kennan hissed, looking around swiftly. At the very moment of his cousin's outcry, however, a great swell had crashed against the boat, and the roar of the sea drowned out his words. A sailor on watch hastened to trim the sail. The other men barely stirred in their sleep.

"Yes, I killed Ithmar." Kennan smiled at the memory. "He deserved worse, but I didn't have the time for it. Why do you think I set up the exact time of our raid on Bryne, right down to the very hour?"

"What of the men on the docks? You told me that you tied them up. Did you kill them, too?"

"Yes. Dead, every one. Softly, deliciously dead. You should have been there." Kennan heaved a tremendous sigh and leaned back, smiling broadly at Eric. "So, you see, your loyalty is more that a cousinly favor... it has become a survival skill. As it is for both of us, I assure you." He smiled boyishly, with all of his wit and charm.

"But these men with us... our friends from Bryne," Eric stammered. "They're innocent." Hearing this, Kennan's eyes focused and he leaned forward, suddenly angry.

"Don't you utter a word about it," he said sharply. "I'll tell them when they need to know."

"Oh, no," moaned Eric, sinking deep in despair and slumping lower in his seat. "This is a nightmare."

"My dear fellow," Kennan replied with an infectious smile. "Don't get discouraged. You are my only cousin, after all. I have great things planned for us.

"I promised you an adventure," he added, his eyes glinting with sadistic glee. "And the fun is just beginning."

Liberty

"Do you have any more cheese?" Julian asked, howling with laughter. The moon came out as they topped the hill, leaving the stately country manor and the Council of Wedmore behind them.

"Stop kidding me, Julian. That's enough."

"Oh no, not yet," chortled Captain Julian. "This is just too rich." Their horses proceeded briskly toward their encampment without the need for human guidance. As they traveled down the moon-bleached dirt road, Julian leaned back in the saddle and laughed.

"Do you have any more food, King Alfred… old shoe?" Julian asked innocently.

"Stop it!"

"You, my boy, are a true Viking prince," Julian added, "with an appetite to match. No somber agreement between kings can fill you with awe. You absorbed every crumb in that room, like a seal slicing through a school of sardines. Amazing."

At this, Gunnar fell angrily silent. He stared ahead into the darkness without blinking or smiling.

"Okay, I'll stop it," Julian added, seeing that he had gone too far. He enjoyed tweaking Gunnar's pride when the opportunity arose. And truly, the opportunities tended to arise with great frequency.

The narrow road wound through open fields spotted with huge trees that cast ponderous sable blots on the moonlit landscape. For some time they did not speak as they walked their horses quietly along the roadway, savoring the peace and quiet.

"Hey, Julian. What did you think about what happened back there?"

"The treaty? I'd call that a lucky stroke of the pen."

"No, not that. What do you think about the speech from the

holy man… the speech about God?" This was a big question, but a big universe surrounded them. The beauty of the night seemed to beg the question.

"I guess it made sense in a way. I mean, if there is a God, and if He's good, why wouldn't He want to help us out? We need all the help we can get. We may not admit it, but that doesn't change the fact." The moon ducked behind a cloud, and they reined their horses to a walk.

"That really impressed me," Gunnar mused. "You know, when Guthrum recognized Tagin, the monk. It was really something. It's hard to see how an incoherent madman could change like that. Whether you believe him or not, the man made quite a case."

Gunnar's horse snorted and tossed his head impatiently, anxious to stretch his legs with another trot. The horse resented the fact that he was being forced to plod from tussock to tussock at such a poor, petty pace.

"You know, Julian," Gunnar added thoughtfully, "it makes me wonder." The Prince had been greatly affected by the holy man's words. In fact, his entire belief system had been shaken. The monk's speech had challenged the concepts on which his identity was built: the Norse code of stoicism, loyalty, love to friends, death to enemies, and revenge of all crimes against the clan… whatever the cost. Most of these values were found wanting when compared to the ideals espoused by the holy man.

They stopped in the road atop a small ridge, considering these things. As their horses rested, a faint clamor of voices, scarcely audible, wafted their way with the scent of distant campfires. They scanned the horizon, enjoying the clear air of a cold autumn evening and listening to the breeze in the trees. After a few minutes, they heard another horse approaching. A voice called out of the darkness..

"Gunnar-val? Julian? Is that you?"

"It's us, all right. Who goes there… is that Roentner?" The big man reigned in his horse beside them.

"It's me, all right. I'm glad I caught you. What went on in that house? Are the rumors true? Has peace broken out? My men and I were keeping watch on the hill above the manor," he added by way of explanation. "I saw you go in there with Guthrum. What happened? We've received orders to stand down, and we don't know why." He paused, awaiting a response. "Go ahead, speak if you can," he urged, exasperated by their silence. "Are the rumors true? Has a treaty been signed?"

"The rumors are true," replied Julian. "A full agreement has been reached. Guthrum and Alfred left some time ago, but we stayed to... well... to help clean up the refreshments."

"We have peace!" Roentner exclaimed. "No kidding? Peace." He repeated the word wonderingly, as if its sound surprised him.

"Yes. But what will we do with no armies to smite? Where will we strike with the hand of our wrath?" Julian asked dryly.

"I don't know. I can't think about that... it's too soon." Roentner let out a loud sigh in the darkness. "Peace. I never thought that I liked the word," he added in a subdued tone. He shook his head slowly. They sat there together for quite some time, not saying a word. The ponies champed and stirred impatiently and their riders corrected them absently, automatically: lost deep in their thoughts. "Peace." The previously unappreciated word had developed marvelous implications.

"Well," said Gunnar finally. "I don't know what you men are going to do without any English to fight, but I know what I'm doing. I'm going home." The distant shout of many men told them that the good news was spreading. Over the hill, back toward the estate, they could see the flare of bonfires beginning to light up the sky.

"Hey," said Roentner, "I'll go with you, if the king will give me his leave. You might need another sword hand."

The unspoken, essential matter of vengeance and recompense for the murder of King Vigmar was, for now, foremost in their minds. The concept was so deeply ingrained in their culture that no explanation of Gunnar's next course of action was needed. They knew where he was headed, and what he must do when he returned. The murderer must be found and utterly destroyed... both he, and all who stood with him in the fight.

"Thank you, Telgar. I appreciate that. And you're right about the sword hand. I can use all of the help I can get."

"I know where I'm going," said Julian soberly, "and that's with my friend, to Bryne. If you can come with us, it would certainly help." They all understood the unspoken truth. The return of the Prince would turn Bryne upside down: the more so because of the prominent social status of King Vigmar's betrayer, Lord Haruk the Cruel.

The struggle for justice that would ensue after the return of Gunnar would lead to bloody travail. They were sick of blood, but there seemed to be no helping it; by their ancient code, the murder would have to be avenged. And yet... something troubled Julian... the words of the holy man, spoken earlier today, returned to him.

"Jesus taught that we should forgive our enemies," the monk had said. As he remembered, the words gave Julian pause. *These are all noble sentiments,* Julian thought. He looked at the darkened silhouettes of his friends, whose features could be barely discerned in the darkness. *I hate to admit it, but I think that man was right. To do good at all times, to all men... this is far superior to warring with one's enemies. But I'm not good enough to do this, and I can't afford to do it now... not when my friend needs my help.* Julian tried with difficulty to push the man's words out of his mind, but he fought a losing battle.

"I've got to get back to my company," Roentner said suddenly. "Listen, if I obtain permission from King Guthrum, I want to go with you to Bryne." He smiled in the dark. "Peace is wonderful," he added. "But I'm a warrior. Besides all of that, you know my wife is from Bryne... I'd like to take a look at the city." *She'll kill me if I don't go home right away, but what do I know about peace?* he reflected. *Once she learns of the murder of King Vigmar and our mission of vengeance, she'll forgive me. She is Brynish, after all.*

"Meet us at Grimsby," replied Julian. "We plan to sail there by way of Hamwic. I'll be preparing my longship in dry dock at Grimsby for the voyage." He looked out over the crest of the next hill, thinking of the journey that lay ahead of them. "After that, we'll take sail for the City of Gold." He raised his head and looked into Telgar's eyes. "And by all means, if you run into any more of that whiskey along the way, do pick up a keg or two."

"I'll get as much as I can lay my hands on."

"Good man. But when you find it, look out," Julian intoned ominously. "Beware of the Weir-Huns."

"What's to be afraid of?"

"They swarm at that stuff like blowflies to blubber."

"Like bees to mead," Gunnar added with a smile.

"Or thieves to gold."

"Well, if they want my gold, that's negotiable," Roentner said blithely. "But they needn't bother trying to get their hands on my whiskey." He rattled the reins and sneered. "Some things aren't for sale."

The Secret

They had sworn the guards who accompanied them to secrecy. After a long search led by Seng, they found Ithmar's broken body in a small cave, wet with salt spray. Raising him in the dark with a litter lowered from above, they had carried him home unnoticed, hidden in a wagon.

Ithmar was alive.

With haste, they called Ivan Redbeard to minister to the feverish Ithmar. Ivan gently removed the cloth plug from the wound and poured in a powerful alcoholic brew that he had prepared against such an occasion.

"We developed this in Kiev," he told them. "It cleans out the wound wonderfully, and can help with the healing process."

As Ivan worked, Ithmar grew delirious in the grip of a raging fever. He sweated and moaned and gnashed his teeth, oblivious to their presence, lost in the free-fall of delirium, plummeting downward in an unending abyss of colorless dreams. From such an abyss, he might never return. He mumbled incoherently as he tossed on the bed, his red, bloated face covered with delicate dew: discolored and tinged with an unnatural grayish sheen.

Their de facto physician hardly fared better than his patient. Acting as weary doctor to his favorite former pupil, Ivan looked sorely out of place and desperately frail. His skin hung loose on his wrinkled face, his eyes large and rheumy, trembling with exhaustion. His hand shook as he treated the wound, but he somehow persevered. When he had finished, his patient lay on his back with the gaping wound bound up securely, covered with a clean white cloth.

The depth and width of the wound shocked Katla. It hardly seemed possible to her that anyone could survive such a gash. But Ithmar clung to life, and so she clung to hope like a drowning woman might cling to piece of driftwood, struggling to stay afloat.

That night, Ilse sat by the warm fire and slept, breathing lightly. She had stayed awake for a day and a half, since the alarms had first been sounded in Bryne. Now she slept the too-deep sleep of a war-weary soldier.

At Ilse's feet, the elkhound Seng lay quiet and still, with his face between his paws. His nose tested the air, so full of the odor of alcohol, salt, and blood. His eyes, reflecting rich red firelight, steadily made a dutiful patrol: to Ilse, to the fire, to the window, to the door, to Ilse, to the fire, the window, the door, Ilse, fire, door... a closed circuit that Seng did not grow weary of.

Ithmar was alive.

Rollo was alive, Gunnar-val was alive, Kennan was alive, and Haruk was alive. But the greatest of their kings, Vigmar the Great, was dead.

The people of Bryne did not know it, but the trajectory of their dreams would soon intersect with their nightmares. Trouble would come to a head in their little corner of the world.

In an age when brute force ruled, women often became the prize when warring factions clashed. Wicked men wanted to rape and abuse them; decent men wanted to work side-by-side with them, building homes and communities as enclaves of peace... refuges of civility in a cruel and barbarous world.

The long-running battle between evil and decency showed no sign of ending, and soon it would escalate into all-out war. Ilse, her mother, and the people of their city would have to take a stand... to vote with their souls as well as their swords.

They did not know it, but their battle had already begun.

The Docs of Grimsby

"This is one sweet ship, gentlemen." They looked up from their work and saw a giant lumbering in their direction in the half-light of dawn: none other than Telgar Roentner. Captain Roentner walked up to their dry-docked ship, closely followed by a shiny-scalped, wrinkled, stoop-shouldered old man. The old man's face resembled a peeled onion used as a seat cushion by a walrus, crushed and compressed into a soggy explosion of toxic wattles. He smiled so broadly, they did not recognize him.

"Captain Roentner!" exclaimed Gunnar, ignoring his aged companion. "It's good to see you." Gunnar and Julian climbed out of the boat and shook Roentner's hand. And then, to their amazement, they recognized his grinning friend.

"My word!" exclaimed Julian. "It's the hairy barrel-troll from the whiskey tent!"

"In the flesh," added Gunnar.

"Me, a barrel-troll? Well said, I say – I've been called much worse. It's good to meet your noble captains again," the man rejoined. "I bear the brunt of greeting your exalted highnesses with a mighty royal pain, if I may make fresh with it. For as you know, the barrels of whiskey have been emptied for good… or for bad, as it were. Such excess simply staggers the mind. I beg your high and lofty pardons for this vile outrage"

"Not at all," Gunnar replied quizzically, lifting his eyebrows as if to ask what manner of being confronted them. The barrel-troll, ingenious at mangling the common tongue, refused to be stifled.

"Not at all? Indeed! In your lordship's grandiosity, if I may be so bold, you both resemble your own better natures, and that not at all. As we saw in the whiskey tent, you are indeed most fierce and violent thanes: uncorrupted by the plague of deep thought that burdens less noble minds."

"By your troth?" Julian replied archly.

"By my trots, canters and gallops. It's as plain as your red nose... or your long face, good sir. Allow me to introduce myself."

"Do we have a choice?" Gunnar interjected hopefully.

"Ha!" the barrel troll croaked, contorting his face into a smile. "My name is Wiglaf Longarms. I've been a servant to my good Captain Telgar Roentner since he was just a babe, before he was the captain of his own crib. Indeed, I do resemble a troll, sir. I'm not ashamed of my looks, since I came by them honestly. They're a gift from my dear father, the very face of my inheritance."

"Are you sure you have no more of that strong Scotch drink?" queried Julian, attempting to change the subject.

"No such luck," interjected Roentner. "The Danes dried up that river."

"And you bravely assisted in the effort, if I recall correctly," added Wiglaf the barrel-troll. "I seem to remember that your brains served as willing sponges for the fateful brew. And you look greatly the worse for wear to this very day, if I may darn with so bold a needle."

"Well, don't just stand there," Julian responded heartily. "Get some caulk and join us." The two men followed his advice, and soon were all finishing the job of meticulously caulking the longship, a job that had been started several days before. The boat, in dry dock, rested on wide wooden rollers.

This was the last of the many tasks to be completed before they took to sea in Julian's ship. His was one of the finest crafts that had ever sailed the North Sea – or any sea, for that matter. They had done most of the work themselves since Julian's men, like Roentner's, had decided to stay in England with the occupation forces. Julian knew of no sea-hands in the Port of Grimsby that he trusted to do the work unattended.

"We added a couple of hands for the trip," Julian mentioned. "The brothers Morris." As soon as he finished speaking, a loud juvenile voice could be heard on the docks.

"Give it to me, will you?"

"I found it," a deeper voice answered. "It's mine."

Two young men shambled into sight on the docks. They were

brothers, orphans awed by the mighty Vikings. They had sailed the coasts of England in fishing boats since they were barely old enough to scrub a pot, serving first as deck boys and later as full-fledged sailors, but had never imagined they would be leaving at such a tender age to cross the sea on a Viking longship. They were sixteen and seventeen respectively: ruddy, rough-and-tumble, and properly British in every way.

"We found it, Captain," said John, the older of the Morris brothers. Over his shoulder he carried a long, heavy coil of fine rope, a much-needed commodity that they had sought for days. Good rope was at a premium with so many Danish ships moored in the harbor.

"Good job, boys," Julian said. "Now grab a brush and help us finish before dark," If they finished caulking the ship before nightfall, they might be able to leave as early as tomorrow morning.

They caulked the last seam just before sunset. After rigging a berth for Telgar and his troll, the men donned clean clothes and left the docks, bound for the only nightspot in town.

They planned to dine at a dangerous, harbor-side hospitality house: the Red Rooster Inn, an infamously boisterous roost of bad birds of every feather. At the Red Rooster, the wrong sort flocked together on a nightly basis like a raucous murder of crows, prepared to fly in the face of sound counsel as well as the common good.

Night at the Red Rooster Inn

"Give me some more of that chicken," Ryan Morris interrupted. "Come on, give me that leg." His brother, worn down by Ryan's persistence, frowned as he passed another roast drumstick to the rambunctious squirt.

"So then, our boy here," Julian said, continuing his narration, "without as much as an 'excuse me, my lords,' began to scour the mead board for uneaten dainties. He sucked them down like a seal in a fish market. You should have seen the curious expression on King Alfred's face." Julian contorted his flexible mug into a look of somber, morbid fascination. "Not to mention old Guthrum.

"It was as if our friend had emerged famished from battle, like a hero of old. Like Beowulf fortifying himself in heroic fashion... stanching his ribs with a hogshead of sweetbreads before his fight with the worm of the gold hoard!"

"Whatever that means," Gunnar interrupted sourly. The men laughed raucously, and Julian frowned at the Prince in mock disgust as a loud noise from the next room interrupted them.

"What's that fuss about?" asked Ryan. Loud voices, blaring through the open doorway, evidently announced the advent of trouble. They could hear the words clearly from where they sat, just on the other side of a thin wooden wall separating them from the main entrance.

"Look, we don't want to start a battle here," a man declared loudly. "We just want to eat."

"You're kind are not welcome here," a thin voice querulously replied. "I don't want any trouble."

"I say," Julian asked brightly. "Does that accent sound familiar?"

"I think so," answered Gunnar.

"We're not leaving this place until we get a bite to eat," the man continued forcefully.

"I told you, I can't let you eat here. You'll have to find another inn. Didn't you see the sign? No Weir-Huns allowed!"

Julian, Gunnar, and Roentner sat up and looked at each other.

"Do you think?" asked Captain Roentner.

"No!" replied Julian. The voices in the next room grew louder.

"Look, friend. My men and I just got back from Wessex. You English gave us a good fight, but you learned the hard way to give us respect. I'd suggest that you reconsider your position."

"Please, sir," the voice replied, beginning to crack. "I could lose my job if my master knows I let you in. Please. He's a Dane, you see... they're all a bit daft, you know." The speaker sounded beside himself with dread as he fumbled for an adequate excuse where none would suffice. He paused. "Please, sir, just leave peacefully, master, uh... master..."

"Ixtalaban."

"Master Ixtalaban," the innkeeper repeated carefully. Hearing the name, Julian looked at his companions and smiled broadly.

"Well, old chums," Julian said, lifting his eyebrows. "It appears that we have company." He leaned over conspiratorially in the direction of the two brothers. "You've heard of them, now see them in person: the dreaded Huns of the Northern Weirs, fabled inhabitants of wildest Teutonia." He smiled sarcastically and looked across the table at Gunnar. "I can easily guess what they're doing here. They've obviously come to help you reclaim your crown... or your hoary, horned helmet... or whatever you barbarous kings wear in the icy extremities of the uttermost North.

"I have no doubt that our Viking friend, the future King Gunnar, will append them to our curious crew. And with the introduction of such questionable influences," Julian added with a knowing nod, "the City of Bryne will never be the same."

Preparation

On the docks of Grimsby, in the first glow of dawn, they took final stock and prepared to depart. The longship had slipped into the ocean smoothly, and she rode lightly on the water.

The two young English sailors stood in the bow, preparing to cast off at the Captain's command, stamping their feet and rubbing their hands together in the early morning chill. Ixtalaban and his men were asleep in the bottom of the boat, having hiked for two days and nights without rest, hoping to catch up to their new friends before they disembarked. Julian was busy counting the water bags stored in the stern.

Interrupting his count, Roentner tapped Julian's shoulder and cleared his throat loudly. Julian looked up and followed Roentner's gaze to the dock, surprised at the sight that greeted his eyes. There, on the rough-hewn dock, stood a slight, balding young fellow dressed in the dark brown robe of a holy man. He squinted myopically in their direction, clutching to his chest a broad leather case of unknown purpose and origin. His mouth was open, as if he were trying to say something.

For a long while the stranger stared as they stared back without a word exchanged. Finally, he spoke in a dry, husky voice that sounded as if it had rusted fast from disuse.

"I say, my dear fellows... Vikings all, I see. And not ashamed of it, eh?" he rasped in rather stilted Royal Danish heavily colored with a refined English pronunciation. "Tell me, if you will... are you headed north?" Julian looked around at Gunnar, who had come walking from the bow to see this curious sight.

"Gunnar," said Captain Julian. "Could you tell this fellow... "

"Brother Timothy," the monk interjected.

"Captain Gunnar, could you tell our new family member – our brother named Timothy – where we're going?"

Gunnar stood and stared solemnly at the thin, slight man who confronted them so earnestly. At the sight, he had to smile.

"We're sailing north by northeast," he answered. "Why do you ask?"

"Well of course, you don't know me at all, now, do you?" the man replied, rather flustered. "I'm Brother Timothy, a friar of the Justinian Order. I live... or rather, I lived until this morning... back down that road." He pointed toward the south. "Our abbey is about eight miles' walk from here. I left before light. I've come to take berth on a ship sailing north." He bowed courteously. "I can pay for my passage, of course."

The men in the boat looked at one another questioningly as Julian mouthed the word "no" to Gunnar. Julian was still trying to avoid dealing with the memory of the last holy man he had met. His conscience was not prepared to handle another.

"Brother Timothy," said Gunnar. "We have a long and difficult voyage ahead of us. We don't need your gold, and you could become a liability. Why on earth should we take you with us?"

"God has sent me here. He told me to sail north."

Hearing this, Gunnar turned to Julian, who raised his eyebrows and looked around at their other companions. Smiling wryly, Julian cleared this throat.

"You come with excellent references. Do you know how to handle a rudder?"

The Augean See

He sits on an ebony throne, unhinged from time and space. Patterns congeal in the air around him, a coalescence of lights that dances and sways and transforms into sharply focused, impossible shapes. The patterns jolt him with crackling bolts of adrenaline that thud and sweep across his body like storm surges slamming the bow of a dragon ship in the midst of a tempest... like the tempest they encountered a few miles off the coast of Francia.

Francia is nice, Kennan remembers. *That's where I am now.*

I'm Kennan the Great, he reflects. *I'm a prince among the slithering Frankish vermin. I'm doomed to rule their hideous race and to use them for my pleasure.*

Kennan has become shipwrecked. Lost on an island in time, he has turned into an insane, hallucinatory version of himself... or of his multiple selves.

The potions of sorcery are strong in Francia... stronger than those of my father. His mouth feels impossibly dry, and he begins to regret his decision to seek the powers of magic on this lonely, lightless night.

No one enters the room. Past midnight, the palace lays silent and still.

In three short weeks, Kennan has become a favorite of his Frankish sponsor, a longtime ally of his father. His host, Lord Henri of Volei, is a confident of Louis the Stammerer who seeks to harness Kennan's Viking expertise in war. Most importantly, the corpulent Lord Henri wants to learn how to build the greatest wonder that the shipwrights of Francia have ever encountered: the Viking longship. These deep-water ships can span oceans with ease, venturing far from the coast, as none dared sail before.

Longships give power to kingdoms. They provide the ability to strike with relative impunity, plundering the wealth of the nations. Lord Henri wants this power for himself.

A tremendous roar, a rush of sensation akin to a thunder of the bloodstream, begins to sweep over Kennan the Terrible, threatening to carry him away. He digs in with bleeding nails and tries to hold on, clutching the armrest of the throne desperately. He waits until it is time to let go... time to lose himself in the evil mist rising toward the nascent moon.

Kennan releases from his body and arises to join the swarm of evil spirits. He climbs into the discordant chorus of foul demonic passion, hallucinating wildly as he wanders through flowering clouds of darkness – lost in the mist of his poisonous dreams, here in heart of the night.

Tower Watch Before Dawn

"Katla," Dannig exclaimed looking over the railing. "What are you doing, out alone after dark?" She stood at the foot of the stairs, looking up at him.

"Wandering. May I join you in the watchtower?"

"Yes, my lady... of course!" He hurriedly opened the heavy door in the floor of the watch room to grant her entry.

A light snow, the last of the spring, had dusted her furs with large, glistening flakes. After entering the watch room, she stood for a minute in the center, as if disoriented by the darkness.

The man keeping watch was a friend of Ithmar's, an elder who insisted on serving his turn in the watchtower in spite of the depredations of advancing age. She knew in advance that he would be here tonight standing watch, honest and true: a faithful friend in a time of trouble.

He glanced at Katla and looked away, staring out over the open fjord to the sea beyond. The sea seethed in the distance, immense and mysterious. It seemed a palpable presence, one that could be felt more than seen at this hour of the night.

The room at the top of the watchtower was a circular structure. On the bay side, it featured a fortified wall that included wide, semicircular window that began several feet from the floor. The open windows provided an easy means of viewing the great swath of seascape that the watchman was charged to protect.

A person could pace in this tower to get warm when it was cold or could sit on one of the tall stools with a clear view of the great panoramic sweep of sea, cliffs, and sky. The view took in the harbor's waters, the wide bay, and Blackwater Sound, the unplumbed abyss that lay just past the broad mouth of the bay. The mysterious depths teemed with seals, orcas, whales, and wheeling, shrieking gulls. In the winter, floes of ice could sometimes be seen drifting past in the open sea beyond the sound.

If one stared too long at the blinding cliffs of jagged blue ice and dazzling white snow, the reflection could burn the eyes.

"It's just like I remembered," Katla said.

"It's beautiful, isn't it?" he answered. The low fire in the center of the room popped loudly, casting sparks onto the smooth stone floor.

The snow had stopped, and the sky had begun to clear. They stood in front of the window silently, watching as the clouds dispersed.

The moon suddenly broke through the clouds, bathing the entire scene in a subtle luminosity that defied description. They marveled at the beauty of the cliffs of their city, wrapped as they were like encircling arms reaching out toward the bay's open mouth, the fjord with its startlingly deep sound and the distant sea. With its soft, golden glow, the drowsy moonlight seemed to ennoble as much as enlighten the scene spread out beyond the safe circle of the watchtower.

As she watched, an elongated shadow, cast against the moonlight by a fast-moving cloud, ran across the cliffs near the south entrance of the bay and skimmed lightly across the waters, heading north. Its shadow temporarily darkened their tall stone aerie before sweeping across the jagged tumble of sheer rocks to the north, topping the lofty peak of Falcon Rock. The first cloud was followed within minutes by another high-flying shadow-giver, a wispy cirrus cloud sailing at astral heights that raced silently across the moon. The black band of shadow slipped rapidly from south to north: across the fjord, the cliffs, the bay waters and the city, following the quicksilver path traced by the first.

Soon, cloud after narrow cloud passed across the face of the moon and soared northward, sending bands of darkness skimming and dipping across the illuminated landscape. The rippling waves of darkness – followed by waves of delicate moonlight – raced across the cliffs, bay and city, creating a pulsating, ethereal interplay of shadow and light.

"So lovely," she breathed, unable to think of anything else to say. After more than an hour, the last thin cloud passed before the moon. The sky grew clear, finally empty of the dark silver clouds that had sailed northward with such speed and grace. The moon illuminated the landscape fully now, setting their universe awash in a steady glow of mysterious beauty.

As he watched her standing there, staring out of the window with her face in the moonlight, Dannig could see the glint of tears on Katla's cheeks. He finally ventured to speak.

"Katla," he said softly. "I'm so sorry." No other words were spoken for quite some time as they stood and gazed at the waves far below, watching them surge against the rocks that bordered the span of the moonlit sea.

The tears streamed down her cheeks freely. The crashing sea, so far below, roared rhythmically, hypnotically. The cold south wind pushed the mist into their room, bringing with it the strong scent of salt – as keen and crisp as the lines of the luminous cliffs. The wet cliffs glittered, washed clean by the bright moonlight.

As the beautiful music of the senses punctuated her prayers, Katla fought to stand strong. And yet, she yearned to collapse and sob, like a lost and wayward child.

Katla stood in the watchtower all night, immersed in the encounter: mercifully lost in the surge of tidal powers, the pulse and breadth of this cold borderland at the boundary of earth, sky, and sea.

Seize the Night

Haruk paced weightily across the hall, taking great solemn strides, periodically pausing to shake his head sagaciously. His visage seemed at once wise and perplexed, like the face of a loving uncle, creased with care.

"You have asked, me, dear brothers, and I will give you an answer," he said smoothly, sizing up the members of the council. "Your question is fair. Why, indeed, should we sail to war? Why should we raid the rich coasts of Francia? Why follow the path of the former days in the golden age of our glory? Why follow the steps of our fathers to pillage the kingdoms of the south?

"The answer to your question is written in blood… the blood of our fathers, the great warriors of the ancient days. The answer cries aloud from the memory of those who fought with King Vigmar the Great.

"Many of us gathered here are old enough to remember the raids led by my noble brother when he was young and hungry for glory." He looked around the room, sizing up these men that he knew so well. They did not give their allegiance lightly, and would not be easily persuaded.

With King Vigmar at their head, they had served as brothers and friends. His greatness had ennobled their efforts. With Ithmar at their helm, they had endured stoically, walking in the image of his faithfulness, keeping the city in Vigmar's stead as they had hoped against hope that their Prince might return. They had nursed that hope until it had sickened them, souring in their stomachs: until it seemed that hope herself strove against them like a hoary sea-witch from a bad Norse poem.

Haruk stood before the council of Bryne, intent upon persuading them that their long-standing dream, this hope of the Prince's return, was something to leave behind; and that their very hope had become a detriment to their city's best interests, mere smoke in their eyes to blind them as they sought to see the future.

With the death of Ithmar they needed a new vision for their city, and he, Haruk, was prepared to provide it. He would charm them into swallowing his plans: root, stem, and seed. He would compel them to receive abundant happiness from his sword hand, up to the very hilt. This was his hour, and he prepared to seize it tightly and squeeze for dear life.

"We are the sons, not the daughters, of the mighty men who claimed the northern wilderness," he continued. "We grew up in a city that was purchased, enriched, and defended not with harpoons or women's needles, but with the bloody swords of our noble ancestors.

"Our grandfathers, and even our fathers, understood the joy of the warrior's life. They understood the joy of battles well-fought, the bite of the pike, the thrill of the hunt, and the spoils of victory. Their golden jewels, hard-bought and dearly earned with rich Brynish blood, hung heavily around our mother's necks. Their women also (our dear, faithful mothers and granddames) adorned their lives like rings upon the hands of their men, full of respect for the noble lords who had made them the richest women in the Northern lands.

"Our ancestors showed what it means to be men. They raised their children to be wolves of the mountains, always ready to devour the fawns. They lived with one hand on the sword and the other in the throats of their adversaries. Their ships raised fear like a flag over every coast, whenever their shadow neared the shore. These were true men. Great men! Heroic men!"

Haruk warmed to his subject. He had long dreamed of this moment, and as he paused, waiting for his words to sink in, the realization hit him: *I have them. With Ithmar dead and the morale so low, with the desertion of so many young men from the city... look at their faces... they are waiting to be told what to do.* He began to speak again, but before he did, a thought raced through his mind. *Slowly now,* he mused, *lest the fish throw the unset hook.*

IV.

Haruk the Cruel, strong grandson of Bjorn,
Shaped subtle words when he faced our grave Council.
Parading among us, he charmed like a serpent
That slips through the nest without stirring a feather,
Soothing the chicks for the banquet to come.

The people were ready to vote him their king
Until one man rekindled the breast-flame of duty.
Ancient Ivan of Novrogod, old Ivan Redbeard,
Stood up at last after Haruk had spoken
And stretched forth his hand to give warriors sound counsel,
To cool their hot greed, and so keep them from harm.

"We must remember that once, years ago,
The ways of the warrior were all that we knew.
Beside those here who have now grown old
I too fought with Vigmar, our lord, long ago.

"King Vigmar led hosts by the time he was twenty.
Lord Haruk, a tot, wounded thanes made of clay.
As our King grew in wisdom
Vigmar turned from such ways…
Long before Haruk grew hair on his face.

"The old men among us know war and its mistress –
The Siren of Death – on more intimate terms.
We've learned that Dame War, like any fell harlot,
Is dainty and fair when viewed from afar.
Seen through smoked amber or glimpsed through a window,

War offers delight in her glory and grace.

"But behold her up close – in the clear light of day –
And she reeks of her madness,
Her hair shows her worms.
Her glory flees, leaving the bones in the berm.

"The swords of the wise do not seek war:
Far easier to wake than to lull that cold dam.

"It takes two to make peace, but one man to break it.
If a city attacks us – and so breaking peace –
Leave us no choice but to wake the wild wolves,
Let axes and death rain on all who would dare
To trouble our homes and the people we love!

"But let us save war for the fools who would seek it –
A bitter reward from the sword's iron edge.
Not without wisdom King Vigmar directed us
Into the pathways of rest, hope, and peace.
Today our great city, once known for its widows,
Is home to old men and warriors alike
Who sleep every evening with untroubled dreams.

"For the sake of King Vigmar let's cease from this haste.
Leave war in its den and continue the peace.
Let's strengthen the guards, but not leap to our fate.
The wild wolves of war should be left fast asleep
To be wakened if fools dare to break our strong peace."

Cat's Paws

Late at night, they drifted upon the quiet sea. Most of the men had fallen asleep after a day filled with hard rowing. The boat creaked quietly as it rocked on the gentle waves.

This was Julian's watch. He manned the windless sail with the assistance of Ryan, the younger of the Morris brothers. Together they watched and hoped for a breeze. Brother Timothy sat at the tiller. To his shipmate's surprise, Timothy had shown considerable expertise in the fine art of sailing. Having come from a noble sea-faring family in Wessex, he had captained a ship before his decision to enter the Justinian Brotherhood.

Gunnar voluntarily shared the watch, filled with excitement at the prospect of his return to the city of Bryne. He reclined against the gunnels and marveled at the subtle beauty of the night, savoring the preternatural hush of the glassy, becalmed sea and the clear bright light of the full moon. Tonight's quiet was so deep, so rich with nuance, it could be felt in one's bones.

They had been stuck in the doldrums for days, trapped in that peculiar state of windless suspense that comes on all sailing ships eventually: a prolonged state of mindless inertia and mind-numbing inactivity in which they had manned the oars by day and prayed for wind during the watches of the night. The ship sat still upon the glassy water, which seemed more like a land-locked lake than a great and perilous waterway.

Toward the end of their watch, they sensed it.

A change had begun. Although they could neither hear, smell, nor taste it, they were roused by the unified action of some sailor's sixth sense that awoke them from their sedentary torpor and sent new life surging through their veins. They had been trapped for three days in this stultifying calm. Now, they caught wind of a sweet transformation.

They heard it first: a long, drawn out sigh, as if the air itself

groaned with relief, glad at the chance to stir. And then they saw it
coming: the leading edge of a fresh breath of breeze.

The gentle wind sighed as it flowed toward them across the top
of the water, etching delicate ripples that caught the moonlight
and launching swirling clouds of mist as it passed across the tops
of the listless swells. Reaching their boat, the breeze breathed life
into the midst of their company: filling the sail and snapping it
taut. The wind pushed the ship into motion, raising a diaphanous
cloud of low-lying mist in its wake as it skimmed across the sea.

"Cat's paws," breathed Ryan Morris, uttering the sailor's term
for the clean new wind and its effect on the quiet water. He and
Julian trimmed the sail – glad to be freed from the pernicious calm
and hungry to travel again. Soon the ship cut through the low-
lying mist on a perfect sea, slicing the water with a clean, sharp
hiss. It creaked deeply as it sailed north by northeast, straight
toward the golden city of Bryne.

They traveled for more than an hour without speaking, reveling
in the sheer joy of movement and the beauty of the night. Then,
Julian spoke.

"Tell me, my brother. Were you praying to the God of Heaven
for that breeze, or did it surprise you, too?"

"Yes, and yes. The sheer beauty of the moment, you see."
Timothy stopped speaking, at a loss for words.

"I must admit that you're quite a sailor," Julian continued. "So
tell me. Why did a talented man like you give up the sea, with its
action and adventure, and move to a castle filled with robed men?
What did that offer you that you couldn't find here?"

Brother Timothy pondered his question. He answered not with
speech, but with a song in the ancient tongue of the Saxons:

> Why do the youths cry, "Make way for the King?"
> Why do men run together to hear this man speak?
> They say he's a poor man; but friend, have you heard him?
> If you saw him, or heard him, you'd follow with me.

Timothy's voice sounded smooth and melodious, mysteriously
intriguing. Julian listened closely, wondering at the beauty of the

words and their meaning. In England, he had heard the story of Jesus of Nazareth. It had seemed too good to be true.

Big questions troubled Julian. Did God care enough about fallen humanity to take on flesh and blood and enter a world filled with pain? Would God give his own life to save us from death?

Had God made Himself manifest in the man, Jesus Christ? Could there be such a God, so noble and compelling – innocent enough to pay for our sins, yet bold enough to walk to his own death? Did He endure bloody murder without lashing out or turning back... all for the love of His own?

"That was beautiful," a rough voice rasped. Timothy turned in surprise to see that the barrel-troll himself, Wiglaf Longarms, had spoken the words. Julian answered him.

"Did you like that song, Wiglaf?"

"I sure did. It was... well, it was real nice," Wiglaf replied, embarrassed by his emotions.

"I didn't know you were possessed of such tender sensibilities," Julian suggested archly, lifting an eyebrow.

"I guess that shows that you don't know everything, sir, if I may be so bold. That song, it was beautiful. I may be a fool, but I ain't made of stone."

"Of course not, dear fellow. That would make you the statue of a fool instead of the genuine article."

"Exactly, sir. But I would be even less than a fool, or less than a statue, to be untouched by such a song." He turned to Brother Timothy. "Those lyrics make me wonder."

"About what?" Julian snorted in surprise. "You? Wonder about the mystery of life? You surprise me, Wiglaf. Do you wish to become a Christian? Aren't they supposed to be wise? But you've just admitted that you're a fool."

"Well, noble master, I suppose I am a fool, and so I've always been. My father was a fool, and his father before him. It's served my family well though the years. We have prospered from our foolishness, and we've been paid dearly for it.

"But a Christian, now, that's a different sort of fool. We saw some of them up close in England. A real mixed bag they were:

genuine articles and devilish fakers all mixed together until their judgment day comes to weed them out, I suppose. The fakers were the worst sort of fakers. But the real Christians, they were something special.

"Real Christians are counted as fools, but they're wiser than kings."

"Really?"

"Yes, really. Think about it! They pray for their enemies and treat everyone with kindness. They're good to their families, as anyone should be, and generous to both friend and foe alike. It's as if the whole world is a field, and they're out there throwing good seeds in every direction, come what may. Even a fool can see that their harvest is bound to be sweet.

"People have called me a fool, and by the letter, they're right. But I'll tell you the truth; I like the sound of the Gospel. If the Christians will have me, I might lend them my sword hand."

Brother Timothy smiled at Wiglaf. "I appreciate the thought," he said. "And if you're serious about it, you can give God your heart. He doesn't need your sword hand."

"You know, I just might do that," Wiglaf answered him seriously, ignoring Julian's rolling eyes, which could be plainly seen in the moonlight.

"Well, that's fine for Wiglaf," said Julian. "But I'm not a Christian yet, and I don't think I'll be one anytime soon. The lifestyle is simply too wholesome. How could I abandon the beautiful women who accost me in every port? They'd be heartbroken, and so would I!"

"Tell me this, Wiglaf," Gunnar-val interrupted, leaning forward from his seat near the stern. "Do you really believe that this man, Jesus of Nazareth, rose up from the dead? Do you think that he's the Savior of the world?" Wiglaf fell silent. For a minute, the rhythmic creak and hiss of the ship was the only sound they heard. And then, he turned to Gunnar.

"Well, now, I think I do," he replied. "No, I'm sure I do! I believe that Jesus is the Son of God. I don't know what to do with it, but I believe it, and that's a fact. So there!"

Brother Timothy almost leaped from his post at the tiller and danced for joy when he heard these words. But he managed to stay seated, thereby avoiding a sailing calamity.

"Uh, Wiglaf," Timothy offered. "About that faith." He smiled endearingly. "If you don't mind, I think I can help you figure out what to do with it."

The Mutton of Future Feasts

"Give me that beast," hissed Kennan, reaching beneath the gelding's glistening neck to snatch his reins from the groom. Kennan swung a leg across the horse's back and settled into the saddle, carelessly kicking the man in the head for good measure.

Viciously applying the spurs, Kennan took off in a dead run, leaving the stunned servant gaping in his wake like a wounded cod drifting behind a departing dragon ship. The haughty Viking lord and his tall golden mount quickly coursed through the open gates of the castle and clattered out onto the crowded cobblestone thoroughfare.

Soon, he had left the city behind. Enjoying a glorious morning in the pristine Frankish countryside, he savored the touch of a cool breeze on his cheek, the warm sun on his back as he rode past filthy peasants slaving over filthy fields.

Kennan felt like a well-fed wolf casting about a fold filled with fat little lambs. With a sneer, he cantered his gelding past the trembling members of the Baron's closely sheared flock, enjoying the moment. Kennan felt confident that the hapless peasants would some day serve him as the mutton of future feasts. He would have plenty of time to ravage them at a later, convenient date.

As Kennan reflected on his recent good fortune and settled into the rhythm of the countryside, he slowly – almost subliminally – became aware of an irregularity in his rhythm. To be more precise, he became aware of a hitch in the gait of his horse. At the exact moment when he noticed the problem, an unexpected sound jolted him from his musings.

"Having a problem, sir?" a low voice asked loudly. Kennan gave a start and turned about to see a big, burly, hairy fellow, mounted upon a stout, rough-coated draft horse.

Where did he come from? Kennan wondered. The dense forest

to the right of the road appeared impenetrable, and during the past few minutes the plowed fields to his left had looked as empty as the desolate roadway.

As one might expect, Kennan kept track of his environment with the wariness of a hunting wolf. But apparently, this man had come out of nowhere… suddenly appearing behind him. It seemed to Kennan as if the man had been conjured, transformed from a tree or stone into a full-blown, rustic ape-man ambling down the roadway, breathing down Kennan's neck with a friendly comment and inanely courteous smile.

"I see that your horse is limping," the man offered.

"He's fine," replied Kennan curtly. He hoped that if he ignored this bumpkin, he might ride past and proceed on his way, but he was to be sorely disappointed. Like a properly servile peasant, the man stayed just a few paces behind Kennan, smiling whenever he glanced back. And, to make things worse, Kennan's horse had begun to come up lame. He struggled to walk in spite of all attempts to spur him on.

"Your horse is in trouble," the man observed. Kennan sighed. *He's right,* he thought.

"Well, it's at least an hour on foot back to where I came from," Kennan observed in exasperation, stopping the horse in the path and glancing back at the commoner with curiosity mingled with proud disdain. "I suppose I'll have to return that way, leading the beast on a leash like a dog, or risk ruining one of the Baron's best hunters." He did not care about the horse but he couldn't afford to displease the Baron in any way… since, for the time being, he abode by his grace and under his powerful protection.

"I could help you sir, if you'd like." Kennan reined his horse around and closely studied this man, who was now less than ten feet away. The stranger's broad, honest face was pockmarked with the ravaged remnants of some childhood infirmity that had long ago passed like a storm across his visage, leaving scalloped indentations like holes from uprooted trees in its wake.

"How can you help?"

"I'm a smith, my lord. My shop is over there, in those trees."

He pointed to the left, across the broken ground, to where a large cluster of treetops could be seen over the top of a low hill. To get there by the most direct route, they would have to cross the wide field and pass over a low hill. It was flat terrain comprised of newly turned earth, damp and heavily furrowed: ochre ground that would be clothed within weeks in a swirling garment of thin, green wheat stalks.

It was now mid-morning, but if Kennan had to walk back to the castle, the entire day would be lost. He swung down off of his horse and straightened his cap. He was sour and upset, but there was no helping it; a good smith might save the day for this horse, and for Kennan himself, for that matter.

If he had been possessed of more tender sensibilities, more appreciative of the splendor around him, he might have been struck with awe at the incredible, almost mystical beauty of the fertile countryside. The cloudless sky almost seemed to vibrate with intense blue light, its cloudless span mellowing to a gentle pastel at the edge of the horizon. To Kennan's left ran a line of low, rolling hills framed by a distant line of dark green trees. The forests offered a vivid contrast to the brown of the freshly tilled earth and the vivid blue vault of the sky.

The scents seemed as powerful as the colors. A faint, acrid hint of smoke from an unseen hardwood fire mingled with the smell of freshly turned earth and the delicate scent of spring wildflowers.

All of this beauty, this infinitely intricate, subtly colored handiwork – the mysteriously complex design of life pulsing in the core of the cosmos – could not penetrate Kennan's heart of flint. He cared only for his business in a village down the road.

In his own way, however, Kennan was a romantic. Or rather, he was a sentimentalist. Kennan was a man who appreciated the warm and fuzzy glow of gold-lust, the gentle sway of hair hanging loose from heads impaled on pikes, the mellow music of coins clanking into overflowing coffers: life's finer things. In spite of his sentimental bent, however, Kennan gave little heed to natural wonders. He took the glories of the heaven and earth for granted, as if he had somehow created them.

"Lead on," he told the blacksmith, oblivious to the beauty above his head and beneath his feet: before, behind, and around him.

At Kennan's command, the brawny yeoman veered from the well-traveled path and struck out across the field. As he followed the man leading the Baron's horse, struggling over the rocks and mud in his ridiculously expensive riding boots, a strange sensation resonated through Kennan's being. He felt a nebulous trill, a high-pitched vibration of the soul that startled him... as if he had somehow suddenly heard his heart beating for the very first time. What, if anything, did it mean?

The man's gigantic horse plodded slowly ahead. Cursing his luck, Kennan struggled across the rock-strewn field, following the man up the slope, toward the top of the beautiful hill.

Rollo

"What are they doing down there?" To accentuate his question, Rollo pointed toward the city gate at the foot of the gently sloped street. He sat with a friend in front of the empty mead hall, basking in the light and enjoying another quiet day.

By mid-morning, all able-bodied men of working age had trudged to their fields or taken to the water, where they busily engaged in productive activities. Rollo and his friend, however, enjoyed no such obligations.

Rollo was still recovering from his wounds. His companion – a gentleman of years named Melgaard the Bald – had comfortably retired, and was making the most of it.

"Melgaard, look. See Haruk standing by the gate? It looks he's adding some blubber to his plan for a new, improved watch."

"Of course. Haven't you heard?" Melgaard answered.

"Heard what?"

"Haruk has championed your cause, dear boy. He's been using your injury to add weight (considerable weight, I must say) to his oversized reputation as the most massive defender of Bryne."

"My injury? What do you mean?" Rollo did not like the sound of this.

"He's been using your wounds and Ithmar's murder and the deaths of the men who manned the dock that night. He's using it all as fodder to fuel his ambitions. It's enough to make a sailor sick, seeing the monstrous old blowhard spout off about how sad it is that murderous outsiders got away with such a crime. He's turned it into a political kick-bladder. He's hawking the defense of our city as if he were selling bad medicine out of the back of an ox cart. It's Haruk the Cruel's serpentine balm, guaranteed to heal every pustule that erupts on the body politic.

"You should have heard him the other night before the council. He stunk up the room like a pod of orcas. He blubbered away and spouted such sincere concerns for you and Ithmar, groaning all the while. You'd think he was about to calve an iceberg! Disgusting!" Melgaard paused and stretched, leaning forward and scratching his ankle where an opportunistic insect had begun to feast.

"Your words are like riddles. Do you mind speaking Brynish? What do you think he's up to?"

"Oh, he wants to be king, of course. And his motives are unselfish, as you might guess. He's had a complete personality change in the dotage of middle age. Three of his men have been assigned to strengthen the dock watch, and you can find them there at all times, openly demonstrating the high-minded magnanimity of our city's new defender: Haruk the High-minded, the Giver of Gifts to the Politically Powerful.

"He's spreading gold fever, talking about the good old days and reminding our men of the glories of war. Haruk's a changed devil! He really cares about us now. He's seeking the good of our city all over the place."

"Nobody has told me a thing about this," Rollo replied impatiently. "Where do you get this stuff?"

"Oh, I know a few things," Melgaard sniffed in reply. "I wasn't born yesterday." *I'll say,* Rollo mused. *You must have been born about a hundred years ago.*

"Well," Rollo finally said, leaning forward on his cane and struggling to stand. "Haruk may be using all of this for his own gain, but he's got a point. Somebody assaulted me. Somebody killed Ithmar." All at once tears came to his eyes and he felt a jolt of anguish. *Ithmar saved my life.*

"Yes, somebody assaulted you and murdered Ithmar," continued Melgaard, studiously avoiding notice of his companion's tears. "Not to mention poor Yordan Longtooth and Filt, Delf's Son. So many young men from our city disappeared on the same night, along with Eric Far-Eyes. None of them have been heard of since." Rollo was beginning to wish that Melgaard would stop, but the old man forged ahead without pausing for a breath.

"I'm not a suspicious man, mind you. But this mess smells like a vat of sour mead. It isn't easy to pull off such a raid as was done against our city. You just don't walk away from Bryne, you know. You have to cross the mountains or sail away on a longship. As for those Brynish boys, they must have left of their own free will. That means it was an inside job, coordinated by a citizen of our city. And I'll wager ivory to ice that Eric Far-Eyes wasn't the only insider involved. Mark my words.

"Someone who knew those boys talked them into leaving, and killed our men on the same night… someone hungry for warriors and ships. Someone hungry for riches, or I'm not an old man."

"A citizen of Bryne? Who?"

"Well, now, how many men do you know who used to live in Bryne, but now they don't? Can you think of any Brynish men with the skill-set needed to kill Ithmar, navigate our fjord in the dead of night, and avoid capture after we gave chase?"

"I can think of only two. Maybe three at the most."

"Who are they?"

"Barad-zur, the scop… Kennan, who was exiled… and Gunnar, if he's still alive."

"Well now, let's think about it. Barad-zur didn't know the boys who left the city that well. He was right in front of us, entertaining us in the mead hall that night. And he's a hero of our city, besides. He saved King Vigmar at risk of his own life, and was never known to be greedy. We can rule him out. That leaves two young men, Kennan and Gunnar. You knew them both. Which of them could have done such a thing? Put it together, man!"

"No!" Rollo cried, finally managing to rise shakily to his feet. "But, if it was Kennan, Haruk must have known about it. Then this thing, this big political move by Haruk to protect us from outsiders, this whole campaign…" he paused.

"Haruk's whole campaign is a gigantic pile of rotten, flyblown walrus cheese!" cried Melgaard, finishing Rollo's thought with typical, pungent aplomb. "And don't tell a soul that I'm saying this, but I think he's up to his elbows in the pile along with our dearly departed Kennan Whitefang. That Kennan's a sneaky little cheese-eater if ever I knew one, if you'll pardon my Scylfing. It's just too perfect! Kennan kills our brothers, and then his father uses the murders to gain political clout.

"Haruk the Cruel has closed the circle. Ithmar's murder was too convenient, and Haruk stood to gain more than anyone else. I wouldn't doubt that the whole bloody mess was arranged by that Bulbous Blast of Northern Wind, Haruk the Cruel, otherwise known as Haruk the Kindhearted, the Faithful Defender of Bryne!"

In the Heart of the Furnace

Kennan awoke flat on his back with a painful, pulsating headache. He found his limbs twisted into unnatural, contorted positions. When he tried to move, excruciating pain stunned his senses. He opened his eyes and looked about frantically, desperately trying to identify his surroundings.

"You needn't attempt to leave us, sir," a rough voice rasped. "We've arranged for you to linger a while." With a sickening shock of understanding, Kennan felt the tight ropes on his arms and legs, the gag in his mouth, and the iron pincers locking his head into place. *I'm locked into some sort of torture device,* he realized. The thought sent a jolt of adrenaline crawling through his belly like a nest of electric eels.

As he strained to move his head and look at his tormenter, Kennan began to regain his memory. *That voice – it's the blacksmith. The last I remember, I was walking into his shop.* In a flash, he remembered the blow to the back of his head. *Oh, no!*

"I'm sure you'll find your bed comfortable," the voice continued. "You slept so well in it, all night long… like a plump little wolf after a bloody kill. I just made that bed by special order of the Baron himself. I'm sure you'll find it sufficient for your needs." The big man stepped into Kennan's line of sight. He towered over Kennan, his rumpled clothes stinking of fire. The blacksmith's frantic, wide-open eyes looked lifeless, like polished pearls with onyx cores. They stood out against his smoke-blackened face like lunatic moons staring down from a smut-stained sky.

"Mmph," Kennan replied through the gag.

"Now, now, let's not try to talk." The blacksmith stretched his face into a madly incongruous smile. He reached for something on his workbench. "Whoops!" he cried, knocking a heavy iron bar off the stone slab. The metal bar narrowly missed Kennan's head as it thumped to the floor. "Look out!" Turning his back to Kennan, the smith began to pull on the billows with his left hand as he turned a long, glowing rod in the heart of the fire. He hummed happily as he worked.

"Mmmm!" Kennan cried, struggling against the rotten cloth of the gag. Hearing the sound, the smith whirled around and knelt on the floor beside him, thrusting a heavily furrowed face next to Kennan's as he seized him by the hair.

The man smiled. His eyes burned brightly with madness, fueled by a heat exceeding anything his forge could offer.

"Don't speak to me," he spat fiercely. With all of his might, he butted his forehead hard against Kennan's, causing the tightly-bound Norseman to writhe in agony as the head-butt slammed down on him: once, twice, a third time.

The blacksmith slowly stood and stepped away, returning to his work as if nothing had happened. "Let me tell you a story," he said, speaking loudly but unemotionally. "This is the story of a little princess.

"Let me continue!" he hissed for no apparent reason. "Shut up! Don't interrupt!" He shook his head as if flies buzzed in his ears. And yet, no flies could be seen in the little blacksmith shop.

"Not so long ago, and not so far away, a little princess grew up in a poor, common household. Her own dear mother died during her birth, and she was raised by a father who loved her more than life, or breath, or heaven, or hell, or death, or the grave, or iron, or smelting, or heat it up, burn it up, sear it, you dog! Kill the stinking pig!"

The poor smith, you see, had gone utterly mad.

Driven by rage, the smith's hot hammer slammed emphatically against the side of the stone forge, showering Kennan with sharp chips and brittle dust from the shattered, fragmented granite. His voice had risen to a scream, but now he stopped talking and regained control of his madness, methodically pumping the bellows, uttering a flat, humorless laugh.

With his powerful grip, the smith held a pair of tongs in his strong right hand and turned the tip of the superheated iron rod in the white-hot center of the fire, slowing pumping the billows with his thick left arm as he stoked the heat to unbearable levels. The hair on his right arm began to singe: one hair at a time popping and shriveling from the terrible heat in the pulsating heart of the furnace.

"You need to know all about this little princess," the smith droned to Kennan with his expressionless monotone. "It's very important. You see, I taught the princess that she was precious and perfect: that she was worth more than all the gold in the world. She loved her Papa, and he loved her. But when she grew up, she wanted to see the world. Young girls sometimes do, you know.

"Her papa did not like the idea, but he loved her more than his own life. And so her vile, stupid, idiot father spoke for the princess. He got her a position as a servant in the castle of the great Baron of Volei. She was happy there for a while. Then something happened." The blacksmith lifted his great hammer and brought it down upon the pulsating tip of the red-hot rod with a heavy, resounding crash.

"Something happened, you see. Some... some... some thing. Yes, that's it... a thing, that's what it was. This thing... this monstrous thing... gripped my little princess in its hungry, bloody claws. It was thing, you see: not a person, though it could have been, should have been a person. It chose to become an animal: a devil, a wolf. This thing that should have been a man seized upon my little princess." Again he raised the heavy hammer, and again it whipped down with a resonant crash, sending a shower of hot sparks in every direction.

"This man-thing attacked the little princess, and he dragged her off, and he raped her. He devoured her for his pleasure: devoured her flesh and her innocence, her little dreams, her tender feelings. He devoured her like a wolf slowly sucks the life from a tiny, bleating lamb." The hammer fell and the sparks flew. The wildly resonant crash made Kennan's ears ring noisily in his aching, spinning head.

"He raped her, I said! And then, what's almost worse than the rape, you see, is that this man told the little princess that she was ugly. He told her that she was bad, disgusting, not a princess, not even a servant, just a whore for his pleasure, and a sorry whore at that! He beat my princess, and he almost killed her!" The blacksmith's voice ended in wail, a thin hopeless shriek of despair: the unspeakable cry of a maddened heart, bereft of hope.

The hammer smashed down again, exploding against the stone as it fired a fountain of cascading sparks into the air, smearing them smoothly across Kennan's field of vision. The blacksmith suddenly whirled and thrust the hot iron close, too close to Kennan's face. The heat crinkled Kennan's eyebrows and painfully tightened the skin on his cheek.

"There, there, don't answer me, my dear man... or man-thing, or monster, or whatever you are. Don't answer me. Don't say a word. But, tell me... do I have the story right?"

"Mm!"

"I said don't answer me!" the smith shrieked, spontaneously whipping the heavy iron rod against Kennan's arm. The blow broke the bone inside his bicep with a loud crack, instantly burning his skin to a cinder where the iron touched it. The sudden pain almost maddened Kennan. He began to convulse in his bonds like a wolf spasmodically thrashing in its death throes, caught in a cruel iron trap.

"God forgive me!" the smith cried. "God forgive me!" The tears flew from his eyes as he fell to his knees, dropping the iron rod on the ground beside him and covered his face with his hands as he began to sob uncontrollably.

The smith suddenly stopped crying and dropped his hands from his face, staring blankly at Kennan as he picked up the long poker. His emotionless, smoke-blackened face, streaked with broad, hopeless rivers of icy white tears, floated like an apparition in Kennan's field of vision.

"God forgive me, I won't kill you," he said evenly. "But you will never look on another little princess, you man-devil, to eat her up like a wolf, you violent pig!" He raised the long rod and brought it near Kennan's face again, shriveling the remains of his eyebrows.

"Look at this burning iron, man-wolf," he said softly. "I have lost my religion because of you. Jesus wants me to forgive you, but I refuse. God is kind, but I am not. He would have me forgive you. But you serve another master, so why shouldn't I?

"Your evil master will rejoice when I sink this hot iron into your sockets and cook your bubbling eyes like two little blobs of candy snapping on a spit. You have served the devil, man-wolf, and he hates you for it. Don't think that he can deliver you from death, or that he will even try! Does he love you enough to come down to earth to save you? Would he suffer death for you, or even lift a finger to save your miserable life?

"But no more waiting. Here, let me show you what I mean."

On this quiet day, no one passed by the little blacksmith shop on its narrow country lane. But if anyone had ventured down the peaceful byway after the blacksmith began his work, they would have heard no screams, garbled or otherwise. They would have heard only the familiar muffled sobs of the forlorn, grief-maddened smith, whose poor little daughter had so recently committed suicide.

No cries of anguish sounded from the tiny shop, or choked in the throat of the blacksmith's victim. Pain had rendered Kennan Whitefang – the merciless Wolf of the Northern Seas – most mercifully unconscious.

Land of the Northern Star

The next week passed quickly. The days grew longer as they sailed north, drawing nearer to the city of Bryne. A severe storm hit them mid-week, but the fast-moving front quickly passed on, leaving little damage in its wake.

After the storm, the wind remained perfect for sailing; forty-five degrees off their tack, holding steady as she went. The Morris brothers and Gunnar manned the sail while Julian handled the till, allowing the others to enjoy a rare time of leisure.

"That was quite a blow the other day," offered Ixtalaban to Andrew. "I thought you were going to let the tiller go in the worst of it."

"You noticed? I thought you slept through the bad weather."

"I was faking it. I have to keep up my image, you know. But you're dodging my question, Brother. How'd you manage to hold onto the tiller in the midst of that storm?"

"I was too scared to let go."

"Scared? I don't believe it. You must have nailed yourself to the deck. I never saw a pilot keep his feet in such seas."

"Okay. To tell you the truth, I lashed myself to the crossbeam," Timothy whispered conspiratorially. "Please, don't tell a soul."

"Hey, Wiglaf," called Ixtalaban. "Come over here." The wrinkled, sawed-off stump of a man joined them in the bow.

"Yes, my lord of the Weirs," Wiglaf rasped. "How may I help your grand Teutonic highness?"

"Tell me," asked Ixtalaban, ignoring his jibes. "How do you think Brother Andrew managed to steer the ship so well during that storm?"

"That's obvious, my boy," Wiglaf replied, clapping him vigorously on the shoulder. "He took advantage of a plentiful ration of my good advice and the gracious help of our Lord." In the last two weeks Wiglaf had become the unlikeliest Christian in the history of the North. He seemed intent on hammering the point home at every opportunity.

"What advice, Sir Longarms?"

"I told him that if he fell into the water, he should jump right back into the boat." At this, Wiglaf clapped Ixtalaban on the shoulder and humming loudly, swaggered back toward the stern.

Ixtalaban shook his head. "That man is without a doubt the most unusual fellow I have ever met," he reflected aloud.

"This, coming from a Weir-Hun," interjected John Morris, who had listened to the conversation. He hastily ducked a missile of loose line and followed Wiglaf toward the bow. He sat on the deck and began to whittle on a piece of walrus tusk. Several of Ixtalaban's men lay sound asleep, scattered throughout the boat.

Gunnar carefully watched the sail and the sea for signs of a change in the wind. If the good weather held out, they would reach his city tomorrow.

He could hardly believe it. He had struggled and dreamed for so much of his young life... for almost three years as a slave, then during the long months of fighting in the cold and the rain during the bloody English campaign. They had fought their way through Wessex, into the very heart of the beautiful island of Britain. Through all of these things, Bryne had remained in his mind as a stronghold of peace and refuge.

At times, it had seemed as if he would never again see his city: the cliffs of the falcons, the familiar pier, the fortified gate and watchtower, the village packed with brightly painted, steep-roofed houses crowded together for warmth. He had left with the memories of a child, but now he was a man. Though he longed for home, his longing was mixed with trepidation. Somehow, the thought of returning terrified him.

The Prince stood and stretched, keeping a watchful eye on the sail. He had changed during the past few years. His face was wind-hardened and tan: a heavy, chiseled face with a light brown beard ruffled by the wind. His hair had been burned white by sun, wind and sea. His laughter, when it came, was boisterous and free.

He had left his city a tender boy, with his hopes and innocence intact. He was returning as a warrior blooded in battle, tough and careworn and jaded and lost… at twenty years of age. He struggled for hope, striving to recapture his golden, stolen past.

Gunnar lifted his eyes to the horizon, searching for a thin blue smudge of mountains at the uttermost edge of the horizon. His intensity was complete as he focused on his goal, as if by the thought alone he could hasten the journey, bringing his homeland nearer by the wishful power of his gaze.

He stood as in a trance, straining to see. Hoping against hope, he sought to somehow defeat the miles with his stare and to behold, with sudden joy, the trembling mirage of distant peaks that would tell him – at last – he was home.

A Blind Beggar at Almsgate

He lay without moving in the dust, unceremoniously dumped at the intersection of two busy roadways in the middle of the night. By the time he awoke, a fever raged within his broken body.

Kennan did not know that he arrived here in a wagon after a three-day trek across the countryside. A state of drunken delirium had plagued him for days, removing him far from reality – sealing him tightly in a hot, sickly-sweet world of swirling sparks, senseless ranting, and shivering, senseless dreams. He had been cared for well, or at least as well as the pitifully mad blacksmith knew how to care for him: force-fed water regularly and protected in dense forest shade from the heat of day. He lay inertly beneath a broad, leafy tree, wracked by deadly fever. Curled in a fetal position and wrapped in a thin brown blanket, he quaked in the grip of a delirium that exceeded mere pain.

The blacksmith had deserted his victim at a busy intersection named (in the translation) Almsgate, a crossroad in the center of an unfamiliar duchy within the domain of another Baron who was decidedly not Kennan's patron. He did not know the dialect of the locals, and given his tin ear, he would have understood none of it, even if he had been conscious. Almost none of them spoke English, or Latin, or Danish, or even the Common Frankish tongue of the coastal cities. To state it succinctly, Kennan had little chance for survival.

He lay all day in the shade of the tree, lost in his fever while a pre-medieval assortment of men, women and children walked past, shaking their heads to see a man reduced to such a pitiable estate. Hard black flies tried unsuccessfully to crawl beneath his tight bandages. The cauterized wounds sent daggers of unbearable pain into his delirious mind: merciless pain that battered him like waves of fire. The pain shot piercing daggers into his soul and pounded his head with hot hammer blows: tormenting and maddening him whenever his consciousness tried to raise its wounded head.

He lay there for most of the day, weak and moaning, lost and shivering with fever, until an old man found him. This particular passerby was a kind and gentle soul.

The old man put a cool hand on Kennan's bright red face, and shook his head slowly. He brushed back the long black hair and looked carefully at the bandages. As he examined him, he smelled the faint odor of burnt flesh and took notice, with quiet understanding, of the grotesquely blackened flesh surrounding the tight, clean bandages.

The old man recognized the signs of torture. *This is how they bruise around the burned areas.* Living in the midst of an oppressive regime, he had seen such victims before.

The short, stocky stranger bowed down and picked up Kennan as if he were a child, placing him tenderly on his own donkey, lashing Kennan's scarred body to the gentle beast's saddle and neck.

He softly led him away, walking in the direction of home.

The Oppressive State of the Sea

"Tell me, Gunnar," Julian queried. "When we get to your city: what do you want to do first?" The Prince did not answer immediately. The sharp wind, pressing powerfully against the full sail, caused the wooden ship to creak deeply, as if in reply to Julian's question.

"I don't know," Gunnar answered. He sighed deeply and shook his head. "I'm not sure of what to expect. It won't be the same city; I know that much." He passed his hand heavily across his face. "I had a dream, Julian. My dream was like a precious jewel; and wherever I went, I carried it with me… the memory of Bryne the way I knew it. For years I thought I could return to Bryne, the city I knew. But I can't. Not really. The city will be changed, the people will be changed… some of the people I love may be dead. My teacher, Ivan Redbeard… my father's best friends, Ithmar and Katla, my friend Rollo… even Ilse.

"Is she okay? And if she's well, does she care for me the way I care for her? Has she married? Whatever Kennan did to her… I hope that she's well. I mean," he stammered, and then he stopped.

"I'll wager she's fine." Julian responded reassuringly. "You don't have to worry about that. I'm sure of it." Yet Julian sounded more confident than he felt. He had never spoken of these things with Gunnar, and he knew without even looking at him that his friend had come to an intensely agitated state… not that it could be detected easily. Gunnar was nothing if not stoic, offering a facade to the world that effectively concealed any inner turmoil. If Julian hadn't known better, he might have blamed his friend's sleeplessness on the oppressive clouds and the turbulent state of the sea.

The surface of the sea had grown in size. Huge swells, closely followed by abysmal troughs, rolled rapidly across the face of the dark green water. These were massive, wet mountains, more than mere waves. Their ship scurried up the waves like a tiny wagon desperately scaling a series of relentless, oncoming aquatic ridges.

The fast-moving hills slid swiftly beneath them, triggering a series of precipitous plunges: nail-biting sleigh rides, each leading to the next sheer climb up the next mountain of water. This was a familiar pattern to experienced sailors: so familiar, in fact, that some of the men not currently assigned to the second watch had fallen sound asleep.

"We're still ahead of the storm," Julian offered, changing the subject. Gunnar nodded his head thoughtfully.

"But not for long, I'm afraid," he replied. "Do you feel it?" The southwesterly wind, unseasonably warm for these northern waters, had become heavily saturated with moisture. A cold cross-breeze was beginning to stir, leading to the kind of buffeting gusts that could quickly give birth to waterspouts.

"Yes. It looks like we're in for a blow. Poor timing, eh?" They sat for a while and thought about their situation.

"Maybe it's a bluff."

"I hope so," said Julian wryly. "But don't bet the ship on it."

Earlier in the day, before the dark clouds had crawled down from their heights and perched low above the roiling waters, Gunnar had said that landfall could occur sometime during the night. An extra sailor had been appointed to each watch tonight due to his prediction, and for good reason. Experience had taught them that his ability to correctly calculate their location, using only a Norse navigator's shadow-dial and his own internal sense of time and direction, was uncannily accurate.

They had assigned a lookout to watch, listen, and study the sea carefully for any indication that the cliffs and mountains of the Norwegian peninsula drew near. The black clouds now lowering in the flat, lightless sky made it doubly difficult to find the harbor. If they drew close to land, they would take no chances; they would drop a sea anchor and wait for daylight.

Gunnar stared at the sea and reflected on Julian's question. What would he do first when they returned to his city? Finally, he decided to answer him.

"I'll tell you I want to do, Julian." he began. "When we walk into Bryne, I want to kiss the people I love. I want to greet my friends. Then, I want to find Lord Haruk the Cruel. When I discover his whereabouts, or when I see him, I will act." Gunnar's voice, usually so calm, sounded pressurized... as if he had become trapped beneath a fully loaded wagon, with the leaden heft of it planted squarely upon his chest.

"I will kill Haruk." he continued, matter-of-factly. "If his men stand with him, I will kill them all... or die trying. If you wish to help me, we will fight side-by-side.

"We will slay and live – or fall and die – as one. That's my plan, such as it is," he added with a sigh, shaking his head like a sleeper struggling wake up. "But whether we kill or are killed, one thing is certain. I intend to slay Haruk the Cruel with my own sword-hand.

"My eyes will see his destruction and the ruin of all he owns. May Haruk's evil return upon his head. May he feast upon misery, and may he be cursed forever from the face of goodness and light!" Prince Gunnar vehemently spat the words out, as if the very taste of his enemy's name galled him – bitter and unwelcome in his mouth, even as he cursed Haruk's name from the face of grace forever.

Visions of the Wise

Ilse walked hastily into her mother's room and stopped in her tracks. She hesitated for a moment, watching her mother sleep; then she bent over and gently shook her shoulder.

"Mother! Mother! Wake up!" she whispered. Katla passed her hand over her face lightly and tried to roll over for more sleep, provoking Ilse to vehemently shake her arm. "Mother, please!" Katla rolled onto her back, her pale eyes glistening faintly in the light from Ilse's candle.

"What is it?"

"Mother, we need to talk." Katla slowly sat up in bed and slid over to one side, sleepily patting the feather mattress as she tossed back a long strand of hair. Ilse climbed into bed and leaned against her like a little child as her mother wrapped an arm around her shoulder.

"All right, Ilse," she answered evenly. "Tell me what it is." Ilse stared vacantly at the foot of the bed, deep in thought as she replied.

"I had dreams tonight, mother, like the dreams that I had before. You remember… about the king." She felt her mother grow tense. *Don't worry, mother, it will be all right.*

"Can you tell me what they were?"

"I was standing outside of our house, and when I looked up to where the king's house is, I saw the tree again. The same tree from the other dream: the one that the men carried away, but it was still alive.

"I saw this tree as some new men tried to plant it up on top of the cliff." Her mother listened silently, shocked by the portent of such an omen.

"But while they were trying to plant it, men with axes came to cut it down, to burn it like they did to the big tree in the other dream. And then," she continued, "I woke up before I could find out what was going to happen, so I went back to sleep. Then I dreamed it again. And this time, I think I know what it means."

"What is that?" asked Katla. *God help us.*

"I think that Gunnar is coming back, mother. Soon. Right away. I think that some men will try to help him become king, and others will try to kill him. And mother, I'm scared."

Her voice sounded frail and small, as if she were once again a little girl in danger. But she was not, and Katla knew it. She had grown into a strong young woman, not easily shaken.

Katla realized at once what Ilse's dream signified: the certain return of the Prince of Bryne. His return would happen soon, even right away, and would be followed by an attempt on his life. And now, as she thought about the dream and its interpretation, something deep within Katla compelled her to immediate action.

"Ilse, will it be dawn soon?"

"I saw some light at the edge of the sky, just before I came to wake you up."

"Good." Katla's mind raced. *God has given us another sign... and this time we're better prepared to use the knowledge.* "You're the best rider under our roof tonight, Ilse. Go now. Get dressed, and ride into town. Swiftly! Don't stop for any reason. Go to Ivan's house, and tell him to drop whatever he may be doing: that I have an urgent message for him.

"Tell him that the Prince is coming back soon... perhaps right away. If he asks you how I know this, tell him about your dream.

"Tell him that I said he must gather the wisest men of our city immediately for a meeting to discuss this matter. I will follow you into the city, and we will both attend the meeting. Tell him, by all means, to beware. This may spell treachery, Ilse... treachery and betrayal!"

Her daughter, whose mouth had dropped open in surprise at the sight of her even-tempered mother in such a excited state, responded immediately. In accord with her impulsive nature, she began to rise to her feet so she could dash out of the door without another word.

Seeing her reaction, Katla instantly reached out and halted her.

Slowly, she took Ilse's face in her hands. She gazed at her with deep understanding, eyeing her intently with a heart full of a mother's fierce, uncompromising love.

"Be careful," she whispered, giving her a tight hug and a quick kiss.

"And now," she added. "By all means, go!"

Dream-Seeker

Haruk casts dry bones into the ashes and stirs the embers tenderly, waiting for a vision. Dawn approaches, but Haruk does not know it. For many months he has seen his personal power grow in magical leaps and bounds, but tonight the very air seems pregnant with opportunity. Now, it is time to make his move.

He has turned once again to sorcery, seeking a defining vision. He is a well-balanced pyromancer of the Devil's own school. Haruk the Cruel offers no pretense of white magic.

He has long practiced the diabolical arts for a pragmatic reason: they work. For years he has used and been used by the wandering spirits and lustful powers that roam the earth, sky, and sea: fallen angels all, although he does not know it and would not care if he did.

Haruk has learned to sift the spirits for pressure points in the body of the natural universe, seeking fulcrums by which the forces of the natural world may be leveraged. By demonic power, he has bent the world of men to his perverted will.

Tonight he once again seeks the fallen spirits, and from them he will receive his answer. And so, he sits. He stirs the smoky ashes, and silently – remorselessly – he waits.

He does not have to wait long. A brilliant picture flashes across the embers, and within him, a revelation occurs. Both the vision and its message are given with a clarity and power that shocks him. He sees far tonight with his magic, and he has beheld somber omens. Men in a longship are coming. They are mighty, and deadly, and they seek his life. But there is more to this vision.

Haruk Longknife sees power reflected in the fire and the smoke. The men in the longship have something new among them. Someone in the ship, some passenger, is accompanied by something unknown to Haruk.

The ship's passenger carries with him the ultimate power.

The passenger bears the presence of a power beyond all powers, a Being of such might that His faintest shadow shakes and startles Haruk, the necromancer and dream-seeker. He senses an unknown intelligence from an unknown source that cannot be defeated.

This goes far beyond sorcery.

Haruk cannot begin to comprehend the breadth of this Being's power. The One who accompanies the ship has wisdom beyond measure... strength to create the cosmos, to bend time and space, to change the nature of light, heat, and universal forces at whim: to instantly vaporize the entire universe as if it were a speck of wax in a blast furnace. As a cankerworm might feel the breeze from a passing king, so Haruk feels a distant echo of the One's glorious might. And the strength of that echo stuns and utterly stupefies Lord Haruk the Cruel.

In a moment of insight, Haruk sees that he cannot stand against such a power. He cannot deceive such a mind. Even the Devil who owns the open grave of Haruk's lifeless soul cannot hope to win such a fight.

Haruk's hopeless chance to defeat these men, these dream warriors in their vision ship, is to avoid conflict with the One traveling with them. This will be his plan. He must ignore the danger that cannot be helped. He must try to divide and conquer these men, hoping to avoid the great Power.

If this Power stands with them, Haruk has no hope. And yet, in spite of it all, he remains an unrepentant villain. If his deadly plans must doom him, Haruk still refuses to change.

With a plan now settled in his mind, he will attempt to bury the memory of the vision. *I will not die without a fight,* he reasons. *I'll crush those that I can, charm those I can, and to Hell with the rest!* His flawed logic neatly fits into the serpentine pattern of his unseen master, making up with depravity what it lacks in wisdom.

He does not have much of a plan, but it's the best he can come up with. For Haruk, unrepentant to the end, this will have to suffice.

Unwilling

The Prince remained awake. In the bow of the ship, he sat deep in thought, focusing so intently he did not hear the approach of Brother Timothy.

"We may yet avoid the storm," Timothy said.

"What? Oh, it's you, Timothy. Yes, I suppose we might," the Prince replied absently. "It's possible." A favorable wind had continued through the third watch, and the sun would soon rise.

"Do you mind if I ask you a personal question?" In response to Timothy's question, Gunnar turned and looked at him sharply. In a bright flash from distant lightning, he read the little man's expression: unadorned sincerity, mingled with uncertainty.

Gunnar had come to know Timothy well during their voyage. He had watched as the monk performed valiantly in the storm, and he had found him to be, among other things, a man possessed of singular courage and a unique, almost painful honesty.

"No, I suppose I don't mind. Not yet." Gunnar smiled as Timothy hesitated, trying to decipher his answer. "Go ahead, ask."

"I was trying to sleep," Timothy began. "I couldn't help but hear your conversation with Julian. I heard your plans for your return to Bryne." Gunnar stiffened.

"Well, if you couldn't help but hear, I can't fault you for it, Timothy. But what I have said, I have said."

"Gunnar," Timothy continued, "I'm not here to judge you. Your plan is understandable, given the circumstances. To your peers, and to the citizens of Bryne – once they learn the facts – you'll be a hero if you succeed.

"My ancestors are Saxons. I understand the ancient code of honor, although I can't really understand all that you've gone through." At this point he paused, wondering if he should say more. *How can I relate to what this young man has been through? The murder of his father, the years of slavery... how can I reach him?* And then, Brother Timothy remembered to pray. *God help me to love this young man like you do.*

"Timothy," the Prince replied wearily, "it's not your problem. You and I have a different way of looking at life. But I have work to do." His own words sounded shallow and vain in Gunnar's ears, and that fact annoyed him greatly. "I think I know what you're thinking," he pressed on, not one to quit, "and I think that you're probably right about it.

"I know that the best way for me to deal with the situation in Bryne would be to do like that holy man said, back in England. I should follow the example of Jesus. I should love my enemies. But I cannot love such a pig as Haruk the Cruel." He breathed deeply, regaining some of his composure. "No, Timothy," he hissed. "Vengeance must be served!"

Timothy, however, would not give up... not as long as Gunnar was willing to talk and listen. He chose his words carefully.

"Here me please, Gunnar," he began. "I will tell you a story. This is a story told first by Jesus of Nazareth."

"Okay," said Gunnar, sighing deeply. "Say on."

"There once lived a man who owed a large sum to a great king. When it came due, he could not pay, so he came and fell on his face before him, crying, 'O king, have patience, and I will pay all I owe!' The merciful king frankly forgave him all that he owed.

"As he left leaving the palace, the forgiven man encountered another fellow who owed him money. Taking him by the throat, he demanded that the debtor pay in full. When the man could not pay, he commanded that he should be sold to pay his debt: both he, and all that he had, including his wife and his children.

"When the king heard of this, he confronted the man, saying, 'I frankly forgave you all that you owed me; why did not you forgive this man his debt?' The king ordered him bound and cast into prison until his debt was paid in full." Gunnar stirred uneasily as he perceived Brother Timothy's point.

"You see the meaning," said Timothy. "God has forgiven you many times for your sins, the proof being that you are still alive after all of your battles. The Englishmen you killed were slain honestly in open warfare, but did they seek your war? Or did they stand to gain from it? Did they ask for war? They did not, but you waged war upon them anyway, and you gained from it.

"If God, then, has forgiven the murder of West Saxony's farmers and bootblacks, shouldn't you forgive this man, Haruk? Won't your city mete out justice to such a traitor, once your story is told?" Brother Timothy was astonished at his own boldness, surprised by the challenging words that cascaded so effortlessly from his mouth. Gunnar was similarly shocked to hear such powerful words from the meek and unassuming little man.

Timothy rose slowly, taking off his hat and bowing. "Uh, excuse me, your grace," he stuttered, thoroughly befuddled. Without further adieu, he clapped his hat firmly on top of his head and strode purposefully back to his makeshift bed near the stern.

Thunder sounded, closer now. Confused gusts of wind began to strike the heavy sail. The Prince's thoughts swirled in profound turmoil, oppressive and tossed like the wind and sea. He was the victim here! It was he who had been kidnapped! Who was this man, this little man, to insinuate his views and cause him to lose what little peace he still had at the cusp of his hour of vengeance?

And yet, he knew there was more to it. Unbidden, a memory powerfully returned of a night spent in agonizing prayer. He had been a slave for three months when the weight of his captivity had come upon him. For one long, lonely evening he had wept and prayed for relief, crushed beneath the weight of his loss.

He had to admit it. His prayers had been answered, and he had obtained relief. He had served with the armies of Guthrum, gained freedom from slavery, attained the rank of captain, helped win a war, dined with kings, and gained friends. He was returning home in valorous company. Why then, given all of this proof, did he find it hard to believe that God had cared enough to answer the petitions of a poor, weeping slave?

He turned away and looked out across the darkened sea as the pitch of the wind increased. The rain began to fall as he strained for any sight... any whisper of wind, motion of water or sweet scent of earth that might tell him, at last, he was home.

V.

Rain cloaked the ship as the hope of our city
Returned with the wind in the cold mists of dawn.
Strong streams of water, wrung out from the heavens,
Cascaded on thanes manning stout oaken oars.

The regal black warship, her sail bound fast,
Swam up to her berth like a swan to the shore.

In the ship Gunnar-val, the lone son of Vigmar,
Had come to gain honor avenging the blood-crime.

The weight of his fathers pressed down with the heavens
Upon the broad shoulders grown slight in such company.

It seemed, in the storm-surge, that spirits of ancestors
Sounded their thunder and charged his young conscience
To mark his homecoming with lightning-like vengeance
If brethren and hearth-land were treasured at all.

Yet moments of glory can turn, like the sea,
Upon the unwary who trust in the calm.
And now, at the pier, he who sought love and vengeance
Received friendly greetings belying the storm.

Untimely Arrival

"Hello. Who goes there?" The watcher's voice echoed loudly across the foggy water, competing with the swirling rain.

"Hello, hello!" the boatmen answered.

"Declare yourselves!" the dock watchman cried.

Within the past few minutes, the heavens had opened. Great gray sheets of water cascaded torrentially from the sky, lashing the waters of the bay, kicking up tiny plumes of water with each heavy drop. This was a surprisingly intense storm, not at all like the mild, misty showers so typical of this cold northern clime. The men on the ship were glad they had entered the bay ahead of the worst of it.

"We are friends of Bryne," the Prince shouted back above the sound of the rain. He hesitated, not quite ready to reveal his identity.

The ship drifted closer to the long, narrow pier, revealing a unexpectedly large contingent of armed men who were nervously gathered at its end with their shoulders hunched against the wind and spray. Where two men usually manned the dock watch, six men and a young boy squinted into the heavy rain, straining to assess the inhabitants of the mysterious dragon-ship that had suddenly appeared on the roiled waters of their bay.

"Who are you?" The leader asked. As he spoke the great ship heaved sideways toward their dock, pushed by a stray swell, startling the watchers on the pier.

"We are friends of Bryne: travelers from West Saxony come to visit Ivan Redbeard," the Prince replied, thinking quickly. *I don't know who they are,* he realized. *They could be Haruk's men.*

"Come to," Bildad cried with a smile. As the Haruk's slave-master, he welcomed the new arrivals in the robust hope that they might soon fall under his care. "Throw us a line, and we'll tie you up. You are well met, friend of Bryne."

Ivan Redbeard

Ilse knocked loudly on Ivan's door. The rain continued to fall, cloaking the early morning light in a shimmering pall of slick gray water.

Ilse ignored the falling rain. She stood patiently on the small porch, dwarfed by her brown sealskin cloak.

Ivan Redbeard was surprised to see Ilse when he opened the door. Her wet blond locks dripped from her cloak's oversized hood, plastered flat against her pale forehead. She stared at him without smiling, her facial expression showing unshakable determination.

"Ilse! Come in, child. Why are you out in this rain?" She stepped in his warm house and took off the soaked sealskin, shaking out her hair in one swift motion.

"Ivan, you must listen to me. It's important," she blurted. He paused, taken aback by her sharp tone.

"Go ahead."

"Mother sent me. She says you must immediately convene a meeting of the council. She's on her way, and she wants us both to attend. We have something to say to the full council… something they must hear quickly." She stopped and caught her breath, then pressed forward.

"Will you do it?" she asked.

Dockside Manners

"Who are you, friend?" asked Bildad as his men caught their ropes and began to tie up the longship. *Thirteen men in the boat. This could be trouble.*

"I'm a traveler familiar with your city," said the Prince. "My mother was Brynish. We have come to seek counsel from Ivan Redbeard regarding a matter of grave importance."

"How nice!" replied Bildad with a syrupy smile, sizing up the tall, bearded stranger. "I must have known your mother. Our city is not as large as some. What was her name?"

"Excuse me if I keep this matter close," Gunnar answered carefully. "The issue requires some discretion." *A subtle answer, and impossible to challenge,* thought Bildad. *Who is this man... and why does he speak such flawless Brynish?*

The rain began to dwindle to a cool drizzle. As they secured the boat, Gunnar recognized the speaker and his companions. *That's Haruk's slave- master, and those men are his slaves,* he realized, *all except for that sour-faced one. He's Tannig... a good man... but who's the lad?* He recognized the child's face as vaguely familiar, but knew that it was not associated with Haruk or his men *Why, that's Rollo's brother Delmer,* he realized, surprised at how much the boy had grown.

"We must ask that you remain in your boat," Bildad said, showing his teeth again. "We've had some trouble in the city lately, and we are forced to request this for your safety as well as our own. If you would like to choose a man to speak for you to our council, you may do that. But the rest of you must stay here until the council has made a decision."

Gunnar heard his words with some trepidation. *That's a reasonable request,* he wondered. *Why do I feel bad about it?* But he had found himself often in dangerous situations, and had learned to heed such instincts. He needed to try to counter this move. *If this is a friendly proposition, he won't mind negotiating.*

"One man may not be able to convey our message adequately," Gunnar responded. "I'll be the first. Let my crew choose a second."

"No!" Bildad blurted spontaneously. But upon seeing the tension run through the men in the boat, he reconsidered the wisdom of such an approach. *Thirteen armed warriors,* he considered with an unusual surge of fear racing through his system. *Perhaps we should compromise.* "Well, okay. But I'll choose the second man." He pointed to Ryan Morris, the younger of the Morris brothers. "That one there. He can go with you."

"He's just a boy. Pick another, and we'll agree."

"Well, then," said Bildad, his eyes nervously scanning the grim-faced crew of the longship. "I'll take that one." He pointed to Brother Timothy.

Timothy stood warily, shifting his weight uncomfortably, as if he stood barefoot on top of a hot stone. He could not understand exactly what was being said (his recent labors in the Brynish language notwithstanding). His heavy robe and cloak dwarfed his slight form, and his outsized ears trembled as if they were about to collapse in a weary heap against the side of his balding head. Looking at Timothy, Gunnar sighed. *He won't be much help in a fight. But there are two here who are not Haruk's, and none of them have recognized me. We can't stay in the boat, and we can't kill all of Haruk's men... not yet!*

On Bildad's side stood tradition. Brynish custom, whenever a large contingent of strangers arrived, required visitors to send emissaries who could request permission to come ashore. Given this custom, Gunnar had no redress. Bildad was following long-established tradition, and, moreover, was doing it with courtesy. The Prince would have to explain this predicament to his men.

"I accept your terms," responded Gunnar. "Let me talk to my men before we go."

The Telltale Gait

Haruk's men had almost reached the top of the narrow path, carefully following the two visitors to Bryne, when Bildad suddenly recognized the Prince.

Gunnar's walk betrayed him. He had a distinctly rollicking gait that had once been a standing joke in the city, although he had never been aware of it.

Bildad was walking at the rear of the procession when the realization took hold. Nobody saw the slave-master give a start and turn pale, almost slipping and falling down on the stony trail. By the time they had reached the gate, Bildad had recovered his composure.

In single file, they followed the visitors through the gate. As they began to walk down the narrow main street, Bildad took the lead, followed by Gunnar, Timothy, and two of Haruk's slaves. Taking up the rear of the procession were two free citizens of Bryne: Tannig and Delmer.

Three Brynish sailors sat on a bench inside the city gate and gazed curiously at the strangers as they passed. Most of the fishermen of Bryne had not begun their trek to the docks; they had recently enjoyed several weeks of unusually bountiful catches and were getting a late start on this rainy morning.

As Gunnar expected, the watchmen and their charges turned sharply left into the first narrow street, heading towards the common room used for small public gatherings in Bryne. This room was near the gate and only two blocks away from the mead hall's back entrance. It served as a waiting area for visitors to the city on those rare occasions when unexpected company chanced to arrive at their docks.

They paused at the narrow door while one of Haruk's men lit a lantern and shuffled into the long stone room. The young boy, Delmer, entered last.

"You'll have to wait here while we gather the elders," said Bildad officiously, holding his emotions in check with great effort. His hands began to shake, betraying his fear as his mind raced, devising a plan. He knew what he had to do.

"You can hang your cloaks over there," he said, pointing behind them. Gunnar turned to look for the coat hook.

When Gunnar turned, Bildad whipped his heavy watchman's club against his head with a dull, sickening thud. All action seemed to stop in the room as the brawny warrior jerked and slumped to the floor. Utterly amazed, Timothy gazed at Gunnar in shock.

"Why did you do that?" he asked Bildad, shaken.

"You pig!" cried Tannig, Offa's son. "Is this how we greet a stranger who comes in peace?" The lad, Delmer, began to edge carefully toward the door. Something felt wrong... very wrong. He had grown deathly afraid.

"Delmer, don't go," began Bildad smoothly, nodding at one of his men to secure the lad. Before he could act, the boy darted through the doorway and was gone, slamming the heavy door in his pursuers face. "Leave him!" Bildad barked sharply, "but hold on to that one!" He pointed to Timothy, and then turned to Tannig with a disingenuous smile.

"Tannig, you must know that I have a good reason for what I've done. Trust me... I'll explain it. We are brothers, you and I." In the traditional Brynish embrace of brotherly love and good will, Bildad wrapped his left arm around Tannig's shoulder and drew his face near the faithful man's wind-creased visage.

"Don't try to charm me by invoking the brother-bond!" Tannig replied fiercely, staring without flinching into Bildad's blue eyes. "By the gods, what are you trying to do?" The faithful citizen of Bryne had no idea of what, or whom, he dealt with.

Tannig did not see the dagger, but he felt it go in: deep and cruel and to the hilt. Pulling out the crimson blade, Bildad used the knife's dripping haft to push him away. He coldly watched as Tannig tumbled on top of the unconscious Prince of Bryne.

Bildad had torn Tannig's heart open, and death came swiftly, if not mercifully. Haruk's slaves watched transfixed as the honest Bryne-man ceased his feeble struggles and yielded a final, gurgling breath: a whistling sigh that blew a soft emission of blood, like a grisly fig, from the old warrior's heavily scarred nose. They could scarcely believe what they were seeing.

Tannig's betrayal of the ancient brotherhood may have been impulsive, but it was no casual act. The murder would bring the wrath of the city upon the killer.

"Who killed this man?" the slave-master barked to his stupefied comrades. They stared at him dully, their lifeless eyes reflecting no answer. "Who killed this man?" he asked again, running out of patience. Bildad pointed to Gunnar, who lay on the floor under Tannig's bloody body. "This stranger killed Tannig, you idiots!"

"He killed Tannig. This is our story. Do you understand?" Slowly they began to nod their heads as Bildad wiped the bloody blade on Gunnar's right hand and threw the sticky dagger in the dust beside him. "Tie him up! Quickly!"

One of the men produced a skein of rope and they went to work, tying the Prince securely as Brother Timothy, in shock, stared vacantly at the unseemly tableau. Suddenly, Bildad stepped close to Timothy, jabbering at him angrily in the language of Bryne... a language that Timothy, in the heat of the fray, had almost completely forgotten.

"Can you speak our language?" Bildad barked at Timothy. Satisfied with the vacant stare he received in reply, Bildad shouted. "Tie this one up to. No need to gag him... he can't say a word!" He eyed Brother Timothy in disgust. "He's a sorry excuse for a warrior traveling with the high and mighty Prince of Bryne!"

"The Prince?" one of the men asked in confusion. They stopped their work and stared at their fallen sovereign.

"Yes, you fools!" Bildad cried. "The cursed Prince, you children of dogs! Why do you think I had to kill Tannig?" He pointed at Gunnar angrily. "This is the wayward Prince of Bryne, and Lord Haruk will eat our livers if we don't deliver him bound hand and foot to his castle as soon as possible. Do you get it, now?

"If anyone tries to stop us, we'll tell them that he's a Scylfing wild man who killed Tannig right before our eyes."

"Before our eyes?"

"Yes, you swine! Before our eyes! Lie if you wish to live.

"If we have to, we'll kill him right on the spot, before he can talk. But let's get him out of here. Tie him up! Quickly! And the runt, too." As soon as they finished binding them hand and foot, Bildad began to kick Gunnar, his hard boot thudding viciously into the Prince's rapidly ballooning face.

"Stop that!" cried Timothy weakly. At the sound of his voice, Haruk's slaves turned like hungry wolves on the last man standing, smothering Brother Timothy with brute force. They laughed enthusiastically as they manhandled the little man, punching him viciously as they bound him with hard leather thongs.

Timothy fell on his side, and Bildad began to kick him with merciless glee, guffawing uproariously at the monk's pathetic yelps. Time after time, Bildad's great, muddy boots kissed Timothy's misshapen face.

The slave-master and his men loved to play, and the opportunities arose so seldom. This was the way they liked it, with no petty concerns about kindness or decency... and plenty of good, mean fun.

Sound Counsel

Ilse and Katla sat patiently in front of the council. Ivan smiled at them warmly from his seat at the long oak table, his eyes flashing encouragement. Katla felt relieved by what had transpired so far. *Ilse was so convincing,* she thought. *Who could fail to believe her?* But none of them were prepared for what happened next.

The double doors slammed open, and Delmer, son of Ekbar, burst into the room dragging a man twice his size. He cried out loudly for all to hear.

"Stop!" he cried as he struggled against the grip of a council guard. "You have to listen to me. I saw something... you have to listen!" Ivan, now standing, extended his open hand toward Delmer and turned to his fellow elders.

"I don't know what this lad has to say," he offered. "But considering how our morning has developed thus far, I think we should hear him out." Severn the Gray, leader of the council, nodded at the sergeant-at-arms, and Delmer stepped tentatively into the main hall.

"Come here, son." Severn gestured at the excited lad, motioning to an empty chair. "Sit down and tell us what you saw."

The War-horn

The peal of the great war-horn rang out, clear and bell-like, across the broad plateau. The unusual sound scattered falcons from the cliffs to wheel high above the bay, watching as the men gathered in the streets of the city. The rain had stopped, allowing the sun to send the first exploratory rays along the tops of the steep-gabled roofs. In the pale sunlight, the tall houses cast long shadows across the damp plain.

In the street below, the council of Bryne had just shared the news with the gathered men. Someone had murdered their friend, Tannig, whose body had just been discovered. A longship full of strangers had arrived, and two ambassadors from the boat had been carried captive to Haruk's castle.

They would need every man today.

Delmer's eyewitness account left no doubt in their minds that Bildad must have slain Tannig after bludgeoning one of the visitors to their city. Bildad was a subtle man, but one given to glaring errors. The boy's escape had ruined any chance for Bildad to blame Tannig's murder on a Scylfing wild man. Bildad should have known this instinctively, but in the heat of the moment, he had missed it altogether.

Bildad had overreached, and he had made the worst mistake of his life. Ancient Norse society, which glorified warfare, neither allowed nor condoned the abuse of visitors who came seeking hospitality. In addition, the Norse code of fraternal brotherhood strictly forbade murder within a family, city, or clan.

Tannig's murder would not go unpunished.

The war-horn sounded again, startling a wild hart that had bedded on the mountainside above the plateau of Bryne. The handsome beast quivered in fear, his delicate nostrils trembling as he tested the wind. Far below, on the western side of the verdant plateau, the creature heard the distant tumult of angry voices.

"Yes," Ivan was saying to the men gathered in the street. "We must pursue them. But they have a large head start; we won't be able to catch them before they enter the castle." Haruk's fortress was barely a mile away.

The members of the council reeled from the impact of the fast-moving revelations. Ilse's portentous dream, Delmer's account of Bildad's assault on the strangers, the discovery of the body of Tannig: these incidents hurtled through their minds like geese rising from the rushes. They could barely track them, much less discern their import.

Could Ilse's dream regarding the return of the Prince be prophetic? The apparent confirmation of her vision by the arrival of the strangers only increased their uncertainty. The words of Ilse had turned their city upside down.

"Luban," shouted Ivan. "Come here." The young man left his friends and trotted up to the venerable elder.

"Yes?"

"Is your horse nearby?"

"Right there," he answered, pointing at the dark brown, shaggy-haired pony tied to the post in front of the mead hall.

"Good. Now, listen closely. You've already heard that Haruk's slave-master and two of his slaves left town a few minutes ago, and we know that they had two visitors in their custody."

"Yes?"

"Go now, ride after them to Haruk's castle. When you get there, raise a cry at the door. Tell them that you come in the name of the council. That will throw a scare into Haruk and bring him to his gate." Luban looked at Severn, who gestured impatiently.

"You must ride quickly, Luban," Severn interjected. "Or the captives may be dead by the time you get there." They all knew Haruk's reputation for cruelty. Haruk's fear of Vigmar's sword had long ameliorated some of his worst tendencies. But now, with Vigmar and Ithmar gone, there was no telling what he might do in the secret confines of his stone fortress.

"When Haruk comes out to hear you," Ivan continued. "Tell him that he must not harm the two strangers. Tell him that they are visitors who came in peace. Say that his slave-master has murdered Tannig. Tell him that the two ambassadors to our city, together with Bildad, must be delivered to us immediately.

"Tell Haruk that your words are the words of the council, sealed by Severn and Ivan Redbeard with the support of the people. Tell him that, if he gives heed to our words, we will accept his gesture as one of peace. But if he defies us, the city of Bryne will declare war upon him. We will utterly consume his household and burn his flesh with fire." *That's the only thing that might stop him... fear for his own skin. He knows he would have no chance against the entire city.* "Now, go quickly." They turned away as he ran to his pony.

"Men of Bryne, come here!" Ivan Redbeard cried, and the men in the street gathered together. They were unsettled, unsure of what was happening, or what they should be doing. Ivan pointed to a group of fishermen clustered to his left.

"You, men, go down to the docks. Bring the visitors into the city and set food in front of them at the mead hall. Perhaps they will be able answer some of our questions."

"The rest of you," he added, sweeping his gaze over a multitude of Bryne-men, "go to your houses and gather your weapons. Kiss your children good-bye, and then meet us in the mead hall.

"If Haruk does not deliver the captive strangers to Luban, we will march to Haruk's gate. By Haruk's hand, or by our own hand, we will receive custody of the men he has captured. Then we will see who they really are. We will see whether our sister's dream was truly an omen regarding our lost Prince."

A few men had already armed themselves. They milled about aimlessly in the street, itching for a fight.

Ivan did not say it, but the man that Delmer had described could well be their long-lost Prince. As hard as it was to contemplate, it was possible that Gunnar-val had returned to their city... only to be taken captive by Haruk's slave-master.

If this were the case, they may be able to intervene in time to spare him the kindnesses of Haruk the Cruel. In doing this, the promise that the city of Bryne had failed to keep in their defense of

King Vigmar might be redeemed by the deliverance of his son.

Dragon's Den

The greedy slave-master – himself a slave in the service of Haruk the Cruel – arrived out of breath at the castle. With mixed emotions, he rang the bell at the absurdly gigantic gate.

The towering, leaved gateway that led into the castle was made of rich, mottled hardwood bound with iron. The gate was greatly treasured by the castle's chief resident, having been imported at great cost from a vanquished southern kingdom by the father of Haruk. Responding to Bildad's ring, the heavy prominence slowly swung open, and the men hastened into the fortress.

Giddy with their good fortune, Bildad the Base and his enslaved companions left their horses in the courtyard (including the ponies with bloody bodies across the saddles) and rushed boldly through a series of doors into Haruk's private suite.

That was their undoing.

Haruk was seducing a young slave girl when they burst into the room. He had drugged her with magical aliments, charmed her, and wooed her almost to the point of voluntary submission when his servants, Bildad, Argob and Delf, stormed into the suite, bursting with their incredible news.

"Guards!" Haruk cried, apoplectic with rage. He hissed and pointed towards the three pitiful miscreants as they gulped and whitened instantly, reduced in an instant from glory to terror.

Haruk's guards raced in pell-mell, swords at the ready.

"Kill them!" Haruk commanded. The guards knew better than to question an order from Haruk the Cruel.

They immediately struck the three slaves with mortal wounds. Their victims collapsed together on the floor, struggling against death in a thick pool of blood. Their last sight on earth was the blood-purple, hate-contorted countenance of Lord Haruk, to whom they had rendered such evil service… and from whom they had received the same, with interest.

Social Graces

"Nils, be careful," said the watchman from his perch in the tower. "There are strangers on the other side of the gate." The man leaned out from a narrow window, gesturing to Nils as he pointed to the steep path on the harbor side of the gate.

"Good. That'll save us a trip to the dock," called Nils with a tight grin. "We've come to get those fellows. The council has asked us to treat them to a little mead and feed in the old town hall."

Informed of the death of Tannig, the watchman had grown understandably wary. Tradition, however, demanded that he maintain a cool façade. He was determined to stay calm, even if it killed him – quite literally. In a similar manner, the men with Nils shrugged off today's grim events with studied casualness, smirking in the face of calamity. They would deal with their grief later.

"Go ahead, boys; open the gate," replied the watchman. "I wish I could join you, but I've got four more hours on watch." With his assent, the huge iron bar was pulled back. The gate slowly swung open, revealing an unusual sight.

On the other side stood a diversely arrayed group of battle-hardened thanes from every corner of northern Europe. Without a doubt, this was the most culturally eclectic assemblage of warriors to ever set foot in Bryne.

Julian and Roentner towered in the forefront of the group like huge, unmatched bookends. They presented a study in contrasts: one so thin that his clothing flapped loosely on his bony frame, the other a powerfully built, well-proportioned giant.

Behind them stood the tall, lanky, red-haired, freckle-faced Weir-Huns, as fierce a crew as ever set boot in a Teutonic dingy. And behind them all, at the rear of the procession, the Morris brothers peeked around their cohorts warily, crowding in front of Haruk's two slaves, who were trying their best to put a good face upon the unexpected turn of events.

"We hereby deliver these strangers for incarceration," exclaimed Emor the Younger, an able slave determined to make the most of the latest developments.

"These men are visitors, not prisoners," Nils replied. "We were sent to escort them to the town hall and give them food and drink. You and Hygelac can join us, if you wish." Nils turned to Julian and Roentner and addressed them courteously in Danish, the tongue of commerce and industry in these regions. "Please, follow me," Nils suggested. They fell into step behind him and began the walk toward the mead hall.

"By the way," Nils asked, still addressing them in Danish. "Who are you, where did you come from, and what on earth are you doing here?"

Right of Refusal

"Haruk Longknife!" Luban cried, standing nervously outside of the ridiculously huge gates that provided the only entrance at the front of Haruk's castle. The last remnants of the morning's misty drizzle had dispersed, but the stones were slick with water, and Luban's feet were wet. He had no desire to linger in this dank, unfriendly place.

"Haruk Longknife!" he cried again, and patiently waited. After several minutes he heard the sound of iron rattling on the other side and the great wooden wall swung slowly outward, putting him unexpectedly face to face with Haruk the Cruel himself. Haruk had been up all night, and he looked simply awful.

His skin had blanched white like a fish from a hidden cavern: a sickly, lifeless shade of white that offset his stringy, jet-black hair. Haruk's dull red eyes stared at Luban angrily, pulsing relentlessly in their inflamed sockets like coals burning a hole in the pasty, paper-thin pudding of his damp, bloated face. He exuded the faintest tang of bitter odor, a delicate scent that hinted of decay. *Is that blood?* Luban wondered, unnerved at the possibility. The aroma troubled Luban as much as Haruk's ghastly appearance.

As always, Haruk had no time for trifling matters. He was rude and impatient, ready to roll over anyone who stood in his way.

"Why are you here?" he asked brusquely. "And who are you to trouble me here, at my private estate? Have you come to offer me the renowned hospitality of the citizens of Bryne?"

"I come with a message from the council," Luban replied. Haruk rolled his eyes. He did not know what Luban had come to say, but it was obviously not good news. The sheer unmitigated gall of the citizens of Bryne, daring to send a messenger to his door, particularly peeved him on this busy day.

"My, oh, my," he exclaimed breathlessly. "The council itself? Well, then I must listen carefully. If I were to ignore the message of such a great and noble assemblage, I might be slain by great Thor, or by his trusted companions in the clouds of Valhalla, the councilmen themselves!" He bit off the last comment, and was preparing to slam the door when Luban continued.

"The council says that you must deliver, immediately, the two visitors who were kidnapped and carried here by your slave-master, Bildad. You must also hand over Bildad, who is wanted for the murder of Tannig Oldfather. If you safely deliver all of these men to the council, the city will show its gratitude.

"If, however, you do not deliver these men to the council (and I say this with regret), the people of Bryne will declare war upon you. They who would have been your friends will become your enemies. They will not rest or sleep until you and your house have been utterly destroyed." As Luban delivered this message, Haruk's face deepened in hue, following a pattern familiar to those unfortunate enough to have crossed his path.

"War?" he cried. "They'll declare war, will they?" With all of his might Haruk slammed the heavy door shut in Luban's face.

After Haruk the Cruel locked the door, he leaned against it, shaking: weak and tormented and almost mad with rage and vexation. "War?" he screamed to no one in particular (there being no servant foolish enough to stand within earshot). "I'll give them war!"

But Haruk, in spite of his pride, was too much of a realist to think that he could defeat the men of Bryne in open war. He knew that his current level of armed strength was better suited for the occasional dirk in an innocent back on a dark and clouded night. He had long acted, quite prudently, within the framework of this reality.

The council of Bryne backed their threat with considerable armed might. Haruk could not afford to downplay this fact, in spite of his wounded pride.

And yet, he refused to remain mired in such dour cogitations. Fortune, that fickle paramour of fools, still seemed to support him at this hour, for when he lifted up his eyes and glanced about his courtyard, he received a pleasant surprise.

At the end of his cobblestone courtyard, by the side entrance that led to his cluster of private suites, stood five patient ponies. They waited exactly where they had been left, watching the action at the castle gate as they thoughtfully chewed mouthfuls of hay from the dirty pile at their feet. Draped across the saddles of two of the ponies, Haruk saw the bloody, battered bodies of Bildad's captives: two remarkably unlucky strangers who had chosen the wrong day to visit the fair city of Bryne.

"Oh my," hummed Haruk happily. "These must be the captives brought here by my dear, departed slave-master." He thought carefully for a moment. "Perhaps I shouldn't have killed him, after all. Oh well, one shouldn't cry over spilled blood.

"Thanks to Luban and the good men of Bryne, I now know how important it is to spare the lives of these precious strangers. That is, if they still have any life left to spare.

"Of course," he reasoned, "if they die now, who will know that they did not die before Luban came to my gate with that damnable message from the council? And if they died before Luban came, I can't really be blamed, can I? Especially if that dolt, Bildad, killed them. Let's see," he mulled. "That's right: the idiot Bildad killed them... and I was then forced to kill the dolt, for disrespecting the edict of the Council! That's perfect!"

Haruk laughed aloud at the thought and stood up dramatically, sweeping his arm toward the broken bodies of the men on the ponies. "Haruk," he cried to himself, uttering a rich, throaty laugh. "Your mission is obvious.

"Since these two men are alive for your own, sweet convenience (a fortuitous circumstance given the fact of their recent untimely deaths at the hands of said deceased, yammering dolt), you should fully avail ourselves of this opportunity to serve your own high and noble purpose. You must, against all odds, pursue a gallant quest for the truth. Your curiosity must be fully satisfied.

"To wit: who are these motley fellows? Where are they from, what do they want, and most importantly, how long will they survive under torture?" These were the kinds of questions that demanded answers, and he, Haruk Longknife, was just the man to provide them. He laughed again and pointed at the prostrate forms slung limply over the ponies.

"Onward," he bellowed. "Let us proceed to the inquisition!"

Murder Will Out

The men of Bryne raised a cacophonous, unintelligible din as they thronged the mead hall and clamored for information. They had hurried to the hall after gathering their weapons, and now they pressed together, straining to catch a glimpse of the strangers who stood in the center of the room. The visitors stood awkwardly, gazing quizzically at the crowd of Norsemen who pushed and pulled and called loudly to one another, trying to understand the meaning of what was transpiring before them.

"Men!" called Severn, attempting to be heard. "Be quiet!" Eventually, he grew tired of trying to be heard above the noisy melee. Standing on a table, he reached up and began to bang the flat side of his broadsword against one of the ornate brass shields that hung from the rafters.

"Shut your mouths!" Severn cried. His voice carried surprising volume given his age.

The room became silent, and the men faced him, grim-faced and sullen. "We didn't call you here to waste time!" Severn stated with asperity.

"Nils, stand here," Severn continued, pointing to the top of the table beside him. "You speak the best Danish among us. Get that tall, skinny fellow over there to come speak for the newcomers. He seems to be the talker of the group."

Nils addressed Julian in Danish. After a moment, they climbed up onto the table beside Severn.

"All right, men, you all know Nils," Severn said loudly, looking around uneasily. "This skinny fellow here will speak for the strangers." Having brought order from chaos, Severn climbed down to the floor.

"Tell them what you told me," he called to Nils. "Then let this man answer their questions." Nils cleared his throat, and the room became instantly, uncannily quiet.

Diligent Inquiry

Brother Timothy, late of Fullerton Abbey, could scarcely see through his swollen eyelids. But what he could see, he did not like at all. A hulking form loomed over him, moving with surprising swiftness and delicacy as it busied itself with the business of torture: a diligent spider wrapping them tightly in threads of finely-spun pain. The hulking form was Haruk, and Timothy and Gunnar were the unlucky morsels trapped tightly in the mesh of his web.

"Why don't you speak?" Haruk asked Timothy with a convivial grin. "You're even less helpful than your friend. He was a lively soul, indeed; at least, until he passed out. But, ah, you see," he continued. "Your friend had joie de vivre! At least he cursed me properly. And it was as finely crafted a Danish curse as ever I heard, calling down the wrath of the heavens, as if the heavens had ears! But you... what is your problem? Go ahead... curse me, little man! Have at it with a vengeance!" Timothy, as before, refused to reply.

"Have you no creative instincts?" Haruk sadly shook his head. "Let's see if we can help."

Haruk carefully negotiated an approach to Timothy's hand with a pair of blood-caked pliers. With a dreamy smile, he peeled off another closely gnawed fingernail, provoking a wild convulsive seizure complete with head thrashing, screams, and drawn out moans. And yet, no curses issued from Brother Timothy's lips, frustrating Haruk's efforts to draw the worst from this mousy little man.

Gunnar, waking up on a table nearby, felt distant and strange. *It's amazing,* he thought, *how shock can numb the pain.* At this moment, in such a curious state of the soul, his own wounds hurt less than the punishing sounds from Brother Timothy's wretched sufferings. Gunnar's innermost being vibrated with sympathy for the harmless, lovable monk. Timothy's cries of pain were almost unbearable.

And then, Gunnar remembered God. He had come too far, seen too much, found himself in too much trouble to debate the Creator's existence at this point. He only knew that he needed the kind of help that only omnipotence could give.

God, help us, he prayed. *I know I haven't followed you. When you called, I turned away. I killed the English to earn my freedom... I know that you don't like that kind of thing. I'm sorry, God. Please, dear God... forgive me.*

"You won't talk?" Haruk hissed smoothly at the unfortunate Brother Timothy. He puffed like an adder in righteous indignation, disappointed at the failed promise of his trustworthy pliers. "I suppose we must provide you with further incentives.

"I will ask you once again: who are you, and where do you come from?" The piteous moans of the frail monk offered no answer to his query.

"Oh, well," Haruk continued gaily. "Let us proceed with our diligent inquiry!"

Loose the Wild Wolves

"Be quiet," called Nils to the men. "I'll tell you what I know. After that, you can ask this man all you want. His name is Julian Longstreet. He speaks the Danish language, but he's a citizen of Holland. His father is a close ally of King Guthrum, and he sponsored a company of men to aid Guthrum in the campaigns in West Saxony, which, as most of you know, is located on Island of England."

"Get to the point!" cried a voice from the rear.

"All right," answered Nils testily, "I'll get to it. This man claims that the leader of his group is Gunnar-val of Bryne."

A jolt akin to lightning ran through the entire room full of warriors. There was a universal gasp, followed by silence.

Julian, from his perch on the table, beheld in awe the stunned expressions on the tough, sunburned Nordic faces that suddenly turned as white as chalk, robbed of blood by the force of Nils' words. On their faces, he saw the stirrings of a painful hope they seemed afraid to rekindle: a deep-seated hurt that had never been healed. *No wonder Gunnar wanted to come back. Look how they loved his father, and him,* he thought wonderingly.

The eyes of the guileless men in the crowd searched Julian's face with shock and dismay. As sometimes happens, the unexpected renewal of hope brought with it hurtful memories, and the buried pain of long-forgotten loss.

The prolonged silence was shattered as several hundred men began to shout questions simultaneously. Nils gave them time to calm down, and within another minute they were quiet again.

"I have a question," called Rollo from the floor.

"What's your question?"

"Ask this man to tell you as much as he can remember about the man he says is Gunnar. Ask him what he told them about Bryne, how he met him, what he looked like... you know, anything that might help us to know if he really is Gunnar." Nils translated the question into Danish, and Julian paused before answering.

"I met Gunnar because of my father. My father purchased him from a Scylfing trader in the slave market at Stockholm." Gasps could be heard in the room as Nils translated this sentence.

"I did not know him during the first years of his slavery. I did not live in my father's house, you see. I had been traveling about Europe for years. But when I begged my father to back me with a company of men for the wars in West Saxony, he insisted that I take his young slave along. He dumped him on me, actually. My father had heard of Gunnar's claim that he was a captured prince, and he was convinced that Gunnar was quite mad.

"As for his appearance, he was rather unusual, to say the least. He stood at slightly above average height, but powerfully built. He had a hooked nose that had been broken once, a thick brow, long, pale-blond hair, and very distinctive, light gray eyes. He was quite a hairy fellow. He could grow a full beard in a week. Rather amazing actually," Julian averred, blinking at the crowd and looking very much like a studious scribe who had just been distracted by an interesting footnote.

"Gunnar served as a slave in our company on the journey to Wessex. But he stood out from the beginning as someone who got things done. By the time that our first battle was over, I had freed him. I never, in my entire life, saw anybody who could match him in a fight.

"He was a natural leader, and when he went into battle, the men in our unit fought like angry bears beside him. Within a year, he was my Lieutenant. After that, Guthrum himself promoted Gunnar to Captain, and soon afterward the war ended. And so, of course, he only wanted to come home; he wouldn't even hear of going anywhere else. There was no question that it would be dangerous for him here. I released my men to King Guthrum, who planned on using them in the occupation of Wessex, and we sailed for Bryne.

"During the campaign in Wessex we became friends, and Gunnar told me his entire story. His father was betrayed and murdered by a prominent citizen of Bryne. Gunnar was kidnapped on the day his father was murdered, and he knows who the murderer is. He came back here seeking vengeance."

The noise that erupted in the hall after Nils' translation was instantly silenced by the blast of a war-horn. "Shut up!" cried Nils. "Let him speak." He turned to Julian. "Look, stranger," he said awkwardly in stilted Danish. "We believe you. This man that you describe is our Prince, in truth. But now you have to tell us everything. Who is the murderer? Who killed our lord, King Vigmar the Great?" His voice quavered with tightly checked emotion as he repeated his question in Brynish for the benefit of his audience.

The warriors of Bryne had to know the answer to this question. To all who had gathered, this was not an issue of life, but of death unto death. The murder of Vigmar, their precious Ring-Giver, still festered like an unhealed wound in their souls. With every fiber of their beings they strained to hear Julian's answer, seeking to relieve their pain with the questionable balm of vengeance. Julian's reply was short and to the point.

"Here this, men of Bryne!" Julian cried in the West Scylfing tongue, speaking with his best Brynish accent so they could understand his words. "Your prince knew the name of his father's murderer, and he described him to me. The killer is a great, pasty-faced lout: a foul, smirking hypocrite named Haruk Longknife, also known as Haruk the Cruel."

As the words took effect, their impact was dreadful.

The men stood dumbly... their faces waxen, their eyes gone glassy and vacant, barely seeming to comprehend what they had heard. And then, something clicked within their collective consciousness.

This was treachery most foul: murder, mayhem, and utter betrayal. To make it worse, their own blood relative, their kinsman Haruk Longknife, had betrayed the precious brother-bond. Through an unnatural act of violence, Haruk had fed the dirt of death to a noble man who had loved Haruk with all of his heart.

The infamy, the utter villainy, the perverse, howling depravity of Vigmar's murder had ripped the heart from the city of Bryne. And after all of Haruk's wickedness, by subtle maneuverings, he had almost managed to sell them a new heart... a merciless organ driven by conquest and greed, created in the crucible of his sick, assiduous alchemy.

To make things worse, Haruk the Cruel now held their Prince captive. The son of Vigmar languished in the custody of Vigmar's betrayer.

As the realization dawned on them, they howled with rage. The sound was at once a primal shriek and a revelation to the visitors, showing them the reason for the grim reputation of this city... why these fighting men were feared and dreaded, even among other Norse kingdoms. This was the sound of undiluted, unadulterated, heedless, headlong and all-compelling fury: the battle cry of the warriors of Bryne.

The sound shook the hall and pounded heavily against their ears. The roar went on as if it would never end. All of them, from lads to white-haired elders, were caught up in its spell, as if they acted out an ritual with roots that ran deeper than blood, deeper than kindred and brother-bond, a primeval pulse and a cry for justice from the time before time, from before the natural universe exploded into being.

The men shook their swords and their spears and howled aloud in rage and frustration until their ears turned numb. Ivan Redbeard, driven to drastic action, leapt as nimbly as a lad onto the long drinking table.

"Men," he shouted in a thunderous voice that pierced the wild, delirious din. "At last, we all know what to do. You have your weapons, and you know the order of battle. Now!" he cried. "You men with Nils, take the visitors and hurry to the pier. Sail to Haruk's dock to prevent any chance of escape. The rest of you, come with me to his castle.

"We will rescue our Prince, whatever the cost. Vigmar's murder will be avenged! Death to the traitor! Death to Haruk the Cruel!"

The shout that followed his words was like none that had ever been heard in their city, or would ever be heard again. The men poured from the hall into the street and fell into ranks, shaking with anger, hungry for battle. Some of them hastily began to assemble an impromptu battering ram.

The main body of warriors left the streets of Bryne in a single pack, hot on the trail of Haruk. They began to run, streaming across the plain in rank order: silently, relentlessly traversing the face of the fertile earth.

They loped like lean wolves over the fresh-planted fields and lush pastures of their narrow coastal plateau, leaping stone walls and skirting hedges, their eyes fixed immutably upon their objective: the castle of the Dragon of Kuzbi, the source and goal of their rage. Like eagles selecting their prey from afar, they set their minds on the man, Haruk Longknife. Falling from high with their wings folded tight, the falcons of Bryne aimed to strike the source of their hatred.

Less than a mile away, up the steep hill due north of their city, Katla and Ilse stood in the doorway of their house on Falcon Rock and watched as the warriors streamed out of the main street of Bryne like drops of human mercury poured from a heated bowl. From their vantage point, the distant figures seemed to swarm in boxed ranks like orderly human insects, crawling across the plain in a single, united cluster.

Ilse leaned against her mother and wrapped her arm around her shoulder. Sharing her daughter's melancholy mood, Katla sighed heavily.

"Let's go inside," she said to Ilse. Without another word, they turned and walked into the house.

Edification

"Do you hear me, Gunnar?" Timothy called, barely managing to speak.

"Yes."

"I thought you'd passed out," panted Timothy.

"I did pass out. I think I did," the Prince added. "Maybe it's all just a wonderful dream." For no good reason, this struck Timothy as hilariously funny. He began to laugh in spite of the searing pain from his broken ribs. The pain stabbed him with every guffaw.

"Heh, heh. Ow!" Timothy chortled, infecting Gunnar with his mirth. The Prince began to laugh, each guffaw accompanied by a mind-numbing blast of pain from the aftereffects of the multiple abrasions, contusions, cracked bones, and deep bruises.

They laughed together, painfully, for over a minute, and then, they mercifully paused. After another minute, Timothy spoke.

"Listen, Gunnar, you've got to do me a favor."

"Okay."

"I know what this man plans to do next. He wants to use me against you. I heard him mumble something about it before he left. And listen, Gunnar… "

"Yes… "

"… if he tries to hurt me to get to you, don't let him do it."

"No problem. I'll just let him kill you."

"Listen, I'm serious!" Timothy replied with uncharacteristic force. "Do you hear me?"

"Don't make me laugh!" Gunnar had begun to convulse in laughter again, and he really did not want to have to deal with that level of pain.

"I'm serious! Listen," Timothy was growing desperate. "I've got to tell you something important." Timothy continued to speak quickly. "I have a message from God."

"What do you mean?"

"The King of heaven, the great Creator, gave me a message for you. He visited me just a few minutes ago, during the worst of the torture."

This instantly sobered Gunnar. *The King of heaven? The great Creator? Those are the words my father used to describe the Maker of heaven and earth.*

"What do you want from me?" Gunnar groaned. *This is real... Timothy couldn't have known to use those exact words... and why speak them now, at this moment, when we both face death? This has to be the very voice of God.* The thought terrified him.

"This is the message. Your prayers, and the prayers of your father, will be answered. Moreover, God will give you more than either you or your father ever imagined. He will not only deliver you from your enemies, he will deliver you from death, both today and forever."

"How?" Gunnar breathed, shocked by Timothy's words.

"By the power of his Word, through faith in his holy Name. By his Word he made the worlds, and by his Word he will save you. Only hear me now, Gunnar, and do not allow Haruk to subvert my wishes. Don't tell him your name, Gunnar. Trust me. Let me take the lead.

"Now is the time to give your heart, your life, and your all to the One who made you. Let Jesus of Nazareth, the Son of God, be your King. God is your Father; now, honor him."

"What should I do?"

"To honor the Father, honor the Son. God will save you from death. Obey Him now like you once obeyed King Vigmar.

"You once told me that you can read Latin. Use that knowledge to learn the words of God. A living faith in Jesus of Nazareth – the belief that He is God, the Son of God – will save you from death.

"Obey Christ, for love's sake. By the gift of His innocent life you have been saved from death forever. Now, follow Him. Obey Him. Seek out other believers and grow strong in their company. In God's shadow, in the arms of the mother Church, you will find peace and rest.

"After you are freed, retrieve my books from the boat. I give them all to you. In those books, you'll find the words of eternal life. Hide them in your heart."

Gunnar finally understood Timothy's message. *God wants me to follow him? To heed his words and obey his Son? All right, I can understand that.* He whispered a response directed to the heights of heaven; a reply that could hardly be heard.

"I will follow you... my Father," Gunnar breathed softly to the God who just wouldn't quit.

Suddenly, they heard Haruk shouting angrily in the hallway outside of the torture chamber. To Gunnar's surprise, a cold sweat broke out all over him, and he almost fainted with dread. He had thought himself immune to fear... but now, under Haruk's torture, he had learned about his own vulnerability.

"Be strong, Gunnar," called Timothy loudly. "Remember my words." Timothy sighed. He felt a weight suddenly lift from his spirit as a peace beyond description rolled softly into his soul.

Gunnar, on the other side of the room, began to experience something also. He felt the first stirrings of the same peace... a deep-seated quiet of mind and soul. "I believe," he said softly.

"What?"

"I believe you, Timothy!" shouted Gunnar, seized with a surge of unanticipated joy. "I believe that Jesus is the Son of God. You've finally convinced me," he mumbled through cracked and swollen lips, smiling painfully. "Brother Timothy, you're an English bulldog. You just never quit."

"Quit what?" Timothy replied with a wan smile.

The door slammed open and Haruk stalked into the room, caught up in a deadly fury.

"The idiots," Haruk screamed, beside himself with rage. "There's not a servant to be found. Not even my bodyguards!"

"I tell you," he fumed to no one in particular, radiating anger. "Good help is impossible to find!"

Gunnar couldn't help himself. He began to shake with unbridled, exceedingly painful laughter.

"No." he gasped. "Oh, no." But he just couldn't stop himself.

Haruk turned slowly and looked at the Prince with a pale, deadly smile defiling his flour-dough face. He drew a well-sharpened dagger from its sheath and crept close to Gunnar, almost forgetting what he was doing in the heat of the moment. And then, he remembered his plan.

"Oh yes, let's laugh now, shall we?" Haruk said through clenched teeth. He had not been able to find his servants, but Haruk was certainly capable of proceeding on his own, with or without a willing servant and a smelter of molten lead. He stuck the knife in the table and turned back toward Timothy, heading slowly in his direction.

"Master Fool," he called over his shoulder to the Prince. "Laugher, what is your name?" Gunnar stopped laughing and tried to move his head to see what Haruk was up to. "I'll tell you, Laugher. Your laughter has condemned your friend to death. If you don't tell me your name, I will now kill your friend. Slowly. Do your understand?"

Kill Timothy? Slowly? Suddenly, a fiercely protective love surged in his breast for the meek little man, driving unwanted tears to his eyes. Gunnar almost answered Haruk, but stopped when he remembered what Brother Timothy had just told him. *Timothy said that I should let him take the lead,* Gunnar recalled. *But how can I do that? This is too hard... oh, God, help me!*

Hearing Haruk's words, Brother Timothy knew that his time had come. His fervent plans, his preparations, all of his earthly dreams had ended. He had to fight this final dragon without turning back. He had to follow in the footsteps of his Maker.

Cocking his head, Timothy addressed his tormentor. "You will fail, you know," he said fearlessly to Lord Haruk the Cruel. Too surprised to answer the frail man splayed out helplessly before him, Haruk stared at Timothy, gaping in unadulterated amazement.

"What?" he asked.

"You will fail. You are fighting an unbeatable opponent."

"What do you mean?" Needless to say, Haruk Longknife was deeply in denial.

Haruk had suppressed the smoky vision received while chasing dreams in the early hours of the third watch. He had buried the startling glimpse of warriors bound for Bryne accompanied by an unbeatable, unutterably awesome power. He had denied it, and had even scoffed at it. But now, the memory returned and flooded Haruk's being.

"I'm talking about you and the choices you're making," Timothy replied. "If you fight us, you will lose. And if you continue in your wickedness, you will lose your very soul."

Haruk shrieked in anger, scrambling desperately for something with which to strike the helpless Brother Timothy. "You pious pig! I'll kill you!" His eyes caught sight of an axe hanging by the door.

Seizing the blunt instrument, Haruk raised it high above his head. Without further delay, he swung it down with all of his might. In this manner, Lord Haruk the Cruel brutally ended Brother Timothy's earthly life.

And then, it happened.

Haruk heard a thunderous sound.

A great, booming crash rang out, sending shockwaves that rolled through the outer walls of stone and caused the wooden floor to tremble beneath them.

With a vacant, uncomprehending stare, Haruk turned from the carnage and concentrated, trying to decipher the source of the sound. At that very moment, the war-horns began to trumpet beyond the thick walls. Their grim music echoed across the broad plain of Bryne, at once haunting and terrifying. The ominous wail of war-horns had not been heard on this coastal plateau in Haruk's lifetime, and the sound sent unwelcome chills down his spine.

"What on earth?" He hastily strode out through the door, slamming it behind him as the war-horns again lifted up their voice, inviting Dame War in her hot, wanton cruelty to visit her grisly bower and wed dear Bonnie Lord Harry. The horns sounded continuously, without pausing, importuning the heavens to rain hot fire upon the source of their rage: the worm known as Haruk the Cruel.

Water Works

"Let them pass," Nils ordered tensely. The men of Bryne carefully rowed their broad-beamed fishing boat up to Haruk's docks as the last leaky dinghy full of fleeing servants slipped past them. "They're slaves... hapless victims of Haruk. It's good that they should escape.

"Kronin and the sons of Salkar are the only freemen who serve Haruk. If they stand and fight, we'll kill them. But I wouldn't be surprised if they sneak out like rats, hiding among these ragged slaves."

They did not speak another word. Julian stood in the bow beside Roentner and Ixtalaban, eager to leap onto the dock as soon as the ship touched. The remainder of the crew sat quietly, watching intently as the oarsmen propelled the boat to the side of the long, narrow pier.

These men had readied themselves for the fight. As they waited for the onset of war, their stomachs wreaked havoc within them. Their inner regions had abandoned their iron wills... almost as if the fearful organs had made a mass, gastro-intestinal defection.

"We'll take the lead up the path," said Nils to Julian. "Once we make it to the top, your group can try to get into the castle. We'll make sure that Haruk doesn't sneak out the back way.

"As for you, and yours," Nils added grimly, "happy hunting. We'll keep the badger in the trap." He tied his scabbard to his thigh with a grimace. "You go inside and exterminate him."

View from the Top

Concerned by the volume and power of the sounds that had flushed him out of his torture chamber, Haruk hurried to the top of his castle wall to discover the source of the crash and clamor. He left a dreadful mess in his wake.

In the darkened heart of Haruk's windowless torture chamber, the very walls were flecked with encrusted clumps of gore. Battered and bruised, bound tightly to a table, the sole survivor struggled to orient himself.

Timothy must be dead, Gunnar thought. He couldn't see Timothy, but he had heard the axe crashing into flesh and wood. He knew what to expect. He wrenched his throbbing head around, his eyes swiftly scanning the room, desperately searching for a way out. Then, he saw the knife.

In Haruk's haste when he turned to murder Timothy, he had left his dagger buried in the table beside Gunnar. It was almost within reach.

Gunnar strained against his bonds and reached, inching closer, clawing desperately until he managed to grasp the wooden handle. He twisted the knife, pried it loose from the splintered wood, and began to cut his leather bonds.

Within moments, he was free.

Gunnar rolled to the side of the table and fell onto the floor. The pain was incredible, and for more than a minute he could not move due to the sheer, overpowering brunt of it. But somehow, fighting against the agony, he managed to rise to his feet.

After a quick, sickening glance to confirm Timothy's death, he stumbled toward the door. He lurched slowly down the hall and stepped through a narrow doorway into a well-lit room. As he entered the chamber, he received a pleasant surprise.

Gunnar had just walked into Haruk's armory.

Light streamed into the room through four tall, narrow

windows. Gunnar limped over to the nearest window and looked out. Below the window, to his right, he saw something he would never forget.

An angry army of men rolled a battering ram back up the straight, steep road that descended to Haruk's front door. The front of the ram, which consisted of a long, massive bundle of tree trunks resting on two wooden wagons nailed together end-to-end, was already broken and splintered where it had suffered a run-in with the iron-clad gate.

In spite of his pain, Gunnar smiled deliriously, filled with a sharp, sudden joy that almost took his breath away. They had arrived at last! His friends had come to save him.

Gathering his wits, he looked one more time at the ram and the roadway leading to Haruk's front gate. *That's a poor design, with the road running downhill toward the gate,* he thought wryly. He glanced down into Haruk's moat and saw that it was almost dry, containing mostly dirt and rocks and a few, shallow pools. *Haruk's most glaring fault, besides his depravity, is his unmitigated laziness.*

A mountain stream passed just north of the castle, but Haruk had never bothered to divert it into his moat or to repair the drawbridge in front of the huge front doors. The permanently open drawbridge, like the waterless moat below it, offered only an ironic hint of protection – a toothless and doddering defense against the angry swarm of armed intruders.

The Prince's eyes returned to the armory. The weapons stored there were obviously of the highest caliber, stolen from some of the finest kingdoms of Europe. *I'll take this one,* he thought, painfully reaching for an ornately wrought sword in a jeweled scabbard. He slid the blade out and looked at it closely, noting the heft and feel of the handle. *This will do nicely.* He stiffly tied it to his thigh and picked up a small dagger, tying it to his calf, visibly wincing as he did. He had been thoroughly tortured, beaten and bruised, and the pain mounted by the minute. *I'd better keep moving, or I might give out,* he realized.

Unsure of his next move, Gunnar stepped out into the hallway and bumped into Haruk the Cruel.

Invasion of Piracy

Ixtalaban slipped over the rampart and dropped stealthily onto the wooden walkway that ran around the top of the stone walls. As the best fighter of their group pound-for-pound, he had been chosen to climb into the Castle of Kuzbi.

Haruk's castle had been built, like Bryne itself, with the cliffs as the first line of defense. Wending its way up the cliffs from a stony spit of shore, the treacherous trail from Haruk's dock seemed scarcely navigable. If the shallow, boulder-strewn waters of Haruk's inlet had allowed sufficient draw for a longship, his position would have been strategically superior to Bryne's.

Haruk's defensive advantages included the height of the cliffs and the exposed nature of its near-vertical path. If invaders ever attempted to struggle up Haruk's exposed cliff face, the strategy of the defenders would be obvious: riddle the fools with arrows and then roll stones until the falling bodies of the foremost rolled the rest of their comrades back into the sea.

His castle jutted into the bay on a narrow peninsula. As a result of these natural defenses, Haruk had spent little time fortifying the castle's sides and back. The fortified front faced the open plateau, but the walls on either side overlooked steep cliffs with sheer drops to the water below. The castle's back faced a small patch of uneven ground between the castle and the perilously steep path.

The rear of Haruk's fortress was protected by a pathetic excuse for a battlement: an uneven, shabby stack of mortared stones that hardly seemed high enough to qualify as a respectable castle wall. Since Haruk's men had abandoned the turrets, negotiating an entry was only a matter of using human resources effectively.

Five stout fellows stood on the bottom of a pyramid, three stood in the next row on top of their shoulders, two in the next row, and finally, Ixtalaban slowly but surely climbed the trembling tower of humanity until he managed, just barely, to gain a finger

hold at the top of the wall. From there, he clawed his way through
the low opening of the rampart and dropped onto the wooden
walkway.

The men had no way of knowing that the castle was virtually
empty. Haruk's men, both bond and free, had fled at the sight of
the Brynish advance, rushing to the docks and packing into every
leaky vessel that could float. The bulk of these men in their wide-
bottomed boats had barely managed to slip past the point before
Nils and company had rowed into sight, sealing off the escape
route.

On the wooden catwalk just below the top of the wall, Ixtalaban
moved slowly, carefully watching for any defenders who might be
found in this cold, windy, deserted-looking castle of wind-pocked,
blood-smeared stone and creaking, splintering, gently-swaying
wood.

Mortal Deftness

Haruk the Cruel and Prince Gunnar of Bryne stood face to face without exchanging a word. And then, Haruk reacted with brutal quickness, plunging his knife deeply into... nothing.

Gunnar spun away, slamming Haruk's chest with a blow that knocked him back and stole his breath. Dropping the dagger, Haruk drew his sword and slashed, only to have the well-tempered blade broken cleanly in two by a lightning strike so fast, he scarcely saw its arc.

As Haruk stared deeply into the maddened eyes of the stranger who stood before him, terror melted his resolve. His knees began to fail. Without thinking, he threw his broken sword into Gunnar's bloody face and ran for his life.

Gunnar chased Haruk, hopping awkwardly on his best leg. Given the state of his swollen knee, cracked ankle and broken toes, the Prince could not move very quickly.

Haruk beat Gunnar to the top of the tower steps, where he slammed and bolted the door in his face. Gunnar paused for a moment, deep in thought. At the sound of a footstep behind him, he whirled instinctively, almost passing out from the agony that the sudden move provoked.

Ixtalaban stared at Gunnar as if he did not recognize him. The Prince's altered appearance shocked Ixtalaban to his core.

Gunnar's eyes squinted through grotesquely swollen, purplish lumps. His forehead and chin showed deep gashes smeared with dark brown streaks of recently dried blood, and his neck was embossed with the twisted imprint of bruises left by heavy twine. Gunnar's left hand, the one that in better days might have carried an iron shield, looked bloody and contorted, and his left fingernails were missing. Ixtalaban winced at the sight, yet his heart surged with joy to know that the Prince still lived.

"Gunnar!" he cried, dropping his sword and spontaneously

embracing him.

"Ow! You're killing me, brother," Gunnar replied, trying to smile. He jerked a thumb at the tower door. "The pig's in the trap." His eyes narrowed. "Get an axe so we can finish the job." As soon as the words came out of his mouth, Gunnar knew his plan was a bad one. *I promised to obey God, and I know that He wants me to show mercy.* He realized now what his promise would mean. *But Haruk killed my father!*

"I will be your father," a still, soft voice spoke deep within him.

What? he thought. *Who was that?* The voice had definitely not emerged from his thoughts. The words had been gentle, but strong and clear... without equivocation. This was a voice he had never heard before. *Is that you, God?* he asked in his heart. *Timothy said you would be my father. Is that you?*

"It's me." He heard the words clearly, deep within him. And then, the voice fell silent.

"Gunnar! Gunnar!" cried Ixtalaban dashing up the steps. "Here's an axe." Gunnar looked at him dazedly, as if he had just been awakened from a deep and lonely sleep.

"What?"

"I found an axe."

"Oh," he replied absently. "Good." His eyes wandered to the window and the pale blue of the clean morning sky.

"Stand back," Ixtalaban shouted as he prepared to assault the door.

Sea of Tranquility

From the beauty of his surroundings, Haruk the Cruel would never have suspected that this was the day of his death. He left the enclosed doorway and stepped out into the full sunlight, blinking in the brightness like an unnatural bleached thing unaccustomed to such dazzling, uncompromising celerity. He felt like a creature of the caves and grottoes that had just crawled into the light of day.

The sky had cleared, and it seemed to quiver with vibrant blue light. Below, in the rich green countryside, birds swooped from tree to tree. A sweet-scented breeze pressed coolly against his cheek, ruffling his hair. He paused for a moment, taken aback by the beauty.

A resounding crash from the front gate made the tower tremble, and a horrible, astonishingly loud roar broke out from the armed men massed below. The massive gate had almost been breached. One more blow of the battering ram, and they would enter the castle. Haruk stared at the swarm of angry warriors below, gazing in open-mouthed dismay at the incontrovertible proof of his own, incipient demise.

"You don't have to die," a voice beside him said clearly. Haruk's head snapped around, but there was no one to be seen.

"Who are you?" he asked. "What are you?"

He heard no answer. His gaze returned to the roadway in front of his gate, where the ram was being pulled, slowly and painstakingly, to the top of the hill. He heard another crash to his left, at the bolted tower door. "Oh, great!" he snarled. "The Laughing Fool has found an axe!"

"You don't have to die," the voice repeated. It was as if a man stood there beside him, the voice was so clear and unmistakable. Suddenly, for no good reason, Haruk decided that he hated this voice.

"What? I don't have to die?" railed Haruk. "Why not? Will you save me? Go! Get out of here, whatever you are! Do you want me to grovel, to beg?" he cried, rejecting the outstretched hand of mercy. "I will not beg for your mercy!" The chopping sound at the tower door changed in timbre as the wood began to yield to the expertly wielded axe.

Haruk heard no answer to his evil outburst. But the methodical smash of the axe and the snapping sound of breaking wood brought home the import of the moment at hand.

At that point, the action accelerated.

The tower door exploded into pieces, scattering splinters and shards and jagged pieces of wood as a heavy boot smashed through the lock. For a moment, the action seemed to pause as the wood chips drifted away from the doorframe.

Ixtalaban knocked the door in, blowing it off its hinges and falling down on top of it right at Haruk's feet. Haruk kicked at Ixtalaban's head. Dodging the blow, Ixtalaban grabbed Haruk's supple boot and wrenched it sideways with all of his strength, straining mightily until the corpulent nobleman fell to the floor with a thunderous thud.

Through the splintered doorframe limped the Prince of Bryne.

Gunnar's impassive face belied his emotions. Only his eyes revealed the powerful feelings that tore at his soul like a deadly riptide swirling just beneath the surf. At the sight of Gunnar, Haruk's internal organs seemed to melt into jelly. His knees, quite literally, began to knock together.

Through wave upon wave of unbearable pain, the Prince pressed toward his mark, sword drawn in his good right hand. Haruk turned and scrambled up the corkscrewed wooden steps that led to the top of a small, elevated platform on the front side of the tower. He had built the platform as an observation post situated high above the ramparts of the battle tower. From its airy escarpment he could clearly seen the mouth of the fjord and the open sea past the top of the cliffs that marked the entrance to the Bay of Bryne.

As Haruk climbed to this penultimate vantage point, followed by his slow but relentless pursuer, a soldier below spotted him. A cry was raised, and soon all eyes were riveted on the two men high above them, climbing onto the shaky platform that rose above the top of the tall tower. One climber could be clearly seen to be Haruk, even at this distance, but the other could not be identified.

A voice called out from among the warriors: "Gunnar!" In that moment they all – from the least to the greatest – recognized their Prince.

The men of Bryne, hoarse from yelling, raised their voices in a howl of salutation and fury. The Prince heard their shout as if from a great distance. He struggled to climb the slender steps, his whole will focused on the task. He wanted to stop... to howl in pain, not in rage. But an unrelenting drive within him compelled him forward, agonizing step after step, with his own ragged breath roaring like thunder in his ears.

Ixtalaban stood and watched from the bottom of the steps. Seeing the end draw near, he began to smile.

The Pinnacle

Haruk had run out of plans. He had no chance left, no roll of the bones: no lot with which to redeem his life. His dagger was lost, his sword gone, and his men... all gone. An enraged warrior pursued him, determined to inflict vengeance. Given the speed and power that his pursuer had already demonstrated, Haruk knew that he had no chance of defeating him.

The small platform, nothing more than a flat floor surrounded by a narrow handrail, swayed in the breeze and shook with every step of Haruk's bloody pursuer. Again, the fear slammed into him, sapping his strength as the stranger's bearded face came into sight at the head of the steps. In spite of himself, Haruk collapsed to his knees and lost control of his bodily functions.

The bruised warrior stepped onto the platform. He towered over Haruk, his swollen eyes alight with deadly fury.

Then, the warrior spoke.

"Do you not know me?"

Haruk could not answer him.

"Do you not know me?" he asked again. Haruk said nothing.

The man seized Haruk's hair and dragged him to his feet in a single, swift motion, as if he hoisted a sack of potatoes. Haruk began to weep with fear as he gazed into the man's blackened eyes.

"Look at me!" the man hissed. "You know me, don't you? Who am I?" Haruk looked at him without comprehension.

"Look at me!" the warrior cried. "You know me!" Haruk stared at him blankly. "Look!"

A dawn of belated understanding – a blossom of horror within his nascent consciousness – began to stir, spreading cruel wings to dominate Haruk's mind with sickening, demonic fury. In an instant of time, with a prolonged, mind-racking blood rush of soul-rending horror, he recognized the identity of his pursuer.

"Mercy," he breathed, turning so limp that he hung loosely like a three-hundred-pound sack of debris, upheld solely by the Prince's strong right arm and iron grip. In the silence that followed Haruk's moan, Ixtalaban could hear the pop and crack of tendons in the Prince's forearm.

"Who am I?" the warrior yelled, framing his query in a monstrous booming shout that further unstrung the ligaments of Lord Haruk.

"Please," Haruk blubbered, "I beg you. Forgive me, most noble Prince."

"Who am I?"

"You are Gunnar-val, Son of King Vigmar the Great," Haruk sobbed. "Forgive me, O mighty Prince." Gunnar dropped him, and Haruk collapsed on the platform in a quivering, gelatinous heap. "Forgive, forgive," he blubbered limply, a profane puddle of flesh who now whispered his words with a weak, bubbling hiss.

"I don't think so," Gunnar retorted dryly.

As he raised his sword to kill Lord Haruk the Cruel, Gunnar suddenly became aware of a roar from below. For a moment, his warrior's training almost lapsed. But with a concentrated effort of the will, he wrenched his mind away from the mob.

Gunnar fixed his attention on the man who lay at his feet. Haruk had grown deathly white. He had prostrated himself, face down, and he groveled like a maggot as he tried to kiss the Prince's feet.

"Spare me, O Prince," he moaned. "Have mercy according to your greatness."

"Traitor," Gunnar spat. "You must die." He lifted his sword high above his head; higher than was prudent for a warrior to lift a blade. But after all that he had endured, what did he care for the niceties of prudent sword-craft?

At this moment, to his astonishment, he heard the voice again in his heart. *Blessed are the merciful, for they shall obtain mercy.*

Unexpectedly, Gunnar experienced a flood of memories. His mother, his father... Ilse, Ithmar, Ivan, Rollo, Captain Rurik, Julian, Roentner, Ixtalablan, Brother Timothy... wave upon wave of poignant memories surged through his being. The images rolled across him like a pent-up river that had burst its banks: rushing through his mind, sweeping everything else away by its sheer, unstoppable power.

The words from Brother Timothy had returned, unbidden, to his memory. *Blessed are the merciful, for they shall obtain mercy.*

Suddenly, Gunnar saw the weeping Lord Haruk with fresh eyes. Haruk deserved death... but he, Gunnar-val, was not the ordained executioner.

As he paused, Gunnar realized that he would not kill Haruk the Cruel. Slowly... very slowly... he began to lower his sword.

"I will not dishonor the pledge I have made to my King," he whispered, stunned and surprised at what he was doing. "I will not kill you." Haruk's face, streaked with tears, froze in its place: an unseemly mask that hardly registered a change.

"Hear this, Haruk," Gunnar said wearily. "I have pledged my sword to the Creator of the heavens, the God of my father. Because He has commanded me to show mercy, I will spare you. The men of Bryne may judge you, but I will not."

Haruk's mouth fell open wide, and his eyes narrowed. He felt suddenly strengthened by a surge of mindless, inchoate rage. *God? The God of Vigmar, that pious fool? Will you spare me for the tender judgments of the men of Bryne? Fire and death!*

As he climbed to his hands and knees, Haruk's choice seemed framed with crystal clarity. Unaware of the power of kindness, only evil seemed real to him. Haruk could not imagine a genuine offer of mercy, so he rejected Gunnar's words out of hand. He had been stripped of his dignity, but he was not without resources. He still had his hatred... and his overweening pride.

"I will not have your mercy!" Haruk roared.

Mustering all of his strength, Lord Haruk dove toward Gunnar's knees, driving his body forward and wrapping his arms around Gunnar's legs as he slammed him into the frail railing. The fragile board gave way, breaking with a sharp, dry crack.

Haruk the Cruel, with Gunnar held tightly in his grip, spun off the top of the high platform. Tangled together, they slowly began to fall.

The men of Bryne watched in disbelief as their Prince and his tormentor whirled hypnotically, majestically in the clean air: floating, as it were, toward the earth until the grotesque ballet accelerated suddenly and the two men slammed into the bottom of the moat with an earth-shaking, lifeless thud.

At first, they did not approach the moat.

They stood there, staring. Some of them looked up toward the top of the tower, while some looked toward the moat. Others looked around with a disoriented expression, like survivors of a tornado trying to understand what had had just happened.

It was a full minute before the oldest man among them, with trembling knees, hurried over to the rocks surrounding the moat. With all of his strength he strove toward his goal, picking his way across jagged boulders to the edge of the declivity and looking down into its depths.

"Come quickly," he quavered. "Come here." The fastest were there within seconds, and soon all of the men of Bryne stared, like Ivan, into the bottom of the moat. What they saw was stark and compelling.

They had fallen together, and they lay together. The prince was curled on his side in a fetal position. Haruk lay on his back beside Gunnar with his neck twisted and broken. Haruk's face emptily stared at nothing as a large fly crawled across his right eye. The two bodies lay half-buried in the top of a mountainous pile of rotting garbage.

The gigantic heap of rotting refuse was the final masterwork of Haruk Longknife. The decaying heap had formed slowly over a period of years, like the delta of a river: expanding by a process akin to accretion… growing into aromatic maturity from humble beginnings into its current, majestic estate. Comprised of bits and scraps of cast-off food that had been carelessly tossed into the moat from his bedroom window, it had ripened into the only fully realized work to come from Haruk's wasted, shipwrecked life.

Haruk had been a true pig in every sense of the word.

Now, as the men watched from the rim of the wide moat, Prince Gunnar moved slightly and moaned.

Seeing this, Ivan Redbeard almost fell over backwards.

"Men, quickly!" he shouted. "Bring some rope!"

Standing beside Ivan, a sour-faced Yon the Elder silently stared into the moat. He brushed flies away from his face as he squinted dourly at the unseemly sight.

"Ay, rope," Yon said finally, smiling wickedly. "After we rescue Prince Gunnar, we can string up Haruk by his feet."

Homecoming

On the third day after the return of the Prince, the mead hall was filled with men and women of Bryne. Since his return, they had abandoned their daily routines. On this day, they gathered in the hall with their little ones, eating quietly, awed by recent events.

At the head of the largest table sat their king. The condition of his face, swollen, bruised and battered as it was, and his body, broken and scarred with abuse, had not prevented him from somehow managing to sit here, propped up at the table, sharing their day of rest and gladness.

The seat to King Gunnar's immediate left was left empty in honor of Lord Ithmar, the Steward of Bryne. At his right sat his father's closest counselor and friend, Ivan Redbeard, the city's oldest citizen. Beside Ivan sat the friends of the King: Julian, Rollo, Roentner, the Morris brothers, Wiglaf the Wise, and the dreaded Huns of the Teutonic weirs: Ixtalaban, Schelten, Hanslinger, Belcher, Geltzig, and Glempf.

"A song!" cried Julian, trying his best to incite the subdued citizens to a measure of exuberance more like his own. "We need a song."

The King had to smile at Julian in spite of the excruciating pain. His injuries were severe. He had suffered multiple cracked bones, abrasions, contusions and lacerations. Sporadic blasts of agony besieged him; but the pain could not distract from the joy he felt at this reunion with his loved ones.

To the citizens of Bryne, the bittersweet poignancy of the moment seemed too intense to bear. They focused on small details of the day... details they would recall for as long as they lived.

"Do you have something to say to the crowd?" Julian asked Rollo loudly, teasing him unmercifully.

"I do," a deep voice spoke. At the sound of the familiar voice, the people in the hall turned to face the door.

Ithmar stood in the doorway. Backlit by sunlight streaming through the open door, he appeared thin and wan. Beside Ithmar stood the two wise women who had hidden him during the past months.

At the sight of the Steward, a collective gasp went up from the crowd, and the Prince struggled to his feet. The people had learned only two days ago that Ithmar lived... but they had become so accustomed to the concept of his decease that the story of his survival had seemed like a fable. They had not fully believed it until this very moment.

They watched in amazement as Ithmar, tall and raven-haired, walked unsteadily around the edge of the room, passing the seated revelers as he approached the chair of the King. After some time, he reached his goal. Reaching out, he firmly grasped the armrest of the Prince's chair.

"My King," he said. "Gunnar-val, son of Vigmar." Kneeling at his feet, he bowed his trembling head.

A great cheer arose... not of anger, horror or despair, but of joy and celebration. All of the people wept freely at the sight. Ithmar's lonely service to Vigmar, safeguarding the throne on the hopeless chance that the Prince might some day return, had been rewarded beyond his most desperate hope.

As Katla and Ilse tarried in the doorway, they felt a joy akin to an overwhelming flood. Their prayers had been answered, right before their eyes. Ithmar had lived. And more importantly, he had not lived in vain. Ithmar's friend Vigmar – dearly lost, coldly murdered – had an heir to sit on his throne.

Ithmar had gained strength slowly during the past few weeks. But until the return of Gunnar, he had seemed adrift, like a faded whisper of his former self. He had acted like a man without spirit: a jagged pain wrapped around a wound, scarcely managing to cling to life. Now, his inner wounds would begin to heal.

Gunnar raised his eyes and looked toward the open doorway, where the afternoon sun scattered beams of light into the dusty room. He squinted against the light, straining to see.

Gunnar could barely discern the silhouette of a young woman framed by the light pouring through the open doorway... but he knew she was Ilse. She stood without moving, wrapped in a blinding cloud of dazzling rays.

Ilse's gaze was riveted fast upon him, studying the rugged, swollen, badly bruised face of a brutalized warrior. She had loved Gunnar as only the pure of heart can love... as her first and flawless love.

When she noticed that that he returned her gaze, her reaction was instantaneous. Ilse turned and fled like a doe escaping a hunter's snare. She dashed from the hall, racing up the empty main street of the town, fleeing toward the sanctuary of Falcon Rock on the steep, stony hill north of town.

Gunnar wanted to give chase, to comfort her somehow, but he remained unable to walk, much less run. He could only sit and watch as she bolted from the room in disarray, not knowing where she would go, or what she would do.

The house that Ilse fled to was once a hiding place, a sanctuary... until her safety was shattered by the underlying battle of their time. Ilse the child, like Gunnar the slave, had been unwillingly trapped in a greater conflict: abused and exploited by the worst angels of a lost generation. The kingdoms of the northern pirates had grown rich by trafficking in amber and incense and ships and ivory, slaves and swords and terror and gold, in shattered hopes and the souls of men. They had bargained for gain in a greedy world and had gained greatness at any expense. The cost, in the end, had been unbearable.

Ilse needed time to recover. The sheer abundance of surprising events, both good and evil, had simply overwhelmed her. And so she ran for the house on Falcon Rock, seeking the safety that had been stolen from her on a quiet, snowy night.

Julian may have been the only man in the hall who understood Ilse's reaction. He leaned over to speak to his friend.

"It's too much for her," he whispered quietly to Gunnar. "She'll be okay. It's just too much; that's all."

Gunnar looked at Julian and then glanced at Ivan Redbeard,

two seats to his left, and at Ithmar, now seated at his left hand. His glance swept slowly across the hall: across the faces of men and women, old and young, that he had known from a child. The faces triggered poignant memories.

The people arrayed before him in this hall were his dearest friends. There was Rollo, there were the companions that had followed him here from the wars in England, there Nils the fisherman and Melgaard the Bald, the farmers, the fishermen, the weavers and warriors and wise women, along with all the rest. Gunnar looked back to the doorway and searched the face of Katla. After that, he looked at Julian and responded.

"It's too much for me, too," Gunnar said. He slowly shook his head. "I'm tingling all over."

The Prince of Bryne had suffered a severe concussion. He was beginning to slip into that peculiarly distorted, disengaged state familiar to those who have suffered a hard blow to the head.

As the room grew quiet, the people of Bryne began to sing arm-in-arm, swaying to an ancient song they had learned as children playing in the streets. Their song was a saga that told of the first of the Brynish sea-kings, of their battles and their bravery and the founding of their city. Their song told of war and of peace: of fierce thanes and golden kingdoms passed like smoke-wraiths from a smoldering pyre, gone like amber washed from a stony beach. The lyrics told of valiant lives and peoples and nations that flared like sparks from a sail burning brightly, sparks that fly upwards and are quenched forever. They sang of youth and strength and valor, of honor and vanity, cowardice and loss. But somehow, in spite of it all, their song was filled with gladness and gratitude.

As the words rang out in the hall, Katla approached the throne, skirting the walls of the hall and threading her way past her townsfolk. She stepped up behind her husband and placed a warm hand on his shoulder. Ithmar clutched her hand tightly and pressed it, reverentially, against his cheek.

"They've forgotten their troubles," she said softly. "It's almost as if they never happened. I don't know how they do it."

It was true that the people had already turned from mourning. Yesterday's tragedies were largely forgotten: the funeral pyre of Tannig and the burial of Brother Timothy were things of the past, as if they had happened decades ago instead of only yesterday. They would deal with their grief later, as with today's joy: in pieces, as they were able.

As he listened to their song, Gunnar began to weep great tears of joy and pain and hope and sorrow: emotions so powerfully mingled within him that he had no ability to sort them out or understand them. He stoically gazed around the hall with an expressionless face as the tears streamed down his bruised face and wet his shirt.

As Gunnar's head grew lighter, his tears seemed to swell into a mighty tidal surge that flooded out toward the mead hall door and onward, pulling at him, tugging him away from this unfamiliar city that had once been his haven and his home. The flood of tears threatened to take him out of his body, so he closed his eyes and prayed for strength. He sat there with his eyes closed for quite some time.

When he opened his eyes, Gunnar had begun to leave the hall. He was being swept away on a river of tears, driving ahead of the wind as if his life depended on it.

Drifting with the current, he floated lightly past the crowd and swam out through the closed doors, slipping down the streets of Bryne and beyond. Gaining altitude, he sailed up toward the cliffs, past the wheeling falcons and eagles... climbing higher into the clear blue sky above the city of his dreams.

From the heights he could see the city below... a mere bump on a small, flat patch of greenery framed by mountains and sea. And still the river rushed onward, carrying him higher, driving him northward: catching him up in the compelling force of its current. Like an eagle driven before the wind, Gunnar watched as its force propelled him high above jagged stone mountaintops, past solemn snow-bound fjords and beyond, into dizzying, celestial heights from which the glaciers below seemed like pure white gems set in the midst of a dazzling sea. And still he traveled, climbing yet higher, soaring above the firmament until, at last, he entered into the homeland of rest, beyond the mountains of crystalline snow.

He arrived on a clean green lawn beside a palace brightly lit from within. And here, at last, in the gardens of paradise, Gunnar laid down his head and fell softly asleep.

The Middle Kingdom

The King slept for hours. The people of Bryne continued their feast without waking him. Gunnar had joined them today in spite of his need for rest and recuperation, and they felt it best that he sit there undisturbed: upright in the throne, but safely asleep.

With Gunnar's election as king, a new era began for the City of Bryne. Those who studied Norse history would some day refer to their time as the Middle Kingdom, but the people in the hall were decidedly unconcerned about such things. They only knew that their Prince had returned, their Steward yet lived, and their mourning had been turned into joy. They could not know that they witnessed the beginning of a golden age for their small city.

The coming years would bring trials and battles and times of exquisite joy. Many decades would pass before the last members of this generation would depart from this world to rest, at last, in their long homes. And yet, their lives had changed for the better. In peace the people of Bryne would live, and in peace they would rest at the end of their days.

Two weeks after the election of the King, Bryne's citizens gathered to reason together and to consider his new beliefs... to hear them explained, and to see what significance they might hold. On that night, after a protracted debate, Ivan Redbeard stood and spoke words that would one day become famous throughout the northern lands.

"Men and brethren," he said. "We have heard our king speak of his new beliefs. We have heard him describe how the one true God – the Creator of all – saved him from certain death; and how Timothy of Wessex, a man known by Gunnar for only a few weeks, gave his life to save Gunnar from Haruk the Cruel. We have heard how Timothy's master, Jesus of Nazareth, gave his own life to deliver us from the power of death... and from our many follies.

"In ages past, since the days of our first kings, our mothers and fathers engaged in a consuming struggle. They battled bravely against chaos and destruction, striving to build a circle of safety for their families in a world filled with hardship, disorder, and death. Our fathers and mothers knew that eventually, they must lose their brave war. In spite of this fact, they fought heroically. They fought until death stole the light from their eyes and stilled their tongues… until dust silenced the calls of their children, and the wind-blown peat hid their glorious cities. There they lie to this day, beneath the green moss. They fought hopelessly, valiantly, against a dragon that none could slay. In end, the power of that dragon, which we call Chaos or Death, stole their lives along with their last, valiant breaths.

"They all died without surrendering. And yet, they went to their graves as they had lived – without a single breath of hope.

"Our ancestors prepared their children to fight like they had fought, protecting the flame of family against the darkness of death. They wished that their children would have a chance to fight as hopelessly and bravely as they. Each generation, as the ages passed, fought and lost the same battle.

"Now, in our time, our King has returned with a message of hope. He says that there is a refuge against death; a tower of safety that our people can run to. He says there is no need to engage in our fathers' valiant, doomed struggle.

"Our lives are short. We awaken from darkness and are born; we open our eyes and glimpse the light. For a brief season, we fly about like a sparrow in a mead hall. We flit from place to place, seeking a way out, but not finding it. We have no peace, no safe place of rest, no enduring home in a world that drives us relentlessly toward death.

"For years beyond measure, this is how we have lived, we and our fathers and mothers. If our King now offers hope, we ought not to dismiss it lightly.

"It is not fitting to think that the great Creator, having made us from the dust, would abandon us without hope. Who among us would not provide for the needs of a strange child left at our door?

And are we nobler than God?

"It is more reasonable to think that our Creator has provided more than a cruel demise and a bitter end. If God is perfect and good, it should not seem astonishing to think that He would leave the heavens to become a man… that He would give his own life to pay the price for our folly.

"And if God is not good, why did he craft us from the dust? Why bother to give us food from the earth and sea? Why would he allow us to live, seeing that we blaspheme His name as a mere figure of speech?

"My counsel is that we pledge our lives to the God of heaven by honoring His Son. For I have seen a wonder: our King has returned from captivity to tell us that the Maker spoke to him. He says that our Maker lived among men in Jesus of Nazareth, the Savior of mankind… pouring out his own blood to reconcile justice and mercy. He tells us God rose from the dead to prepare a place for us, so we can live with him forever.

"I will not reject such a Savior. I will no longer live like a sparrow in a mead hall, flitting from light to light. I will accept this faith, with its promise of eternal life. I will believe in this great Deliverer who has outwitted the Dragon of Death. I will pledge my life to Jesus, the Son of God, and I counsel you, my people, to do the same."

Reconciliation

They were married in the spring, three years after his return. The passage of time had not fully healed their wounds; but they had learned the wisdom of silence, and in the space of their silence grew a profound, unspoken trust. They spent long hours quietly together... reading their books, watching the sunset from the watchtower or riding up into the mountains on the cool days of summer. Their pain would heal in time.

The sea still tossed its heady spray within sight of the watchtower. The sun still arose each morning and set in its place each night. The mysterious lights of the North whorled across the sky in their season, and the stars shone clear and true upon those who watched from earth. As the seasons passed, the hearts of Ilse and Gunnar were knit together by the bond of love and the touch of true devotion.

Their children played at their feet in the house on Falcon Rock, a house filled with the abundance of grace. Their life grew rich and multi-faceted, a precious stone in its own right: one that prospered wherever it was turned. They lived into old age, wise and filled courage, and they left behind a legacy of hope.

The end of their lives, it can safely be said, was only their beginning.

VI.

The story is told of the city of Bryne –
The jewel in the mind of the Prince of the realm –
About how that great city learned to be small
And to share the strong joy of a hope that endures.

Stories are stories, and words work their gift,
Lending life to the tales of our age and its kings.
But this story abides of a day that has passed:
A missive, a tale of a time slipped away.

This story is yours, and the Truth of the tale
Now echoes within the fair realm of your soul.

Bryne was made strong on the cliffs of your dreams,
Her cast iron gates and her stones and her kings
Assumed weighty ponderance
By your vested strength.

This is how stories of kingdoms are made.
We spin the story, the teller and hearer.
We spin it ourselves, together, creating.

It is not so with Truth.

Truth is the endless Creator of all.

Truth will endure when our fables have passed.
Kingdoms will fail, but the Truth will remain:
Ascending in smoke from the altar of grace,

Borne to the heights on the prayers of the saints.
The soul that trusts in its Maker will drink
From His river of life
Living waters of Light.

At the end of our faith
Lives the source of our dreams:
The Jewel in the mind of the bond and the free,
The Jewel in the heart of the homeland of peace,
The pure fountainhead of the crystalline spring,
The Jewel in the mind
Of the free.

To the King.

Smoke from the Altar

In the midst of the saints he stands alone, unhindered by time or place. His focus is solely upon the Source, the goal of the clouds of ascending praise.

He has lived here for fifteen years.

Here he found grace one day long ago, when he lay in danger of death. On that bitter day, he was rescued by monks and carried to this monastery, where still he abides, breathing praise to the heavens, tasting pure grace.

The Brothers of Mercy, in this man's case, have truly lived up to their name.

The tears flow freely from sightless eyes as he sings from his heart a familiar song – a chant of love in an ancient tongue that once, as a lad, he dared to despise. But that was when he was only a child, in a land far away, in another day.

He sings his devotion with all that he has, offering thanks and a paean of praise, savoring awesome, unending love. He basks in the warmth of God's wonderful grace.

He can barely begin to realize the grace that God has shown his wayward soul. Salted by tears, cleansed by the blood, his offering of praise burns brightly within. It ascends, with his prayers, to the heights of the throne.

For fifteen years, he has lived here with the Brothers of Mercy. And here, in the midst of the body of Christ, mercy has touched Lord Kennan's soul. Unmerited favor has changed his heart. He is lost in the uplifted clouds of joy, singing his sweet, precious Savior's high praise.

Kennan lifts up his eyes and cries out with measureless joy as his Lord passes by: illuminating the hope of the saints, revealing the Truth and the Life and the Way, lighting the path to the Holy of Holies... here at the top of the mountain of grace.

www.ingramcontent.com/pod-product-compliance
Lightning Source LLC
Chambersburg PA
CBHW070318260626
47160CB00003B/883